Gentle

Like the

Rain

A Heart's Design Novel

JoAnn Durgin

Cover Design: RUTHIE MADISON/MADISON DESIGNS

Cover Photo: MICHAEL JUNG

From the Author

Dear Readers,

Gentle Like the Rain is a spinoff of *Heart's Design*, my 2015 novel set primarily in the fictional town of Evergreen, Maine. While this story features the same New England setting, and shares characters in common, *Gentle Like the Rain* can easily stand on its own with the introduction of two new lead characters, Sidney Prescott and Isabella Caccavale.

In *Heart's Design*, heroine Caroline Prescott's eldest brother, Sidney, was mentioned but never made an appearance. When I was invited to contribute a book to the *Whispers of Love* project, I began to contemplate sharing Sidney's journey. He is a complex and intriguing character. Driven to succeed his entire life, he's a man burdened with high expectations and recent loss.

As an author, I love showing how God can use our human weaknesses for His glory. *Gentle Like the Rain* explores one man's quest as Sidney seeks God's purpose and meaning for his life, even without first recognizing it as such. Along the way, he encounters intriguing individuals who impact his life in unforgettable ways. While *Gentle Like the Rain* is a love story between a man and a woman, it is also the story of a man's journey in discovering the immeasurable grace, mercy, and love to be found in a personal relationship with Jesus Christ.

As always, thank you to my husband, Jim, for putting up with my crazy writing schedule. My family is my greatest source of encouragement, and I praise the Lord for their patience. I am a continual work in progress, just as we all are.

Thank you, dear readers, for supporting authors of Christian fiction. It's my prayer that you'll find a blessing—a word, thought, prayer, or a verse of Scripture—in *Gentle Like the Rain* to carry with you on *your* life's journey.

Blessings,
JoAnn Durgin
Matthew 5:16

Theme Scripture Verses

Psalm 37:4
Delight yourself in the LORD;
And He will give you the desires of your heart.

Proverbs 2:6-9
[6]For the LORD gives wisdom;
From His mouth come knowledge and understanding.
[7]He stores up sound wisdom for the upright;
He is a shield to those who walk in integrity,
[8]Guarding the paths of justice,
And He preserves the way of His godly ones.
[9]Then you will discern righteousness and justice
And equity and every good course.

Proverbs 15:27
He who profits illicitly troubles his own house,

But he who hates bribes will live.

Proverbs 16:9
The mind of man plans his way, but the LORD directs his steps.

Romans 8:28
And we know that God causes all things to work together for good to those who love God, to those who are called according to His purpose.

Philippians 4:13
I can do all things through Him who strengthens me.

1 John 4:8
The one who does not love does not know God, for God is love.

Chapter 1

The landline phone rang. Again.

A sigh escaped Isabella Caccavale's lips. That phone would continue to ring until she answered. When she assumed ownership of Mahoney's General Store in Evergreen, Maine, from her Aunt Clara a year ago, she never could have imagined she'd be explaining the benefits of goat's milk soap to a customer three days in a row. So far, that had been *this* week's topic of conversation with Hattie Nelson. Next week, it'd be something entirely different.

A quick glance at the caller ID confirmed that, sure enough, it was Hattie. Isabella could tell time by the woman's weekday calls—five minutes after her favorite talk show ended. The older woman was recently widowed. If she could help by lending a sympathetic ear, why not?

Isabella grabbed the receiver before it could ring again. "Mahoney's. This is Isabella." As Hattie began today's rundown of questions, Isabella tapped her short, unpainted fingernails on the counter.

A bright flash of orange caught her attention. What was that? Seconds later, little Ned Kendrick peeked around the corner of BAKED GOODS, his brown eyes wide. Already a known prankster at the age of seven, Ned liked to manhandle the large glass jar of dill pickles on the front counter when she wasn't looking. What was the fascination?

I see you, Isabella mouthed, giving the child a mock glare while trying not to laugh. In a way, Ned's hide-and-seek routine had become a game between the two of them. The youngster's dad, Marty, sat on a large wooden crate at the back of the store, playing checkers on the top of a barrel with Hank Jergens, same as he did every afternoon. Those two men did more jawing around than playing the game, but they kept things lively and helped around the store if needed, so she had no complaints.

Ned darted over to CANNED GOODS and peeked out at her again. That innocent little face didn't fool her anymore. After a few store casualties, she was up to his tricks and needed to curb the boy's mischievous ways. To be fair, it was summertime, and a child that age should be outside playing, not stuck inside the store every afternoon. Who named a kid Ned these days, anyway? Well, young Ned *was* named after his maternal grandfather. Not to mention this region of the western foothills—with the White Mountains wrapping Evergreen in their majestic glory—was steeped in long-held tradition.

Would switching from a jar to a plastic container dilute the robust flavor and crispness of those pickles? If it didn't affect their quality, she'd make the change. Grabbing her clipboard, Isabella made a note to do some research.

All in a day's work.

Hattie's voice in her ear drew Isabella's attention back to the present. Today's issue? Apparently, the words *alpha hydroxyl acids* in the list of additives for the goat's milk soap had raised red flags in the older woman's mind.

Isabella employed her most reassuring tone. "Yes, Hattie, I understand your concerns, but remember how Marijane said your skin looked luminous after church last Sunday? That's why." She waited as Hattie made another comment before responding. "Well, yes, of course, that glow *could* have been from the uplifting worship service. I'm certainly not discounting that. Listen, I know the word 'acid' is a little scary, but in goat's milk soap, it actually prevents aging. It sloughs off dead skin cells and gives you that beautiful complexion. I promise you, in this case, it's a very *good* thing."

She'd never used the words *slough* or *luminous* in her life. *Just give me a job at the Macy's cosmetics counter already.*

Fourteen months ago, Isabella's days revolved around planning, coordinating, and executing top-dollar corporate marketing campaigns in Hartford. Now, here she stood in her little general store in Maine on a gorgeous afternoon in early June, listening to a widow's questions about goat's milk soap while keeping one eye on a prankster and a jar of arguably the largest dill pickles on the planet.

She'd never been more content.

Marty's laughter carried to her above the whirring of the ceiling fans. Hank was quieter, a single, never-married man in his mid-40s who chomped on root beer candy sticks and sang along whenever a Randy Travis or George Strait song played on the radio. His renditions were decent enough to turn the heads of a few women in town and the occasional female tourist. An amputee as the result of a work-related injury, Hank had his own issues, and the positive attention was good for his self-esteem.

Sing away, Hank.

Listening to more of Hattie's questions, Isabella flicked a fly from her white cotton top. When it didn't move, she inspected it more closely. That was no insect, but a small black ink stain. Oh, well. If nothing else, she'd become a laundry expert in the past year after discovering some of the excellent, all-natural stain removal products sold in the store.

"Yes, Hattie, but the goat's milk soap is also packed with essential nutrients and vitamins." Walking over to COSMETICS, Isabella grabbed a bar of the soap and read from the back label. "It repairs damaged skin, reduces lines and wrinkles, and helps prevent skin cancer. You really can't go wrong with it. I use it myself. What? No, I've never sold Avon."

Replacing the soap on the shelf, Isabella headed to the front counter. "Tell you what. Try the goat's milk soap for another few days and let me know what you think. If you aren't completely satisfied, then you can return it for a full refund. No questions asked."

Wonderful. Now she sounded like an infomercial.

Disconnecting the call, Isabella heard the roar of an engine outside. Her 22-year-old clerk, Tommy, flew around the corner. In his haste, he knocked over a sack of potatoes sitting on an end shelf. After hastily stuffing the bag back in place, he scurried over to the front picture window.

"Sweet Betty, would you look at that!" When he skidded to a stop, Tommy's canvas shoes squeaked on the wooden floorboards, making Isabella cringe.

She glanced out the window at the object of Tommy's affection, a red sports car that looked Italian and obscenely expensive. A Ferrari or Maserati, most likely. From her personal experience, fancy cars like that one usually came with an oversized ego attached.

"Probably a hotshot from the city," she mumbled. She'd seen enough of them since moving to Evergreen, although most arrived for the weekend, not on a sleepy Wednesday afternoon. Tourists often stopped in Mahoney's for a cold drink, to ask questions, or to use the facilities since the store was one of the first major stops near the center of town. At least most of them bought something as a courtesy, even if only a stick of penny candy.

Tommy whistled under his breath. "I gotta take a closer look."

"No problem," she said. That car was like the mother ship beckoning to Tommy. "Have fun, but try not to pester the owner with questions."

"Gotcha, boss. I'll be right back."

Time to get back to work. Picking up her clipboard and pencil, Isabella approached the quilt display racks. She needed to take inventory. Caroline Barnes had called earlier in the day and wanted four quilts in varying sizes for friends. The sale would give her a good start for the month. The handmade quilts were exquisite, each one a unique treasure of heirloom quality, made by a local mother-daughter duo. Most recently, Caroline had commissioned two baby quilts— one for Liesel Mattingly's baby son as well as for her own infant daughter's nursery.

Hmm. Isabella lightly tapped the pencil against her chin. Could the baby quilts possibly be a draw for tourists? The upper-crust New Englanders—and others—sometimes dropped a hundred dollars or more in the store. If she offered gift packaging and shipping, that'd be an added incentive. Another thought popped into her mind. Perhaps she could have Francie or Hilary make some lap quilts in the most popular patterns for seniors. That might also be a draw as a unique gift item. In recent weeks, some of the locals complained they didn't know what to get someone older who already "has it all." With the cooler year-round temperatures in Evergreen, the lap quilt idea had serious potential.

One thing at a time. She jotted a quick note.

A few minutes later, Isabella stole another peek out the front window. Tommy was engaged in an animated conversation with the owner of the car. Her employee was talking with his hands. Nothing new there, but the hotshot seemed equally invested. What was it with men and their expensive toys?

The man had strong, well-defined features, thick dark hair, and looked as though he'd stepped out of the Brooks Brothers casual weekend catalog—attractive and masculine in a well-groomed way that exuded urban sophistication. Dressed in dark slacks, he wore a white dress shirt rolled on his forearms, and his yellow tie was loosened at the collar. From what she could tell, he was medium height with broad shoulders that tapered to a trim waist. Expensive black shades covered his eyes.

City slicker all right. *Buff* city slicker, but whatever.

If he actually decided to step inside the store, she'd offer him a refreshing drink, suggest one of her highest-priced items, and then send him on his way. The likeliest scenario was that he needed directions to The Evergreen Inn, the town's most luxurious overnight accommodations, three miles to the north. The inn hosted a lot of meetings and conventions in the summer months. Ten to one, he was a registered guest.

She wondered if his car boasted personalized license plates. These types of cars generally did. Holding the clipboard against her chest, Isabella inched closer to the window. Massachusetts plate. *Top Dog.* Yep. Totally pretentious.

Aunt Clara's words popped into her mind. "Only the Lord can judge a man's heart." Of course, at the time she'd been referring to Tristan the Traitor. "Like everything else, learn from it and move on," Clara advised after Isabella's monumental breakup with Tristan, both personal *and* professional. "Trust the Lord to guide you because He knows the desires of your heart," she'd said. Part of the fun is seeing how He works."

"Go away, Aunt Clara. Not now," Isabella mumbled. Life wasn't always full of roses and never-ending happiness. Another sigh slipped past her lips. The big 3-0 loomed six months from now, and her dream of having a husband and baby by that milestone wasn't happening anytime soon.

Isabella's gaze fell on a cross-stitch sampler hanging above the front door. *Proverbs 16:9. The mind of man plans his way, but the Lord directs his steps.*

"Okay, I get your point, Lord." Now she was talking to herself? With every passing minute, she was becoming more like Aunt Clara. Scary thought. Eccentricity wasn't a bad thing, but it somehow seemed more endearing in a person of advanced age.

Against her better judgment, Isabella took another peek at the stranger. She could appreciate an attractive man as much as the next woman. She hadn't been on a "real" date since moving to Evergreen—the kind with a little butterfly flutter in her belly where she hoped for a kiss at the end of the evening. Not that Isabella kissed on the first date—only with Tristan. She'd done a lot of "firsts" she shouldn't have with that man. And not that she needed an excuse to ogle the stranger. She was single, and he appeared to be single—no wedding ring—so what could it hurt to appreciate him? The man was only passing through town, after all.

Still, everything about this guy outside the front window of Mahoney's practically screamed *I have a great life and want everyone to know it*. She was well-acquainted with the type.

No, thanks. Time to get back to work.

With renewed focus, Isabella checked off the newest quilt on the inventory list. Another flash of orange near the front counter caught her attention.

Oh, no. Ned! Sure enough, that kid had his arms wrapped around the large jar of pickles. Her eyes widened as the little hoodlum-in-training tugged it closer to the edge of the counter. Glancing over one shoulder, he gave her a *will I, or won't I?* grin.

"Step away from the jar, Ned." Staring him down, Isabella forced as much authority as she could into her voice. She'd show him, the little troublemaker. Marty's voice carried to her from the back of the store. Calling for him now would be a lost cause. Not enough time.

Ned inched the jar along the counter again, making her growl under her breath. He wouldn't dare!

Tossing the clipboard aside, Isabella sprinted across the store. She could only pray she'd make it in time.

Chapter 2

By God's great mercy, Isabella managed to catch the jar at the same time it tipped over the edge of the counter. The wide-eyed boy jumped aside, and she staggered under the weight of the jar. Beads of perspiration multiplied on her forehead, and a sinking feeling soured her stomach, as Isabella fought to keep her arms around it.

She was quickly losing this battle.

The bell on the front door jingled. Within seconds, someone moved to the opposite side and slid his arms around the jar, steadying it. A male someone with a white dress shirt rolled on his muscular forearms.

Top Dog.

"Steady now. I've got it. Take small steps toward the counter." His voice was deep, a little husky. Unmistakably Bostonian. Not that it was a bad thing, especially since he was helping to rescue the pickle jar from certain doom.

Within seconds, the visitor helped her to carefully reposition the jar on the counter. He did most of the work, but Isabella wasn't about to loosen her hold. She'd need to find a new permanent resting place for that jar, but for now, this would do.

"Okay to let go now?"

Blowing out a sigh of relief, Isabella ducked beneath his arms. "I think so, thanks." Top Dog was taller than she'd estimated, at least eight or nine inches taller than her 5'3" height in tennis shoes.

When he released his hold on the jar and removed his sunglasses, Isabella met blue eyes tinged with a hint of gray. Intelligent, intense, and *weary* eyes based on the tiny lines sprouting from the corners. Even so, she figured he couldn't be much older than his mid-30s. A surge of empathy coursed through her. He must work too hard. She knew a little something about that. Hopefully, he'd get some decent rest during his stay in Maine.

Not surprisingly, Ned had disappeared again.

"I think he went into hiding."

Isabella glanced up at the handsome visitor. "Yes, well, so much for responsible parenting." She smoothed one hand down the front of her white top, thankful no pickle juice had spilled.

"Yours?"

Isabella shook her head, momentarily confused. "What's mine?"

"The kid with his arms around the pickle jar?" At least he didn't look at her like she'd lost a few brain cells, although she couldn't blame him if he did.

"No, he's—"

The bell jingled as Tommy came back inside. "Sorry, boss. I was just…" He shrugged with a sheepish grin and gestured to the red sports car.

"I know. It's okay." The need to scold her young employee evaporated. As much as anyone, Tommy had helped maintain her sanity since she'd taken over the store. He'd worked at Mahoney's since he was 16 and knew all the regular clientele and vendors. "Just be glad we won't need to scrub the floorboards to get rid of the pickle smell. That wouldn't be the best thing for business."

"Sorry about that, Isabella." Marty finally lumbered to the front. "Ned, get out here and show your face. Apologize to the nice lady." Best as Isabella could tell, the boy was hiding out somewhere between COSMETICS and HOUSEHOLD GOODS. That territory covered three of their widest aisles.

"Ned Thomas Kendrick!"

A few seconds later, Ned stepped around the corner of HARDWARE but appeared more chagrined to have been caught than genuinely apologetic. "Sorry," he muttered, staring at the floor. "I won't do it again, Miss Carnivore."

Marty collared his son and hauled him toward the front door. "You bet you won't. Wait until your mama hears about this. Come with me." He jerked open the door, making the bell jingle.

Isabella could hear Marty chastising his son as they headed up Elm Street.

Hearing a soft chuckle, Isabella eyed Top Dog with a lifted brow. "You found that amusing?"

"No, but for *your* sake, I hope your last name isn't Carnivore."

"Oh, that." She waved her hand. "My last name's Italian, and a lot of people get it wrong or mispronounce it. I don't even notice anymore. The names they come up with can be creative. Keeps life interesting." Her words slowed on that last part. Why was she telling him this?

"I'm sure it does." He tugged on his silk necktie, untying the knot with practiced fingers. Sliding the tie away from his shirt, he neatly folded it and placed it on the counter beside his sunglasses. "Ever try giving that boy a book to read?" After unfastening the top button of his shirt, he leaned both elbows on the front counter. Whatever cologne he was wearing was deceptively subtle, not to mention downright appealing.

Isabella raised her chin. "The way I see it, keeping Ned entertained shouldn't be my responsibility." Why *hadn't* she thought of that? His suggestion was a good one. When she was Ned's age, her mom usually found her squirreled away in her bedroom of their rambling old house in southern California—or sitting beneath the backyard shade tree—with her nose stuck in a book.

"No, it's not your responsibility," he said. "But if his dad's a regular and doesn't pay close attention, you might as well offer Ned something to keep him occupied and out of trouble before he does something more dangerous than bring down a jar of pickles. You don't need a liability issue. Besides, I'm sure you've got more important things to do than babysit."

She watched as he crossed the floor and retrieved her clipboard from the floor. "I believe this belongs to you?"

"Thanks again." She took it from him. "We have a small selection of books, but they're mainly Christian-themed devotionals, do-it-yourself guides, biographies, a few novels. In other words, nothing for a kid Ned's age. We also have a coloring table in the back for the toddler set, but he's obviously outgrown those. I guess I could borrow a few books from the library and see how it goes. Miss Millicent would be able to recommend age-appropriate titles."

"Since you don't seem adverse to my suggestions, you might also think about adding a coloring table for the senior set," he said. "I've heard those are very popular these days."

So, this guy was the type who wanted to *fix* things. Or suggest ways to do things differently. That could be good...to a point. *Annoying* was another word. She didn't need him telling her what to do with her store. His scrutiny made her squirm a little. While his focus couldn't be called rude, exactly, it made her self-conscious.

"Let me guess," she said. "You're an entrepreneur."

He snorted. "Hardly."

"In any case, I'll take your suggestions under advisement."

"That's all I can ask."

She wondered how this man would react to someone telling him how to run *his* business.

"Now I seem to have lost Tommy. He's disappeared on me." A quick glance out the front window confirmed her employee was examining the car as though it were some kind of shrine. For Tommy, it probably was. As Isabella watched, he dropped to his hands and knees on the pavement and peered beneath the car.

The visitor chuckled. "Do you want me to go out and grab him by the collar like that guy did with his kid? Haul him back in here?"

"No manhandling is necessary. Unless you're opposed to his near idol worship of your car."

"Not at all. The car's meant to be seen."

Smug man.

Isabella cleared her throat. "I should probably thank you. You're making Tommy's summer by roaring into town in only the first week in June. We see a number of fancy cars here, but I can safely say that, hands down, yours would win the prize as the flashiest. No offense."

"None taken."

"How did you find Mahoney's?"

"I spotted your billboard a few hundred yards past the EVERGREEN CITY LIMITS: POPULATION 18,687 sign."

"It's 18,683, not that it matters."

"Close enough. I stand corrected."

"That billboard has been my costliest but wisest expenditure to date," she said. "I'm glad to know someone actually noticed it."

"You made a wise investment."

Isabella tilted her head, studying him. "Work in finance, do you? What brings you to Evergreen, helpful stranger?"

"No, I'm not in finance. I need driving directions."

That made her smile. "Of course, you do. I mean, sure thing. Where do you need to go?"

"Caroline Prescott's home." He shook his head. "Caroline *Barnes.*"

Isabella's instincts told her this man was legitimate, but why not have a little fun? "Depends on who wants to know. I don't make a habit of divulging personal information about the citizens of Evergreen."

"So, you *do* know her?" He'd tripped her up on that one.

"Of our 18,683 citizens, yes, I know her. Caroline is lovely and one of my favorite people. That doesn't mean I'm going to give out information to anyone who asks." She frowned. "No matter how helpful your suggestions are for keeping a little troublemaker at bay."

"Don't forget I helped you rescue the pickle jar from said troublemaker."

Said troublemaker? He had to be a lawyer. She should have guessed when he'd used the word *liability*. "Yes, there *is* that."

Straightening to his full height, he zeroed his gaze on her. "I assure you, I'm not a dangerous person. I only defend some of them," he muttered under his breath.

Isabella couldn't stop her quiet gasp. "Please don't tell me you defend serial killers."

"No." The word was clipped as he turned his head toward the front window. Guess he didn't care to elaborate. His profile was distinctive. His nose might be a little sharp, but he had defined cheekbones and nice lips—not too thin, not too full.

Stop that. This kind of thinking could lead nowhere good.

"I'm obviously not well-acquainted with the judicial system, but I draw the line at serial killers. Or people who defend them." Isabella bit her lower lip. Had she completely left her sense of tact behind when she'd parted ways with the marketing firm? Being politically correct had been a way of life. Sometimes it seemed as though her days in Hartford belonged to someone else's life, not hers.

The man's brow creased. "Glad to know you have such an inherent mistrust of lawyers."

"That's not true," she said. "I have nothing personal against lawyers as a species."

Those steel-blue eyes narrowed. "Dangerous people come in many varieties. You might be surprised."

"Well, I'm sure *you'd* know, but that topic could start a whole new thread of conversation, couldn't it? I'm sure you need to get on your way soon. If I may ask, what is your business with Caroline?"

"My apologies for not introducing myself." He offered his hand. "Sidney Prescott. Caroline's my sister."

Caroline was close to her older brother, Bryce, and he'd visited Evergreen a few times with his wife, Tiffany. Now that she thought about it, Isabella vaguely remembered Caroline mentioning the oldest brother—a high-powered, successful Boston attorney who worked with Bryce in the law firm started by their father. At the time, she'd surmised from Caroline's comments that she wasn't as close to this particular sibling. After talking with him a few minutes, she could understand why not. Intriguing though he might be, Sidney didn't seem especially warm and cuddly.

Then again, maybe *she* could stand to be a little less defensive.

With a smile, she offered her hand. "It's very nice to meet you, Sidney. I'm Isabella." Warmth shot through her when he wrapped his hand around hers. She needed to bury that reaction immediately. "It's Sidney Prescott *Esquire*, I presume?"

"Correct. From Boston. Caroline must have told you about me." He appeared pleased.

"No, not really." His grip on her hand tightened, and Isabella tried not to wince. She liked a solid male handshake, but this was overkill. "Is she expecting you?"

Sidney's semblance of a smile faded as he released her hand. "Look, I wasn't expecting the Evergreen Welcome Wagon to roll out the white carpet for me, but I'm reasonably sure my sister and brother-in-law won't turn me away."

"Well, that might be, but I hope you can appreciate that I don't freely give out information to the first guy who comes into Mahoney's claiming to be Caroline's brother, drives a fancy Italian sports car, and says he's a hotshot Boston lawyer." Isabella drew in a quick breath. "A person can't be too careful these days. I mean, with so much information on the Internet, how can I be sure you're not—?"

"Insane? A serial killer?" Sidney's eyes flashed. "For the record, I never claimed to be a *hotshot*." He parked his hands on his hips. "Exhibit A. Caroline is married to Seth Barnes. A min-er-a-lo-gist." He stretched out the word, saying it slowly, as though she were a child.

Pretentious and condescending to boot.

Okay, so maybe she had an issue with confident, cocky guys who flaunted their wealth.

He reached for his wallet. "Exhibit B." After flipping it open, Sidney held up his Massachusetts driver's license.

Isabella waved him off, refusing to look. "Put your wallet away, Mr. Prescott. I believe you, but I have one more question."

"Fine." Sidney returned the wallet to his back pocket. "Lay it on me."

When he looked directly into her eyes, simmering heat seared through Isabella. *No, no, no!* She *could* not, *would* not, be attracted to this man. She'd been fooled by one self-possessed, high-powered man. After that relationship ended—badly—she she'd vowed to never again be hoodwinked by a handsome, smooth-talking lothario. Going down that road could only lead to heartache, loneliness, and a tear-soaked pillow.

She'd learned her lesson. Never again. *Never.*

Give her a nice, quiet man with a good job who could generate dinner conversation. Proven mental stability would be a plus.

You'd be bored in a week.

Her friend, Joel Haddon, was attractive, funny, and a good man—a respected bank officer in town—but there were absolutely no romantic sparks between them. *None*, a truly tragic fact. But that wasn't *this* man's business.

"Isabella?" Sidney waved one hand in front of her. "You had a question?"

"Um, right." Whatever question she'd been pondering had vanished in the midst of her musing. *Think of a question.* "Who was…Queen Isabella?" Wow. What a stupid question. She felt like slapping herself but fisted her hand by her side instead.

"You?" He hadn't skipped a beat. How did he manage to keep a straight face?

Isabella laughed. *Good answer.* Apparently Sidney possessed a sharp wit hidden somewhere beneath the stoic demeanor.

"If you know Seth's a mineralogist, then I'll give you the benefit of the doubt. Most can't remember that word much less pronounce it. I've stumbled over it a few times myself. Why didn't you just call Caroline and Seth and ask them for directions before driving up here to Maine?"

An odd expression passed over Sidney's features.

"Wait a second," she said. "You don't *have* Caroline's phone number, do you?"

He visibly stiffened. "I have her home phone number on speed dial in my office. But no, I don't have the number on my cell. *Yet.*"

"I'm sure Bryce could help you with that. He was here in Evergreen with Tiffany recently." She hadn't meant to purposely irritate him, but based on Sidney's scowl, she'd succeeded in hitting a nerve.

"Point taken. I could also call my assistant, but I'd rather not. I'd also prefer to surprise Caroline."

"I'm sure *that* won't be a problem."

"Isabella, come on." His voice was edged with obvious exasperation. "Help me out here. What will it take to get my sister's address?" Grabbing the same sack of potatoes Tommy had knocked over earlier, Sidney lifted it as though it were weightless. "How about I buy your entire stock of potatoes?"

Seemed more of that sense of humor might be emerging. Twisting her lips, Isabella shook her head. "Nope. Sorry. Potato bribery won't work with me. Letitia Baldwin will be here soon and her husband, Larry, will be sorely disappointed if he doesn't get mashed potatoes for his dinner. *Sorely.* They're his favorite, you know."

"Then set aside a bag and mark it for Letitia and Larry." He stared at her for a lingering moment. "You're right. I couldn't have it hanging over my conscience that I'd deprived a man of his favorite mashed potatoes."

After replacing the sack of potatoes on the shelf, Sidney strolled back to the counter. Maybe she should give him directions so he could be on his way, but Isabella was momentarily enjoying his discomfiture. She'd tell him soon enough.

"How about I buy Caroline some homemade fudge? Surely there's not some husband who expects a slab of chocolate walnut fudge for dessert every Wednesday night? We went to the Jersey shore boardwalk as kids a few times. Unless my memory is faulty, that's Caroline's favorite. That'd make a good housewarming gift, don't you think?"

Sidney flashed a disarming smile that Isabella imagined would handily win over jurors and more than a few gullible women. That smile completely transformed his features, making him impossibly attractive. A Boston lawyer shouldn't have such natural, healthy color in his cheeks. Didn't most attorneys spend all their time holed up in their offices or a law library researching case studies and studying legal briefs?

Enough with the stereotyping. She had better ways to spend her time than speculating about some guy who'd parked his obnoxious car in front of her store and would only be here long enough to get what he wanted.

Play nice, Isabella.

Maybe more anger than she realized still lingered from the fallout of her relationship with Tristan. "Fudge might be a little cheap but, like you said, Caroline's charitable."

He shook his head. "When did I say that?"

"You said you felt sure she wouldn't turn you away."

"As I recall, I said *reasonably* sure." Their gazes locked.

Isabella pulled out the tray of fudge. "The fudge *is* delicious—some of the best in the region—and I'm sure she'll love it. Here's what we'll do, Sidney. I'll give you some chocolate walnut to sample. While you're enjoying it, if I can coerce or threaten Tommy to come back inside and mind the store, I'll dart to the back and call Caroline."

"No." Sidney stood up straighter. "Don't call Caroline. Like I said, I'd rather surprise her."

Isabella frowned as she cut a small slice of the fudge. Plucking a piece of bakery tissue paper from a box on the counter, she put the fudge on it, and then pushed it across the counter. "Then it would seem we have a conundrum here."

Taking the knife she'd left on the counter, Sidney cut off one small end of the sample. "I don't have a problem, but *you* seem to have one." He put the rich confection in his mouth and made an exaggerated show of savoring it. "Excellent. I'll take a slice for Caroline. Make it a really *big* slab."

"I wouldn't expect anything less." She'd half expected him to want the entire inventory of chocolate walnut fudge. After cutting a generous slice, Isabella transferred the fudge onto more bakery tissue paper.

The bell on the door jingled and Tommy came back inside as she wrapped the fudge and slid it inside a Mahoney's brown paper bag.

"Thanks for letting me sit behind the wheel, man." Tommy tossed the keys to Sidney. "Sweet Betty, that car is beyond awesome."

"Welcome." Sidney caught the keys with one hand and then pocketed them with a satisfied nod, appearing pleased by Tommy's fawning. "Who's Betty?"

Tommy shrugged. "Nobody. Isabella didn't like me taking the Lord's name in vain. Then I started saying Sweet Moses, but she didn't like that either. She didn't seem to mind Betty so much."

"Still sounds irreverent," Isabella mumbled as she replaced the tray of fudge in the case. She seriously needed to get out of the store more often. Now she sounded like Miss Millicent, referred to as *Maid Millicent* by some. The middle-aged librarian chastised anyone for saying anything she perceived as a curse. In Isabella's marketing firm, she'd worked in a perpetual hotbed of cursing the likes of which would make Millicent's ears curl.

Sidney pushed his fudge across the counter toward Tommy. "I need some directions. Want to help me convince Isabella?"

"You got it, buddy. Where are you headed?"

When Tommy reached for Sidney's fudge, Isabella laid a hand on his wrist. "No eating the customer's fudge while you're on the clock." She glanced up at Sidney. "And no bribing my employees."

Sidney and Tommy uttered *Yes, ma'am* simultaneously. Laughing, Tommy high-fived the other man.

"Tommy, did you officially meet our visitor?"

"Nah. We were busy talking about the car."

"In that case, Tommy Morton, meet Caroline's brother from Boston. This is Sidney Prescott."

Tommy grabbed Sidney's hand and pumped it up and down. "Nice to meet you, Sidney."

"Likewise." Sidney angled his head in her direction. "Tough boss you've got here."

Tommy grinned. "Isabella's cool. She keeps me in line."

"I have no doubt." Sidney gave her his best smile. He needed to stop doing that.

The bell jingled and Cynthia Pederson stepped inside the store. She untied the pink ribbons beneath her chin and removed her sun hat. "Afternoon one and all. Isn't it a glorious day?" With one hand, she fanned her flushed cheeks.

"That it is." Isabella felt Sidney's gaze on her as she exchanged pleasantries with the woman. A minute later, she summoned Tommy. "Can you please show Cynthia where we've moved the sewing supplies?"

"Sure thing. Right this way, Mrs. Pederson." Gesturing for her to follow, he asked Cynthia a question about her new car. Tommy was personable, great with their customers, and—at least for the foreseeable future—seemed to have no greater ambition than working at Mahoney's. In many ways, he was the ideal employee.

Isabella returned to the counter where Sidney watched her with a thoughtful expression.

"Seems we're at a standoff," he said. "I'd like to propose a compromise."

Isabella retrieved her clipboard and pretended to study the inventory. "I'm listening."

"Can you get away from the store for about an hour?"

"Excuse me?" She glanced up at him.

"The way I see it, the most logical solution for my dilemma, and yours, is to ride along and show me how to find Caroline's house." This man could certainly turn on the charm when he wanted. She felt his smile down to her toes.

"So, how about it, Isabella? Come with me?"

Chapter 3

Isabella made a chicken scratch on the inventory and then tapped the eraser on the clipboard. "Who said I have a dilemma?"

"You didn't have to *say* anything."

She increased her tapping to a rapid-fire pace and Sidney stilled the pencil. Taking it from her, he laid it on the counter. "I can tell you need to get out of here. It's a gorgeous Maine afternoon. Not too hot with a light breeze."

When she didn't immediately answer, he continued. "The fudge is great. Locally made?"

Now he wanted to be chatty? More than that, Sidney's apparent ability to read her with alarming accuracy was disconcerting.

"Yes. A couple of young mothers who live over in Bethel make it for us." Although grateful for the change of topic, Isabella knew he'd steer his way back to the main topic sooner than later. She figured a lawyer must be quite practiced at that very thing.

"What percentage of the items sold in the store would you say are locally made?"

Why did this man care? "Hard to say, but I'd guesstimate about forty percent, give or take."

"I take it you're the store manager?"

"Yes. I'm also the owner."

Sidney's brows lifted with obvious surprise. "Impressive. You seem fairly young to be the owner."

"Thanks, I guess." *Fairly* young? She'd gotten the same reaction when she'd first moved to town. Maybe she should consider dressing a little older, a bit more professionally. Still, this was a store with hardwood floors, ceiling fans, dust bunnies, and an unfortunate hint of mildew she'd need to seek out and eradicate. Her T-shirts, cotton tops, jeans, and shorts allowed her to climb ladders, scrub and clean, sort through stock in the backroom, and run around the store with freedom. Besides, she'd had enough of high heels and power suits in Hartford to last a lifetime.

"I meant that as a compliment." Sidney's comment broke into her musing.

"My aunt and uncle opened the store back in the mid-70s," she told him. "Uncle Phil died a few years ago, and then a little over a year ago, Aunt Clara retired and sold the business to me. She still lives in Evergreen and pops in on occasion to help out."

"Did you grow up around here? I'm not detecting the Maine accent."

"No. I grew up in California and ended up in Hartford before coming here."

"How long did you live in Hartford?"

She hesitated. "Why do I feel like I'm a defendant on the witness stand?"

"I'm sorry, Isabella." Sidney's cheeks flushed, and he had the grace to lower his gaze.

"Since I finished school," she said. He didn't need to know details.

"I guess I'm trying to figure out why someone would purposely—"

"Move to a little no-name town like Evergreen, Maine?" Isabella leveled her gaze on him. "Because after actively pursuing the corporate dream, I woke up to the fact that taking care of my soul was more important than padding my bank account. Not that my path is for everyone, but it's what I needed to do."

Nodding slowly, Sidney turned and glanced around the store. "It's a rare thing to find this kind of store anymore. We have boutiques and mom and pop stores in the city, but Mahoney's definitely holds its own unique"—his gaze returned to hers— "charms."

Isabella blew out a sigh. If he was flirting, she didn't want to go down *that* path, either. "I'm glad you can see what a lot of people take for granted. I need to make some updates to the store, but I've learned how to make it work for now."

Scooting over to the ancient cash register, she gave it an affectionate pat. "Take Cash, for example."

"You named the register Cash?"

"I didn't, no. If I had, it'd be a more original name, but don't you think it's cute? Uncle Phil named it, and now I can't seem to part with the old guy."

"Why would you? Cash is an antique treasure. You could always give it a place of honor and install a more modern machine. Don't tell me you still run the credit charges through..." With an arched brow, Sidney made a motion as though sliding a credit card through an old-fashioned machine.

"Yep," she said. "You have to understand the locals pay cash for the most part. Or we still allow them to write checks. It's normally the city sl—our, um, *visitors* that use plastic." Huh. She'd adopted the phrase *city slickers* without even realizing it.

"Do you get a lot of visitors in the store?"

"More than you might expect, especially during the summer months. Like I said, that billboard helps. We're also headed into tourist season now." Time to tease him a little. "Why all the questions, Sidney? Are *you* thinking of buying the place?" Isabella nodded toward the car parked at the curb. "I suppose if you sold that fancy car of yours, you probably *could* buy it and still have a decent chunk of change to spare. Not that Mahoney's is for sale, mind you. Please don't start *that* rumor."

"I'm not in the market for a general store today, thanks. As far as the car, it's not mine. It's a loaner from a dealer friend of mine in Boston."

Oh. She really needed to stop the premature judgments. "A *car* dealer?"

"Very funny." The corners of his mouth twitched. "Yes, an *automobile* dealer. As far as I know, Benito doesn't deal in anything else. If he does, I don't want to know."

"With a name like Benito, I wouldn't be so sure. I suppose a short ride in that borrowed jalopy of yours might be a nice afternoon break. One problem, though. How will I get back into town? Normally, I wouldn't mind a brisk, five-mile walk, but I have plans after work today."

"No worries. I'll drive you back." Crossing his arms over the back of Cash, he grinned. "Hot date tonight?"

Her pulse went haywire. "That's not up for discussion."

"I still don't know your last name. That information isn't off-limits, is it? Isabella...?"

"Just Isabella. Let's leave it at that." This man asked too many questions. And she'd been around enough to know the uptight lawyer from Boston was loosening up and...definitely flirting.

Be strong. Resist this guy.

"Have it your way." Sidney began to wrap what was left of his fudge sample inside the baker's tissue paper. "I could just ask Tommy, you know."

"Feel free. For that matter, you should have asked him for directions to Caroline and Seth's house when you had the chance. Could have saved yourself some money." Smiling, Isabella handed him a small bag for his fudge.

Tommy usually stumbled over her last name, too, even though it was on his bi-monthly paycheck. Most people didn't use last names in Evergreen. Liesel and Paul's four-year-old daughter was the only one who shared her first name, but they called her Bella.

"What do I owe you?"

"Nothing. It's on the house. From the Evergreen Welcome Wagon."

"Why, that's mighty neighborly of you."

"I'd say it's more like I'm a pushover."

He chuckled. "Can I quote you on that?"

"No, you may *not*. I only meant you must be good at your job since you're obviously efficient at getting what you want."

"I don't know about that." Sidney's smile sobered.

"Let me rephrase." Isabella's cheeks grew warm. "You work very hard at getting what you want." Maybe that wasn't any better.

"I try my best," he said. "I also want to see Caroline. She's been a voice of reason when I've stopped long enough to listen. You've already called me cheap, so the least I can do is pay you for *her* slab of fudge." Retrieving his wallet again, Sidney whipped out a fifty dollar bill and slid it across the counter.

Isabella bit her lower lip. "I don't suppose you have anything smaller?" Making change for a fifty would seriously drain her supply of smaller bills. If needed, the bank was open for another hour.

In response, Sidney pointed to a hand-blown glass paperweight inside the case. "I'll take that blue and green paperweight."

"Good choice." The piece was a personal favorite of hers that Earl had picked up on Monday morning. After unlocking the case, Isabella placed the paperweight on his waiting, outstretched palm.

"Looks like expert craftsmanship." Turning the piece, Sidney ran his hand over its smooth contours and then traced the delicate swirled design with one finger. "I'm guessing this is also locally made?"

Isabella nodded. "If you look closely, you'll see a small heart design near the center. It's bittersweet, really. The man who makes these paperweights lost his only daughter to cancer a few years ago. In her memory, he puts a heart in everything he creates. It's become his hallmark feature. See? The heart's right there."

Her fingers touched his as Isabella pointed to the heart. How could that brief touch make her senses come alive? Crazy, but they did. Embarrassed by her short, unpainted fingernails, Isabella was thankful she'd at least scrubbed beneath them earlier that morning.

"It's like his father's heart—his *love* for his daughter—carries on in each of the pieces he creates." She turned the paperweight to show Sidney the bottom. "The paperweight is also signed and dated."

"So, as far as you know, Caroline hasn't seen this particular piece yet?"

"Not that I'm aware of since we just got it in earlier this week." What made her think Sidney would be interested in a story like that? This man dealt in facts, not sentimentality. Moving over to Cash, Isabella rang up the sale and counted out his change.

"How old?"

Isabella shook her head. "I'm sorry. What?"

"How old was the man's daughter when she died?"

"I don't know for sure, but I think she was in her early twenties. Would you like the paperweight wrapped?"

"That's not necessary." As Sidney pocketed the change, he appeared lost in thought. "Do you have a gift bag?"

"Yes, but the paperweight's heavy. I wouldn't want it to fall through the bottom and fall on your big toe or anything. I should have a sturdy box for it. Let me check." She held up one finger. "Hold tight. I'll be back in just a minute."

"I'm holding. Take your time. I'll…count pickles or something."

Did I really mention his big toe?

Isabella walked into the backroom, mentally willing her pulse to slow. She scanned the long rows of cluttered shelves, making a mental note to do some more organizing. She'd improved the hodgepodge this room had been since taking over the store, but she had a long way to go. After rummaging around on a shelf, Isabella selected a plain white gift box.

"Does Caroline shop here often?" Sidney said when she returned to the front counter.

"Once or twice a week on average. Friday's the day she usually stops by since she comes into town and has lunch with her friend, Liesel Mattingly." After peeling the price tag from the bottom, Isabella wrapped the paperweight in tissue paper. Sidney watched as she packaged the gift and affixed a gold oval Mahoney's General Store sticker.

"Liesel's the woman from Landon's? The bed and breakfast here in town?"

"That's right." Isabella began to tie a maroon satin bow around the gift box. "Liesel's the daughter of the owners. Caroline and Seth were both staying at Landon's when they first met a few years ago, the weekend Liesel got married. Liesel's folks retired and moved away, and now Liesel and her husband, Paul, run Landon's."

Finished with the bow, she nodded. "All done. Sorry to go into all that. I'm sure that's probably old information to you."

"It's not, although I know Caroline holds great affection for Evergreen and the people here." A slight frown creased Sidney's forehead. "Guess I have some catching up to do. Tell me, what's Caroline's favorite thing to buy in the store?"

"She's my best customer for the handmade quilts." Isabella caught his expression. "Please don't tell me you want to buy a quilt now? You *really* don't need to do that."

"Why not? I don't know how much they cost, but I'm thinking it'd be a good sale for you." This man had probably never asked the cost of anything in his life.

"I'm sure she'll be perfectly fine with the fudge and the paperweight. And I don't need your—"

"I don't consider your general store a charity case, Isabella. Nor am I attempting to throw my money around to buy my way back into my sister's affections." Sidney's gaze settled on her. "I might stay longer than a few days in Evergreen. In that case, I'll need a bigger, more appropriate gift. Something lasting and meaningful. You said she loves the quilts, so that'd fit the bill nicely."

"I'm sure Caroline won't expect anything other than an explanation for showing up unannounced on her doorstep." *Back* into her affections? What had this man done?

"Let me get this straight. Are you *trying* to discourage me from dropping serious money here?" Isabella couldn't tell whether he was more irritated or incredulous.

"I certainly won't stop you if that's what you want, but I have a suggestion."

Sidney squared his shoulders, those very *broad* shoulders. "I'm listening."

"Why don't you start with the paperweight and, if you're still in town next week, come back then and pick out a quilt? As a parting *thank you for your hospitality* gift." She lowered her gaze. "Something like that."

Not a chance this guy would last until Sunday. He'd be stir crazy after a good night's rest.

The corners of Sidney's mouth curled. "Challenge accepted. I'm going to prove you wrong, Isabella."

She met his gaze. "You can't know possibly what I'm thinking."

"I've got a pretty good idea. I can read people well. It's my job."

Isabella suppressed her smirk. "If that's true, then you'll understand that Caroline will place more importance on the opportunity to spend quality time with you. No matter how long you're staying. Exactly how *much* time are you talking?"

Be nice, Isabella. She hadn't meant to sound rude to a paying customer. Sidney's reasons for coming to Evergreen, or how long he planned to stay, were absolutely none of her concern.

"Depends."

She should have known a lawyer would come up with such an ambiguous answer.

"I'm aware it's none of my business, but I'm sure a Top Dog attorney from Boston can't take too much time away from his important clients and cases." Just because she considered him a bit arrogant didn't mean she had the right to be smug. If she were honest, this was the first man she'd allowed herself to be attracted to since she'd left Hartford. The problem was, did it have to be *this* guy?

"I've turned over my current cases to my trusted partners, including Bryce. He's more than capable, not to mention willing." Sidney beckoned for her to come closer. "I'll tell you a secret."

"What's that?" Isabella inched nearer to the counter.

His lips, so close, warmed her skin. A shiver ran through her.

"I'm running away from home."

Chapter 4

Isabella stared at Sidney. "I see." But she didn't, not really. What did running away from home mean to a man like this? She didn't know him, knew nothing about his life. She couldn't help but be curious. He seemed to have it all, so why would he want to leave it all behind? Surely he was joking?

You did the same thing.

Isabella's lovable but slightly dotty Aunt Clara had marched into her Hartford, Connecticut marketing firm in early April last year. Clutching her handbag with both hands, dressed in her Sunday best, Clara announced, "God told me it's time to sell the store, and I should sell it to *you*, Isabella."

Although Aunt Clara quoted her a decent price, why would Isabella *want* to sell her interest in the marketing firm she co-owned, jeopardize a solid relationship with a wonderful man, and leave her beautiful brownstone to move to a little town in Maine? No matter how quaint and charming, Evergreen might as well be Mayberry. Had Aunt Clara gone off her rocker for good this time?

Besides that, Clara had *five* children. Surely one of Isabella's cousins would want to take over their parents' store? She'd thanked Aunt Clara for the gracious offer, treated her to an early dinner at one of Hartford's finest restaurants—where she'd tactfully turned her down—and then sent her on her merry way back to Evergreen.

In an ironic twist, Tristan—in his best placating, coaxing tone—had convinced her to reconsider. "Help your aunt out, Isabella. She's older now and wants to enjoy her retirement, especially since your uncle is gone. Why don't you buy the store and keep it in the family? You can hire people to staff it, or keep the ones that are there, and it'd give you some fun weekends in Maine."

Tristan hadn't said *us*, but *you*, a distinction Isabella should have taken as a sign that her life was falling apart around her, but she'd apparently been too busy to notice. Within a month of signing the paperwork to buy the store, everything in her life had gone south. *Way* south. So, she'd moved north with a small U-Haul trailer hitched to the back of her Toyota Highlander and a *Maine or bust* attitude. In essence, what had started out as a lark turned out to be her opportunity to reinvent herself and start again. All before the ripe old age of thirty.

Sidney retrieved the gift box and two bags of fudge. "Let's do this already. Are you with me or not?"

Isabella didn't bother answering since he'd probably known the answer before *she* did. "Hey, Tommy?"

"Yeah, Isabella?" His answer came from HARDWARE, his second favorite section of the store after AUTO PARTS. They'd received new merchandise this morning, and she hoped Tommy was busy restocking the shelves.

"Can you handle things here for about an hour?"

"Sure. Longer if you need."

"An hour should be fine, but I'll call if I'm running late."

"Sounds good. I'll hold down the fort." Tommy came to the end of the aisle and saluted Sidney. "Hope to see you around town."

"Same here, Tommy."

Isabella darted into the backroom to collect her purse. It would be good for Tommy to take charge of the store for a short time. She'd left him in charge before but not during the middle of the afternoon. Not that it was a test but—as much as Isabella didn't want to admit Sidney was right—she *could* use a break.

She stopped halfway to the front door. "Before we go, would you mind helping me move the pickle jar behind the counter? Even though Ned's gone for today, I'd feel better doing it now."

"Good idea. I'll take care of it." Before she could move to assist him, Sidney set his purchases on the counter and accomplished the task in short order. "I'm surprised you didn't think of that before the near-miss."

She forced a smile. "Tradition. It's my only excuse."

"Maybe it's time for some new traditions. New owner, fresh new attitude, that kind of thing." Following her out the door, Sidney clicked a button on his key fob, and the doors of the sports car lifted in the air like a huge red bird raising its wings.

"That's amazing. I've never seen anything like it." Trying not to gape, Isabella was impressed in spite of her resolve not to be wowed by the car. As a general rule, she detested using the word *amazing*, but no other word seemed appropriate.

"They're called scissor doors," he said. "It's one of the car's signature features."

After climbing into the passenger seat, Isabella smoothed her hand over the luxurious black leather. "I feel like I'm in a James Bond movie and should be wearing a gorgeous, slinky gown to do justice to this car. With sequins and boa feathers." Tossing an imaginary boa over one shoulder, she laughed.

"That's a thought-provoking mental image."

She'd led herself right into that one. After she fumbled with her seatbelt, Sidney demonstrated how it worked and then made sure her belt was secure. Although she felt like a clueless country bumpkin, *he* didn't make her feel that way so much as her own sense of ineptness.

"Keep your arms inside the car until the doors are lowered."

"Sweet talker. I don't think anyone's ever said that to me other than at an amusement park."

With an amused glance, Sidney walked around the front and climbed behind the wheel. "Glad the car brings out your sense of adventure."

She should try to curb the silly talk although Sidney's personality seemed to inspire her natural flippancy. At the marketing firm, her sarcasm and sense of irony had worked to her advantage. In small town Evergreen, some found her amusing. Others, not so much.

After pushing another button, he waited as the doors lowered.

"How long has it been since you've seen Caroline?"

"Four months." He didn't even have to think about it. After positioning his sunglasses, Sidney adjusted his seat belt.

Isabella drew in a quick breath, mentally kicking herself for not remembering that the Prescott family matriarch, Eleanor, had passed away from cancer four months ago. Caroline, Seth, and little Ellie—two months old at the time—had traveled down to Boston when they knew her mother's death was imminent. At least Mrs. Prescott had been able to spend time with her only grandchild and namesake before her passing. Their father, Duncan, a well-respected attorney, had recently been moved to an upscale facility for dementia in the Boston area.

Compassion for the man beside her swept through Isabella. "Sidney, I'm sorry about your mom." Perhaps it was best not to mention his father.

"Thanks." The muscles in his jaws flexed as the engine roared to life.

From her friendship with Caroline, Isabella knew the Prescott family situation had been disjointed through the years. Old money, high expectations, and strained relationships did not make for an ideal family situation. The odds were high that the man in the driver's seat had not experienced the same kind of happy home life she'd enjoyed in California. Not even close.

"Ready?" Staring straight ahead, his voice was even and steady.

"As much I'll ever be." She needed to lighten the mood. "You *do* realize you're not an Indy 500 driver, right?"

"Yes, I'm well aware," he said. "We can do this one of two ways. You can give me the address so I can program it into the GPS, or you can give me the play-by-play as I drive. Your choice."

"It's convoluted, so I'll guide you manually. Have you seen those rural property deeds where the description says to turn at so many feet and mentions pins, trees, railroad tracks, things like that? The way to Caroline and Seth's house has a lot of twists, turns, and odd markers."

"Fair enough. Start by telling me which way I need to go from here."

Isabella settled into the plush seat. "You'll need to turn around, but don't make a U-turn." She pointed to the closest intersection. "Take the next street to the right, by the Grayson house."

"That's one thing I like about small towns." Sidney smoothly pulled the car away from the curb. "You probably know the names of most people in town and where they live. Dropping by to check on each other is considered neighborly instead of invading someone's privacy. People take each other homemade pie, sit on front porches, and talk. *Really* talk, whether it's about important things or nothing. You have church socials and town festivals and, except for the occasional drunk or scoundrel, get along well. You've got each other's backs and are there for each other in times of loss and stress. You mow your neighbor's lawn, collect their mail, and watch over their pets when they're on vacation."

Isabella found his observations spot-on for a city slicker. "You got all that from me telling you not to make a U-turn? And a lot of people in Evergreen don't take vacations."

"Why not?" Following her direction, he'd turned the car around and now sat in front of the stop sign on the side road.

"No big reason except they're content where they are," she said. "No reason to see the world when we get so many tourists, especially at this time of year. A lot of Europeans come into Mahoney's. They chat for a bit, tell us about their country, what it's like to live there. They show us photos on their phones and impress us with their romantic-sounding accents. Okay, from here, turn left," she told him. "Then go about a mile, and I'll tell you where to turn again. You've never come to Evergreen since Caroline moved up here? Not even for a weekend visit?"

"Nope."

"That wasn't a criticism. And you seem to have us pegged, Sidney."

"Nothing that wouldn't describe a few hundred other small towns across America."

She frowned. "That comment totally negated the nice things you just said. If I didn't know better, I'd say—deep down—you like the idea of living in a small town."

"I guess you could say I harbor affection for them. Enough to want to visit, anyway. At the moment, I'm wondering how long it'll take me to get an itch for the city."

He earned points for being honest. "You mean how long it'll take you to *scratch* that itch?" Although she couldn't see behind those dark shades, Isabella sensed she had *Sidney* pegged. As much as she could with someone she'd only met a short time before. "My guess is you won't last until Sunday."

"You're a betting woman, are you?"

"No, not at all. I'm only wondering how much thought you gave to your whole *running away from home* plan." She glanced at her watch—3:45. She'd met Sidney within the last forty minutes, and now she was riding in a car with the man. A serial killer wouldn't ride down the main street of town in a flashy red car, would he?

"Then I guess you don't want to know the wager Tommy made with me."

Trying not to squirm, Isabella stared straight ahead. "You're right. I don't want to know." She stopped her foot from tapping the floorboard. "Although it sounds like you're a betting man."

"I work too hard to squander my money on trivial wagers. I should clarify and call it a challenge since it doesn't involve the transfer of money."

"You seem to like challenges, and I suppose calling it that does help it go down a little easier," she said. *Change the subject. Fast.* "So, what kind of car are we riding in today?"

"Lamborghini. Aventador."

"Aventador," she repeated. "My bad. And here I thought it was a plain old Ferrari or Maserati. Tell me something. Why *do* men like cars like this? Speed, flash, ego, to get a woman? Be honest."

"In some cases, all of the above, I imagine."

"I didn't ask about some cases. I'm asking *you*, Sidney."

He glanced her way for a few seconds before returning his attention to the road. "In my case, it was a nice way to escape Boston."

She shook her head. "No wonder you're a lawyer."

Sidney chuckled. "Be glad this isn't an Egoista."

Isabella leaned back against the luxurious leather headrest. "There's actually a car with that name?"

"Yes, believe it or not. It's a concept car developed for the fiftieth anniversary of Lamborghini." Sidney's gaze darted to her. "If this *were* an Egoista, you wouldn't be sitting with me."

She shifted in her seat. "I appreciate the vote of confidence. You sure know how to deflate a girl's ego...um, make that self-confidence."

"The Egoista is a one-seater car with a cockpit like you'd find in a fighter jet. You have to remove the steering wheel to get in and out. In other words, there wouldn't be room for you.

"Ah, good to know. I thought you were insulting me."

"Sorry," he said. "I should have explained."

"I may not be familiar with many Italian words, but I can guess the name Egoista must have something to do with ego."

"You'd be right. Selfish. Extreme hedonism."

"Lovely. And what does Aventador mean? Or should I not ask?"

"Believe it or not, it's named after a valiant bull in the ring in Zaragoza, Spain in 1993. The Aventador starred in one of those Transformers movies."

"Interesting that a car's named after a bull. Was it the good movie car or the bad car?"

"Antagonist."

"Figures since it's big, bad, and…intimidating."

Sidney shook his head. "I find it hard to believe that you'd find much of anything intimidating, especially a car."

"I find it difficult to believe you know so much about this car if it's not yours." She glanced his way. "And I'm not intimidated easily. I was speaking more in general terms."

"Like the lawyer species comment."

She shot him a wry grin. "Do you think it's possible we understand one another, Sid?"

"Perhaps. If you don't mind, I prefer Sidney." She could tell he was watching her behind those dark sunglasses.

"What's your middle name?"

"Jefferson."

"Sounds fitting. Very patriotic. Landon's Bed and Breakfast is on the right." Isabella pointed to the lovely Queen Anne style Victorian home as he stopped at the corner stop sign. They'd already passed the center of town with the post office, Town Hall, and Evergreen Park with its small gazebo.

He pointed to the top of the three-story structure. "What are those pointy gold things on the roof called?"

"With all of Landon's charm—wraparound porch, lovely stained glass windows, turrets, balconies, beautiful landscaping—you want to know the name of the *pointy gold things*?"

"As far as I know, they're called finials," she said. "That's spelled f-i-n-i-a-l-s."

"I didn't ask how to spell it. I asked what they were." Was that another chuckle?

"And I was firing back at you for the min-er-a-lo-gist thing. So, since I can tell you're dying to tell me, what's this challenge with Tommy all about?"

"I'm thinking it might be more fun to make you wait."

"Stinker," she said. "Continuing with our tour, Landon's original structure dates back to 1856."

"History buff?"

"I like town history as much as the next person, but the welcome sign above the front door also says so."

He adjusted a setting on the electronic control panel. "The temperature all right for you?"

"Yes, but could you maybe lower the windows, or the roof, whatever this car does? Seems a crime to waste all this lovely fresh air."

"I've got an even better idea." When Sidney pressed something else on the control panel, the top of the car lifted up and away from them.

"Up, up, and away!" She ignored his cocked brow.

As he pulled the car into the intersection, Isabella waved at a few members of Evergreen Community Church. She slid down a little in the seat. Crabby old Mrs. Wintersby probably thought she'd sold her soul to the devil and was now riding in his car.

"Where's a pitchfork when you need one?" she murmured under her breath, thankful for the noise of the engine. Why did the expensive cars have to be so loud? "Borrowed or not, Tommy was right. This is one awesomely cool car, but can you eject me if I get on your nerves?"

"Not that I know of, but I haven't investigated all its features…yet." Lifting his sunglasses, Sidney glanced at her for a few seconds, waggling his brows.

Isabella grinned. "I'd better be careful then." She shifted in the seat to face him more directly. "Does Vinnie even know you've driven this car up here to Maine?"

"*Benito*, and yes, he knows."

"Let me guess. You defended Benito in a court trial and now he owes Sidney Jefferson Prescott, Esquire *big* time." Isabella shifted in the seat to face him. "Am I even close?"

"That's not up for discussion. Benito has my Mercedes in his shop for repairs. It wasn't ready, so this is what he gave me." He shrugged and glanced her way. "Would *you* have refused?"

"I get the client confidentiality thing. And no, I probably wouldn't have refused, but I hope you've got great insurance. Did you tell him you're running away from home before or *after* he handed over the keys?"

"Wouldn't have mattered, anyway. He looks at it as advertising."

So, Sidney's earlier statement about how the car was intended to be seen was the literal truth? *Point taken, Lord.*

Isabella shook her head. "A word of advice? You'd better slow down if you don't want Hamilton Watters to come after you. Nice man, but he has a habit of targeting out-of-state drivers."

"If you're talking about *Sheriff* Watters, I already made his acquaintance on the way into town. And law enforcement officials need to be more than a *nice guy*."

"What'd he clock you at?"

"He didn't. He pulled me over to ask about the Aventador. Notice I've been going the posted speed limit and crawled through town. I wasn't sure this car could even go that slow, but I'm a law-abiding citizen."

"Meaning you must have cops in your back pocket?" Isabella waved to a few townspeople who openly gawked at the sight of her in the car. Oh, yes, the gossips would be abuzz tomorrow.

Sidney grunted. "I'll pretend you didn't say that, Miss *No Last Name*. You don't know me well enough to insult me. Meaning I man up to my faults and pay my own speeding tickets. But I didn't get one this time. Don't go spreading rumors about the new guy in town."

"My lips are sealed," she said. "I like a man who can admit his faults. With a car like this, you must have been a target of New England's finest during your three-hour drive up the I-95 corridor. Or did it only take you two hours?"

What *was* it about this guy that made her want to challenge him?

"I'm sure. Okay, my turn. I have a question for you."

"Go for it." Isabella waved to Hattie Nelson walking her black and white toy poodles. "Hey, Hattie!" She giggled when the woman's jaw dropped.

"Why are you working at Mahoney's instead of hiring a full-time staff while you hone your painting talents?" Sidney said.

She balked. "How do you know about my…honing?"

"I saw an easel in the backroom with a painting sitting on it. Granted, I'm no expert, but it looked like the work of a talented artist." When she continued to stare at him, he shrugged. "Can I help it if it's within sight of the front counter? I wasn't snooping, Isabella. You ask me—and I realize you didn't—I think subconsciously you're waiting for a famous painter to come into Mahoney's and discover you."

Isabella mock gasped. "And take me away from Evergreen? No way! You have an overactive imagination for a lawyer, I'll give you that much. That still doesn't explain how you know *I'm* the artist."

"Ever been a defendant in a criminal trial?"

"Of course not. Have you?"

He chuckled. "You'd cave and admit you did it in the first five minutes on the witness stand. At least you'd save everyone involved some serious money."

"I'd never cave because I'd be completely innocent. You're kind of nuts, you know that?"

"Without a doubt. I'll take it as a compliment." Dipping his head, Sidney lowered his sunglasses and fixed his steely blue-eyed gaze on her. "You're quite fetching when you're all fired up."

"That's enough of that talk." Now the man was blatantly flirting? "I haven't even signed that painting yet. I'm only a beginner, and I could never make a living selling my work."

"With that statement, you admitted you've painted more than one."

"So? Why should that matter? Stop being such a…lawyer," she snapped. The unusually warm, early June breeze ruffled through Isabella's hair, tossing it about so that long, dark strands brushed across her cheeks. She searched the pocket of her jeans but came up empty. Usually she kept a hair elastic nearby to pull her hair into a ponytail.

"If Picasso could make serious money, then so could you. I figure a woman who's sentimental about a paperweight might be the sensitive, creative type. You understand nuance and…artsy fartsy things like that."

She smiled. "Did they teach you that in law school?"

"Some of it is common sense. I'm also a people watcher, an observer of human nature. Like I said, that's a big part of my job. So is playing amateur detective. I've also watched Caroline when she's worked on her jewelry designs at home in Boston. She explained a little about the process. I can't paint or draw, but I'm thankful there are those who can."

The Prescott family home in Boston wasn't just *any* house from what Isabella had gathered from her conversations with Caroline. Located in Beacon Hill, one of the most historic and exclusive neighborhoods in Boston, the area featured the backdrop of the Massachusetts State House perched on top of the hill. Caroline never boasted, but most people didn't grow up in homes with servants, tapestries, statues, and marble floors.

"I'm taking lessons from Toby Daniels, a local artist, although he primarily does landscapes," Isabella told him. "Toby works with

Caroline, as a matter of fact. If you stick around long, you'll probably meet him. She designs the jewelry and he makes the pieces. They're a good team."

"Glad to have you to fill me in on *Who's Who in Evergreen.*" Sidney followed her direction and made a left turn. "There's a passion inside Caroline that goes beyond merely doing something she's good at to make money. I admire anyone who follows their dreams."

"Is that why you're running away from home, Sidney?"

"I don't know what you mean."

"Sure you do. This is just my theory, mind you. I realize I don't know you, but I'm thinking you've come to Maine to discover *your* passion. Since it worked for Caroline, you're hoping that maybe it'll do the same for you. To see if there's something that makes you *tick* more than the legal system."

Tapping her fingers on the window ledge, Isabella lifted her face to the welcoming warmth from the sun. Maybe she'd pushed the limits with that observation. Using the word *passion* might not have been the best choice either. Ditto *overpriced* and *tick*. A large part of marketing was capitalizing on key words that garnered attention and potential sales. In everyday conversation? Not such a great idea.

Isabella glanced his way. "Are you searching for that ejector button?"

Sidney was quiet for a long moment. "I imagine you and Caroline get along famously."

"Yes, we do." So, it seemed he intended to avoid or ignore her theory. He owed her nothing, and she shouldn't have imposed her opinions on him. "I admire Caroline very much. She and Seth are a fabulous couple, and I'm blessed to call them my good friends."

"Good to know. Where do I turn next?"

"Oh, sorry. Turn left at Conifer Street. It's two streets ahead. As you might have noticed, most of the streets are named after trees. Pick a tree name and chances are good there's a street named after it in Evergreen. Once you turn on Conifer, you'll go for another half mile or so. I'll show you."

"Where do my sister and Seth live? The boonies?"

"No, just the high-end suburbs of Evergreen. It's a fantastic house. You'll see."

"I've seen photos," he said. "It looks like the ideal place for my escape."

She pointed out the front window after he turned onto Conifer Street. "See that"—she brushed hair away from her mouth—"bus stop shelter ahead? Right past that, you'll veer left at the large fork in the road."

Sidney didn't respond, so Isabella waited until he'd steered the car onto the narrow gravel road. "This leads to their house," she told him. "Stay on this road for another eighth of a mile or so. Then you'll turn left at the blueberry stand."

"Quaint."

"Isn't it? Just wait. It gets even better. After the blueberry stand, you'll go about a thousand feet to the peach stand, and then turn right. Then at the corn and tomato stand the Carlson kids set up last week, you'll take a left."

"What about the apple stand? Don't they have apples in Maine?"

"Yes, but apples are celebrated in the fall, especially at the town's Harvest Festival. After the Carlson's stand, then you'll take a quick right at the kissing booth."

"That's too precious for words."

Isabella laughed at his wry comment. "Hey, don't knock it. That's a new thing the local teens started every Friday night. It's quite popular and raises money for the local ASPCA, but the town council wouldn't allow them to set it up in town due to protests from some of the older, more proper citizens." She'd affected a haughty tone as she'd said that last part.

Sidney tossed a quick glance in her direction. "You're serious? There's really such a thing as a kissing booth?"

"*Egoista* serious."

"Huh." He scrubbed a hand over his jaw. "Any eligible ladies around the age of, I don't know, thirty or so, ever take a turn in that kissing booth?"

Isabella's pulse skyrocketed. "Not that I'm aware of, no." She didn't dare look at him.

"Why? The *proper* citizens of Evergreen don't believe in kissing?"

"I'm sure I wouldn't know." She squirmed a bit. "They don't want to risk the kids getting out of control in the middle of town. You can't blame them, really. What with all the impressionable children around."

"Come on, Isabella. It's summertime. Where's that adventurous spirit?"

"Welcome to Evergreen, Mr. Prescott. I hope you'll enjoy your stay here."

He laughed. "I'm sure I will. Are we there yet?"

Chapter 5

Through the beveled glass oval on the front door, Sidney spied Caroline. Barefoot and in jeans. He still wasn't used to seeing her so casual since their mother and Nanny Regina always dressed his little sister in designer clothes. Her naturally curly, blonde hair was loose and hung well past her shoulders, longer than he'd ever seen it.

She looked good. *Earthy*, as their mother used to call her. Mountain living obviously agreed with her. Ditto being married and the wife of Seth Barnes, mineralogist extraordinaire. That guy adored her and doted on their little girl. As well he should. Sidney could learn a few things from their solid relationship. He didn't know Seth well, but the blame for that oversight sat squarely on his own shoulders. The practice had kept him occupied whenever they'd come to Boston. After Mom passed, he'd withdrawn, preferring to deal with his grief privately.

But now? Now it was time to reconnect. Time to figure out some things. Time to get his life *right*. Maybe it was a mistake to think coming to Evergreen could give him answers. It'd worked for Caroline, so he wanted to try. He figured it couldn't hurt.

Isabella had been more accurate in her assessment of his motivation than she could know. The woman was almost scarily perceptive. She was also incredibly attractive. At first, he'd been more amused by her, but she was witty, bright, and fun. He could use more fun in his life.

"Sidney!" Caroline swung the door wide. "What are you doing here? I mean, what a wonderful surprise!" She looked radiant, happy, relaxed. Confident and self-assured. The epitome of the suburban mom in the remote woods of rural Maine. Slender as ever, she didn't look like a woman who'd had a baby only six months ago.

A rush of deep affection surged through him at her warm, spontaneous greeting. Opening his arms, he wrapped her in a bear hug as though he hadn't seen her in a decade, not four short months ago. Sidney chuckled at her surprised expression as she pulled away. No, it was more than surprise—shock was an apt description.

"It *is* you, isn't it?" Cupping his face between both palms, Caroline studied him.

"In the flesh." He kissed her cheek as guilt seeped into his subconscious. Add horrible communicator to his mounting list of sibling sins. Bryce had always been the doting older brother. Sidney had some catching up to do. Not only because he'd promised Mom before she died, but because—in spite of all his professional success—family was all he really had. Co-workers and friends floated in and out of his life, but Bryce and Caroline were his flesh and blood.

"You're family, Sid," she said, reinforcing his thoughts. "You're always welcome." Something inside him shifted, making him want to hug Caroline again and not let her go.

Stepping to one side, Caroline peered behind him. "Isabella? Is that you back there?"

Why was Isabella standing behind him? Putting one hand beneath her elbow, Sidney tugged her close to his side. He had no idea why he'd done that, and Isabella appeared none too happy.

His sister gave Isabella a warm hug. "So nice to see you, too. This is certainly an unexpected surprise." Caroline looked from one to the other of them with obvious questions in her eyes.

Sidney could no longer ignore the wet spot on Caroline's blouse. He forced his gaze upward. Give him a good court trial and he was perfectly comfortable, but a lactating woman made him squirm like a teenage boy.

And now you're Uncle Sidney. Since he'd been an adult, he hadn't spent much time around many kids below the age of puberty. He'd never changed a diaper or rocked a baby to sleep.

Why did *he* feel damp? Glancing down at his shirt, Sidney barely restrained his groan.

"Sorry. I was feeding Ellie right before you arrived." Caroline's lips twisted as she smoothed one hand over the small spot on his shirt. "Don't worry. You can't even see it. Besides, it's breast milk, and—"

"I'm glad you've embraced mountain living. Nothing's healthier for her. I get it. God's miracle food for babies. No further explanation is needed."

He ignored Isabella's soft laughter.

"I was going to say it'll wash out easily. I can take care of it for you later." Stepping aside, Caroline motioned for them to enter the spacious home. "Please come in."

"Oh, wait. I come bearing gifts." Retrieving the Mahoney's bag of fudge and the box from where he'd left them by the front door, Sidney handed them to Caroline. More like he held them out with a goofy smile as though he were a kid offering a gift to his favorite teacher.

"What's this?" Caroline took them from him with a curious smile.

"Chocolate walnut fudge and a paperweight. Both made locally. What more says lovin'? Go ahead and open them now if you want."

"My brother *and* gifts all in the same afternoon? I'm not sure what I've done to deserve this."

"Thank you for having the grace to smile when you said that. I'll try not to be too big a nuisance." Caroline stepped inside the front foyer and motioned for them to follow.

Isabella nudged him. "You don't do this often, do you? The gift-giving thing."

"Sure I do, but it's the thought that counts, right? You'll note Caroline *asked* what they were."

"Yes, but it was a rhetorical question," she whispered. "For future reference, the element of surprise is always a nice touch."

He abhorred shopping, and his assistant was a saint for doing it for him for birthdays and the holidays. Mikaela knew Caroline's gift preferences better than he did. Speaking of which, Mikaela had texted him three times and counting since he left Boston, but he'd ignored them on the road. Then he'd silenced his cell phone before going inside Mahoney's. What was the sense in running away from home if he was chained to the dumb thing? The world wouldn't end because Sidney Prescott didn't answer his phone for a few hours.

"Thanks for the tip." Reaching for Isabella's hand, Sidney led her inside. Unexpected attraction raced through him at the feel of her hand in his.

With a small frown, Isabella wriggled free from his grasp. Dropping her gaze, her cheeks flushed a pretty pink. Was she actually affected by him grabbing her hand? He found that almost laughable yet also sweet, old-fashioned, and...oddly appealing. Hopefully, he hadn't offended her in some way.

"Isabella was my guide to find the house," he said to Caroline. "Over the river and through the woods, past all the fresh produce stalls, and even a kissing booth. Left to my own devices, and surrounded by the mini-forest out here in the suburbs, I'm not sure I would have found it on my own before dark."

After closing the front door, Sidney followed the two women through the front foyer, past the living and dining rooms on the left, kitchen on the right, and then into a family room at the back of the house. Spacious and welcoming, the house was filled with elegant but practical furnishings in jewel-tone colors, wood and brass accents, well-placed artwork, and family photos. Caroline and Seth's home boasted none of the priceless artwork, sculptures, and marble floors of their childhood residence, and yet it felt much more like a *home* than their Beacon Hill mansion ever had.

By comparison, Sidney's penthouse was sadly impersonal and blasé. It wasn't a showplace, by any means, and he'd bought it for its prime location downtown within walking distance of the law office. Perhaps he wasn't invested because he didn't spend much time at his place, and he didn't entertain anyone. He'd hired a decorator to work her magic with lots of high-end pieces made from metal and astoundingly horrid colors. Served him right for giving her free rein. His home had been featured in some high society magazine— probably *Ugly Penthouse Today*. He hadn't bothered to pick up a copy.

If he had to describe it in a word, his home was *functional*. Served its purpose. Maybe he should add more…paperweights or something to give it more character. Or take the time to explore a gallery and pick out a painting that expressed his individuality. One with vivid colors.

Isabella glanced up at the high-beamed ceilings, tucked her hands in the pockets of her jeans, and rocked back and forth in her tennis shoes. "Isn't this house beautiful, Sid? It's like the perfect combination of rustic and casual elegance, wouldn't you say?"

He sucked in his cheeks. "Sure is, Izzy." That earned him a quick frown. He turned to Caroline, "You have your own mountain retreat here. Great place. Remote and cozy."

"Thanks. I'm happy you like it." Caroline stood beside an antique desk in one corner of the room and held the paperweight on her palm. "This is beautiful, Sid! I'll find a place of honor for it." She turned it over. "Ah, the heart."

"Seems you know about that tradition, too." He'd been too busy watching Isabella and hadn't noticed when Caroline opened the gift.

"We have a lot of traditions in Evergreen," Caroline said, placing the paperweight on the desk. "Another reason to love living here."

"Amen to that!" Isabella shot him a grin.

A low-burning fire crackled in the fireplace even in the early summer. With the massive evergreen trees surrounding the home, it was secluded and naturally cool.

Inching closer, Isabella prodded his right side with one finger.

What are you doing? he mouthed.

"Tell her," she said under her breath, "or I will."

"Give a girl a ride and she gets bossy. I'm getting around to it." Sidney cleared his throat. "The rock doctor around today?"

Caroline had been tossing throw pillows to one side of the sofa but paused at his question. "Seth should be home in about an hour. Is everything okay?"

"Everything's fine, but I've, um… Well, you see…" When Isabella shot him a look, he sucked up his pride. More than anything, Sidney despised being inarticulate. "I've taken a leave of absence from the law firm." He figured stating it as such would be more palatable to his sister than blurting out that he'd run away from home. After all, he was supposedly a grown man, not a kid.

Caroline visibly tightened her grip on a throw pillow but continued her work. "My first response would be to ask if Dad knows, but I guess that's more or less a moot point now, isn't it?" She glanced up at him, her eyes bright. "I know not to expect a change in his condition, but it's hard so soon after Mom's death."

"I know," he said quietly. "Bryce will call if there's any change."

With a nod, she motioned to the sofa. "Come and sit down. Let's talk."

Sidney waited for Isabella to be seated first and stifled his amusement when she curled into the far corner. He purposely sat in the middle of the sofa. Retrieving a throw pillow, he offered it to her. "Pillow?" Something about Isabella clearly brought out his latent flirting gene.

"I'm fine, thanks ever so much." She clasped her hands together in her lap. He'd noticed those hands at Mahoney's—slender fingers with short, unpainted nails. With her silky, long dark hair and soft brown eyes, Isabella was undeniably pretty, especially when she allowed glimpses of her genuine smile. She was the spunky, girl-next-door type. Although she'd mentioned school, living in Hartford, and working in the corporate world before deciding her soul was more important, she didn't strike him as the dressed-to-kill career woman. This woman had layers, and that fascinated him.

Most of the women he'd dated, always on a casual basis, tended to be aloof and distanced. Privileged. The female counterpart of himself, as weird as that sounded. No wonder he didn't pursue anything further. But Isabella? She was the kind of woman—the kind of *person*—he'd like as his friend if he *had* female friends. Most women didn't challenge or tease him the way she'd done almost from the start. Isabella No Last Name spoke her mind, like a gust of fresh air clearing out the musty cobwebs.

Perhaps he should focus on building relationships and developing friendships when he returned home. Did he have anyone he could *really* call on in a time of need? No. He didn't even have a friend he could call up and say, "Hey, wanna catch a movie or go grab a meal?"

You are pitiful, Prescott. No kidding. No wonder he'd run away from home.

Caroline took the seat opposite them in a cozy armchair. "So, how long is this temporary leave of absence?"

"Two weeks, three tops. I'm not exactly sure."

His sister's brows arched. "Forgive me, Sid, but are you going through some kind of premature midlife crisis? I mean, you rarely take a vacation day, much less a week off. And then there's that red sports car parked outside—"

"The car's a loaner," Isabella piped in. Nice of her to speak up on his behalf, such as it was.

"Thanks." He mumbled it under his breath, hoping she didn't say anything about a dealer.

"Welcome," she whispered.

Sidney blew out a sigh and sat back on the sofa. He'd ask Caroline not to call him Sid another time. How to answer her questions? "I needed a break, Caroline. I've been going at a breakneck pace since I joined the firm."

"No one would ever question your work ethic or dedication to Prescott Tate Burnesse."

"Thank you." A small lump lodged in his throat. God help him if he shed a tear in front of Caroline much less Isabella. He'd barely hit town and he was already getting soft? Perhaps he could stand to be more sentimental, but soft was totally off-limits. He had a reputation to uphold.

"Are you planning on staying here in Evergreen the *entire* time?" Caroline's green eyes widened. "I mean, it's fine if you do, but I'll need to wash the guest bedroom sheets and do some dusting."

Caroline did household chores instead of hiring others to do them?

"I might show up on your doorstep unannounced, but I wouldn't impose myself on you that long," he said. "I'd like to stay here a few days or at least until early next week if you don't mind. If I end up staying longer, I can always book a room at a local hotel provided there *is* one. I'm winging it at this point."

"You're welcome to stay as long as you need."

"You should probably check with Seth before you make promises."

That statement elicited a frown from his sister. "Seth will be the first to agree with me. Did something major happen to precipitate your trip north?"

"Not one specific thing, no. It's more a culmination of things over the last year." He figured Caroline could surmise his break from the law firm had as much to do with Mom's death and Dad's regression as anything else. He hadn't stopped long enough to adequately grieve. Who could say how long that would take? The way Sidney understood it, coping with grief was personal and different for everyone. Hopefully, he could do it in two weeks, three tops.

"Do you have any luggage?" Caroline said. "You *did* take time to pack, right?"

Her inadvertent pun amused him. "Yes, I definitely have some baggage. Sorry. Don't mind me." He settled back on the plush cushions of the comfortable sofa. "I have one suitcase and an overnight bag. I'll grab them from the car later. I didn't want to scare you right off the bat."

"Maybe some more of that fresh mountain air is what you need to clear your head and put things in perspective," Isabella suggested.

Sidney grinned. "Patience. In good time."

Caroline glanced between the two of them the same as she'd done on the front doorstep. "You two only met today, right?"

"That's correct. I saw the billboard for Mahoney's General Store on the outskirts of town and stopped in to get directions. Isabella wouldn't give them up until I promised to give her a ride in the car." Sidney felt Isabella's glare from her corner of the ring—the *sofa*—but she remained silent, surprisingly enough.

His sister smiled. "Well, I'm glad you found your way here."

"You look better than ever, Caroline."

She gave him a look of surprise, a reminder that he should pay attention and compliment her more often. He could probably learn a thing or two from Seth in that regard.

"Thank you, Sidney. I appreciate that."

To his regret, he hadn't given Caroline much encouragement in years past. Sure, he'd given her gifts of remembrance for her birthday or for achieving significant milestones—graduation from her private girls' academy, then Wellesley, followed by her acceptance into Harvard Law. Based on Caroline's expression at the moment, his expensive gifts meant diddly-squat compared to a simple but sincere compliment. Why hadn't that concept seeped into his mind before? No wonder she was wide-eyed with disbelief.

"How about something to drink?" Planting her hands on her knees, Caroline pushed to her feet. "Would you two like some huckleberry lemonade or iced tea? An Arnold Palmer?" She hesitated and gave him a pointed look. "We don't have any alcohol here, and I'll ask you not to bring liquor into the house."

Why did Caroline have to say that? Sidney tried to mask his frown. He crossed his arms over his chest while Isabella's gaze bored into him. Great. Now she probably thought he was a closet drinker if not a raging alcoholic.

"Not a problem. Huckleberry lemonade sounds great."

Isabella scooted closer on the sofa. "We have an excellent treatment center nearby," she whispered.

"I don't have a problem managing alcohol," he seethed. An irrational urge to laugh seized him, and at the same time, Sidney swallowed the curse word rolling around on his tongue. He'd never been a big drinker and rarely drank hard liquor. Anymore. Sure, he enjoyed an occasional glass of wine with dinner to help him relax after a grueling day, especially when he'd been in front of a jury.

Surely holy rollers didn't have a problem with wine? And he never got drunk. He'd done enough drinking in his undergrad days to last a lifetime.

Next subject.

"Does Seth golf? I'm thinking there has to be a decent course nearby."

"I'm sure you could convince him to swing a club with you," Caroline said. "The Evergreen Inn has a nine-hole executive course. That's the closest one. I'll have Seth call and get you a tee time for one morning early next week if the weather cooperates."

"A little rain never hurt," he said. "Just let me know." He hadn't been on a course in a few years, but hopefully, he could still play a decent game.

"Make yourself at home while I get our lemonade." Caroline nodded to the coffee table. "There's an album of Ellie's baby photos or feel free to check out the books if you'd like to do some reading while you're here."

Caroline had always shared his love of reading the classics. Sidney glanced at one wall with built-in shelves and smiled to see it was packed full of books. The library in the Beacon Hill house had always been his favorite room, and he knew Caroline felt the same way.

"How about *The Maltese Falcon*? I'd like to revisit that Dashiell Hammett book. It's been a while." The classic Sam Spade detective novel had been a mutual favorite with Caroline, but Bryce and Dad had preferred *The Thin Man*. They'd had a few mock "trials" where each side argued the benefits and drawbacks of each novel. Yeah, he probably shouldn't admit that to anyone outside of the family. A family of lawyers could be nerdy geeks of the highest order, but those times were among his favorite memories.

"I've got the book, but I'm not ridiculous enough to shelve them all in alphabetical order like someone else I know," Caroline said with a small smile. "Happy hunting." She'd never let him live that down. So what if he liked books in order by an author's last name? CDs filed by the artist's name? From his perspective, it made good sense and saved time in the long run.

"Care to join me in the kitchen, Isabella?"

"Love to." At Caroline's invitation, without a backward glance, Isabella jumped up from the sofa and headed out of the room.

Sidney had no doubt the conversation in the kitchen would be lively, but he'd never been one to stoop to eavesdropping. Rising from the sofa, he walked across the room to the bookshelves. Time to go on the hunt for *The Maltese Falcon*.

"Your brother seems nice." Nice seemed inadequate to describe Sidney, but Isabella was at a loss for a better word as they entered the large kitchen. Built to resemble an old barn, the room featured high-beamed ceilings and the latest in modern conveniences. Even a double oven that Isabella secretly coveted.

She glimpsed her friend's befuddled expression. "You okay, Caroline?"

"I think so. Just wondering if that's my oldest brother sitting in the family room or an imposter. I mean, he *looks* like Sidney. Sounds like him, too. But he doesn't *act* like him."

"How does Sidney normally act?"

"Classic Type A. Workaholic. In control. Strong. Capable. Focused." Caroline retrieved the pitcher of lemonade from the refrigerator. "Now he's talking about golfing and reading. What's next? Fishing?"

"That's not such a bad thing, is it?"

"No, not really." After opening an overhead cabinet, Caroline pulled down two glasses. "It's unexpected and surprising, that's all. Sid's not an alcoholic, Isabella. He doesn't drink much at all compared to the past. I'm not sure why I even said that except it's best to set the ground rules from the start."

"Understandable." In truth, she was relieved, although Sidney hadn't exhibited the telltale signs of being a closet drinker she'd noticed in others—ruddy cheeks, nervous mannerisms, defensive or exaggerated behavior. Then again, she'd known him all of an hour.

"I imagine Sidney's an excellent lawyer."

Caroline retrieved a third glass. "I don't brag on him much, but Sidney's one of the best attorneys in Boston. In the entire Commonwealth of Massachusetts, actually. Next to Dad, he has one of the sharpest legal minds I've ever known. He has amazing recall of case law, and his summations are becoming the thing of legend."

"Impressive." Isabella began to fill the glasses with ice.

"I hope he didn't say anything to offend you on the way to the house," Caroline said.

"Honestly, Caroline? I had fun and enjoyed your brother's sense of humor. I'm sure even brilliant minds need a rest and a change of pace every now and then."

"Agreed, but taking a leave of absence even for three *days* is completely out of character for him and doesn't make sense. I can't imagine what prompted him to do it. I'll call Bryce tonight and see what he knows."

"Sidney told me he made sure his cases were covered before driving up here. He also told me he'd run away from home. Exact words." Why did she feel as though she'd violated Sidney's confidence? She'd been friends with Caroline since her first week in Evergreen. Given that relationship, Isabella's sense of loyalty almost demanded she tell her friend what she knew. Right?

Caroline poured the lemonade into the first glass. "Running away from home? That's an interesting choice of words. Do you think he was joking?"

"How do I know? I barely know the man. When you have some time to yourselves, I'm sure he'll explain." Isabella glanced at her watch. "Speaking of which, I can't stay long. Sidney promised to drive me back into town. I need to close the store on time since I'm going to Manelli's Grill tonight."

"That sounds like fun." Caroline lowered the pitcher to the counter after filling the last glass. "Wait. Are you going with Sidney?" A frown flittered over her pretty face. "Sidney didn't already ask you out, did he?"

Already? "Of course not. I'm meeting Joel for dinner." Sidney had grabbed her hand for some unknown reason at the front door, but that didn't qualify as asking for a date. Or anything else, for that matter, unless it was some kind of weird mating ritual. Maybe things were different in his fast-paced world in Boston. She'd heard from friends in D.C. that a handshake was as good as an offer for sexcapades, and similar things from friends in New York. She didn't doubt that Sidney was a mover and shaker professionally, but that didn't mean he was a player. However, Caroline's question made her wonder.

Okay, then. She needed to curb the mental meandering, drink her huckleberry lemonade, and wax poetic to Sidney about the joys of

Evergreen. Then return to the store and hope Tommy had things under control. Pulling out her phone, Isabella glanced at the screen. No messages.

Caroline grabbed a small stack of cocktail napkins. "A word of advice, Isabella? Be careful with Sidney. He can turn on the charm, but unless he undergoes a personality transplant, he's not the kind of man to settle down with one woman. I can admit my big brother attracts women without trying, and—let's face it—he already roped you into bringing him out here."

"No roping involved. Really."

"As much as I love my brother, I wouldn't want you to get involved with him."

"Trust me, I learned my lesson with Tristan. He and Sidney share similar qualities. You don't need to tell me to stay away from him as anything other than a friend."

Caroline's pretty features relaxed. "Good. I'd hate to see you get hurt again, and I wouldn't want anything to stand in the way of our friendship."

Her mind was spinning after Caroline's warning. As much as she loved her, Isabella couldn't help but be disappointed that Caroline held such a low opinion of Sidney. Perhaps running away from home would be good for him. In the short time she'd known him, he'd already relaxed and smiled more, even teased her. She'd liked that more than she wanted to admit.

Isabella reached for the other woman's hand and gave it a quick squeeze. "Nothing could spoil our friendship." At the same time, she appreciated that Caroline hadn't started the spiel about how Sidney wasn't a Christian and the whole unequally-yoked thing. Didn't warn her about the dangers of playing with fire. It wasn't in Caroline's nature to lecture. As a general rule, she was low-key and soft spoken. That's also why she'd decided not to pursue a career in law, and Sidney was one of the best.

"Sid's also very good at reading people," Caroline said, breaking into her thoughts.

"Yes, I know. He told me." *Twice.*

"That's one aspect of his character that makes him such an intuitive lawyer. But it also makes me wonder if he's up to something."

"Like what?" Isabella lowered her voice in a conspiratorial whisper. "Do you have a vial of truth serum to add to Sidney's lemonade?"

Caroline laughed. "No, but that's not a bad idea."

Chapter 6

"Isabella, I can tell something's on your mind. What's up?"

Oh, dear Joel. Such a sweet man, a caring friend. If they *were* romantically involved, this would be the moment when he'd take hold of her hand, stroke his thumb over it, gaze soulfully into her eyes, and say something a whole lot more romantic than *what's up?*

A number of people in town couldn't seem to understand how two people of the opposite sex could be platonic friends without underlying sexual chemistry or physical attraction. What an old-fashioned concept. She'd been close friends with several guys in her undergrad and grad school days. Tristan once told her that all guys subliminally wanted a woman in the physical sense if they were friends. Perhaps that was true to a certain extent, but if a guy ever got too fresh or hinted at anything along those lines, she'd soundly squashed those ideas. Isabella set the ground rules. If a man didn't abide by them, and if that's all he wanted from her, then he could move on to the other side of tomorrow as far as she was concerned.

Since she'd shared dinner and a movie several times with Joel— Dutch treat, of course—there were still the inevitable whispers among the townsfolk. Until either she or Joel officially started dating someone else, those rumors would likely continue.

"It's nothing." Shaking her head, Isabella took another bite of her chicken cacciatore as if the simple act of consuming food could dismiss her thoughts of a certain man from Beantown. Who'd roared into town like a lion. Helped her save the pickle jar. Sparred with her.

It's only a pickle jar, Isabella, not saving the world.

Joel chuckled. "My dad always said that when a woman *says* it's nothing, guaranteed it's something. Spill it."

Isabella pondered her options while taking a drink of her water. Why *not* tell Joel? They mutually understood the terms of their relationship and genuinely enjoyed one another's company. It wasn't like they were biding their time until someone better or more marriageable came along. Well, maybe they were. But she could be honest with Joel and know that anything she confided to him would remain confidential, and vice versa.

"Caroline's oldest brother, Sidney, came into town today. He stopped at the store."

Joel swallowed a bite of lasagna, his favorite dish at Manelli's. "I heard about that, Miss *Cacciatore*."

She laughed and waved her empty fork at him. "Very good. That's a last name I haven't heard yet. So, tell me. What did you hear?"

"I stopped by Mahoney's this afternoon while you were out. All Tommy could talk about was *Sidney this* and *Sidney that*. I guess that car of his is really something, huh?"

"I suppose. Don't get too excited. It's only a loaner."

"Doesn't matter." He chewed another bite. "I hear you got to ride in it. What's it like?"

She sighed. "Like some kind of futuristic, big red bird." How many times would she need to tell the story? And why did Joel's question make her so defensive? Maybe because Caroline had driven her back into town, not Sidney. Logically, it made more sense, but she'd been disappointed. Her disgruntlement stemmed more from the way Sidney had casually waved good-bye and thanked her for her *guidance*. Then he'd turned aside as though dismissing her. Isabella bristled at the memory.

"You like this guy, don't you?"

"I really do, against my better judgment." She swallowed a bite of her roll. "He's intriguing, not to mention a whole lot better looking than I need him to be."

Joel laughed. "At least you're honest about it."

Isabella looked up as she heard a familiar voice close to their corner table. "Darren, please be a love and go get the car. I'll be there in just a minute."

"Yes, dear." Doting Darren nodded in their direction and departed.

Isabella leaned into a quick hug from the plump woman who carried the perpetual scent of roses, as though she'd bathed in a pool of the fragrant blossoms. "How are you, Barbara?"

"Fine, but I hear you're even better." The woman's grin was too sly for Isabella's liking. The grapevine in Evergreen was alive and well. Even in Hartford, it hadn't been *this* fast.

"Bring your new friend up to the store to meet me, and I'll give him a jar of fresh homemade blackberry jam," Barbara said. "I haven't met a man yet who could resist my jam."

Isabella sputtered after taking a sip of water. "You must be talking about Sidney Prescott, but he's not—"

"Oh my yes, is that his name? Pity that, but I hear he's quite a handsome man, a real alpha male." As Isabella coughed, Barbara paused as though seeing Joel for the first time. "Why, hello there, Joel. Forgive my rudeness, but I thought you were dating that sweet Nelson girl from Bethel. Imagine my surprise seeing you and Isabella dining here…together." Barbara moved one hand over her ample chest. "I hope you don't mind my chatting with Isabella about the new man in town."

"Not at all." When Joel gave her a wink, Isabella fought the inclination to kick him beneath the table. Apparently, he'd been keeping something from her. They'd promised to tell one another as soon as they'd met someone new they wanted to date.

"I only met Sidney today," Isabella said. "I'm certainly not dating the man."

"Well, then, you must forgive me," Barbara said. "I must have misheard. From what I know, you looked mighty cozy sitting beside him in that fancy red car of his."

Don't say anything. Not a word. If she knew what was best—and Isabella *did*—she'd leave it alone.

"I'm sure Darren is waiting outside, Mrs. Olander." Joel rose to his feet. "Let me escort you to the entrance."

God bless you, Joel.

"Aren't you such a polite gentleman? Thank you." Barbara swooped down and planted a quick peck on Isabella's cheek. "We'll chat again soon, sweetie. Don't forget what I said." She waggled a finger. "Blackberry jam."

"Oh, I won't forget." Although Barbara was one of Evergreen's busiest gossips, the woman had a kind heart. Her blackberry jam *was* mighty tasty.

"Okay, so what's an alpha male?" Joel said when he returned to the table.

Isabella grinned. "Barbara enjoys her romance novels."

They talked for a few minutes before Isabella broached the subject of the other woman Joel may, or may not, be dating. "Why didn't you tell me about that *sweet Nelson girl?*" Isabella hoped her tone didn't come across as accusatory or jealous. If anything, she'd miss Joel's company. Single men close to her age weren't exactly plentiful in Evergreen.

Before she'd met Joel, Isabella had dined solo in town a couple of times. Doing so had stirred up more trouble than it was worth. Before she'd closed her front door after returning home, the calls had started with well-meaning but nosy townspeople wanting to set her up on blind dates with everyone *but* the butcher, the baker, and the candlestick maker. They'd dredged up every so-called eligible guy from Bethel, Oxford Hills, and anywhere within a 50-mile radius.

"I was working my way up to it when Barbara interrupted." Joel's regret was obvious. "Why don't we finish our dinner and then go over to Barron's for ice cream? I can tell you more about it then."

A short time later, they sat side-by-side on a park bench outside Barron's ice cream shop on Elm Street, a few doors down from Mahoney's. The light summer breeze caressed her cheeks as Isabella licked around the base of her chocolate raspberry ice cream cone. The rich aromas of the flavored coffees from Java Joe's also sold at Barron's were inviting. She'd never been a coffee drinker, but sometimes they tempted her, especially when they wafted down to her store during the morning hours.

The fading sun lowered on the horizon as a few visitors strolled up and down the streets, poking in and out of the boutiques that stayed open late to cater to the tourists. The locals knew to shop first thing in the morning or late afternoon close to the dinner hour.

Joel spooned a bite of his butter pecan ice cream. "Barbara can be dangerous to be around. She's inadvertently let some secrets slip to different people in town. Not that I have any secrets. I *was* going to tell you." The poor man sounded genuinely contrite.

"No worries." Isabella licked around her cone again before the ice cream could dribble onto her dry-clean-only dress.

"For one thing, Barbara spilled the beans to Paul that Liesel was pregnant with Paul, Jr."

"That's a shame. I know Barbara means well." Isabella savored another bite, wishing she could push the woman's alpha male reference from her mind. Joel was so obviously not an alpha male, but Sidney? *Oh, yeah.*

"Some people run in the opposite direction when they see her coming," he said.

Isabella took a bite of her ice cream. "That's kind of sad, don't you think? I hope no one ever says that about either one of us."

"I sure hope not." When Joel took another bite of his ice cream, he inadvertently whacked her hand and dislodged the remaining ice cream from the cone. *Plop!* Right in her lap.

"Oh, no!" She didn't want to sound prissy, but the dress was a favorite and made from linen. Ugh. Chocolate could be a bear of a stain to remove. The saving grace was that it was a floral pattern. If the chocolate *did* stain, it should blend in with the rest.

"I'm sorry, Isabella. I'll be right back." Joel jumped up from the bench and darted inside Barron's. Coming back outside within the minute, he offered her a handful of napkins. A few floated to the ground as Isabella concentrated on removing the ice cream from her dress. Great. Her body heat had apparently managed to melt the ice cream even faster.

"Here. Let me help you." Taking one of the napkins, Joel fumbled as he reached for the hem of her dress. Lifting the fabric, his fingers brushed her thigh. Nothing indecent, but this little scenario couldn't look good. Although he'd caused the spill and genuinely wanted to help, Joel could be a bit clueless.

"Please, Joel. I know you mean well, but *I'll do it*," Isabella hissed under her breath, fully aware of the curious stares directed their way. She snatched the dress out of his grasp. "I'm sure the dry cleaners can get out the stain. Could you please go back inside and ask Becky or Suzanne for a damp paper towel?" Her cheeks burned with embarrassment.

"I'll get it. Hang tight." Taking the empty cone, Joel hurried back inside the shop.

"Lover's tiff?"

Isabella's heart raced. What on earth was Sidney doing back in town tonight?

"Everything's fine and dandy. Thank you for your concern." Isabella glanced up at him, putting one hand over her brow as she squinted into the waning sunlight. "I figured you'd be resting or sleeping off the effects of running away from home. Are you lost?"

"Not at all. Seth and Caroline treated me to a grilled salmon dinner at the house. I thought I'd take a stroll to familiarize myself with more of Evergreen, get the lay of the land. Plus it's good for the digestion." Sidney patted his stomach, drawing her attention to how absolutely *fit* he looked in his untucked red polo and khakis. Nice muscles in his upper arms, too, not that she should be noticing such things. When the evidence was in full glorious view right in front of her, what could a girl do?

You're hopeless, Isabella.

He laughed. "I realize I sound like an 80-year-old." The breeze picked up strands of his dark hair, tousling them. Especially with that five o'clock stubble on his chin, he exuded masculinity. The image Sidney presented tonight was quite different from the put-together, button-down, corporate image he'd presented earlier in the day.

Isabella liked this image even more. Less uptight. Casual. Friendly.

"All the way into town?" She stared at him. "That's no leisurely stroll. It's a five-mile walk."

The corners of his mouth lifted. "I walked fast, so it didn't take me long."

From the looks of him, he hadn't even broken a sweat. The man was in great shape.

"You do realize Evergreen's not exactly a hotbed of nightlife activity, right? Nothing exciting here to offer a man like you."

"A man like me? That's a curious observation."

"Come on, Sidney. Anyone can tell you're the type of man who lives life large."

"Define large." He crossed his arms over his chest. Oh, the irony.

Isabella rose to a standing position so she didn't have to squint in the sun to speak with him. "You don't do anything halfway. You need to be the best." When Sidney frowned, she knew she should stop. "Sorry. I can be a little presumptuous at times."

"Not to mention judgmental." He sounded more amused than offended.

She twisted her lips. "Agreed and point taken, counselor." She felt sure he'd already made some judgments about her. Whatever they were, she probably wouldn't want to know.

"I don't see anything wrong with wanting to give my all," he said. "I try to be the best I can, but I'm not in competition with anyone else. I've tried it, and that's self-defeating. Not worth it. I'll be the first to admit I've failed more times than I can count in both my personal and professional life."

Isabella nodded. This man surprised her with his candor. "Same here."

"Wouldn't you agree our failures make us stronger?"

"Yes, whether or not they're of our own making," she admitted. "But, to be honest, the failures really...*hurt* in the midst of it all."

"I know." They locked gazes and Sidney's eyes softened. "I was hoping Mahoney's was open tonight. That's one of the reasons I came into town."

"We close at six Monday through Thursday, seven on Friday and Saturday. Closed Sunday. Did you need something in particular?" Goodness, she'd spouted her store hours like an automated machine.

"I forgot shaving cream. And a few other things. Maybe I'll stop by tomorrow."

"I'll be there." She liked the scruff on his chin. Made him look more rugged, and maybe a little more like he fit in here in Evergreen. Made her wonder what he'd look like barefoot in old jeans and a T-shirt. But she'd hop all the way to Caroline and Seth's house backwards—on one leg—before she'd ever admit to those thoughts.

Joel returned with a handful of damp paper towels. In his haste to reach for Sidney's hand, he practically threw them at her. "Joel Haddon. You must be Sidney Prescott."

Sidney darted a quick glance in her direction. "Guilty as charged. Nice to meet you, Joel."

"Same here. Did you bring your car into town?" Joel pumped his hand up and down like Tommy had done earlier in the afternoon. "I've heard a lot about it."

Isabella hid her smile as she dropped back down on the bench. *Boys and their toys.*

"Afraid not," Sidney said. "I left the car at my sister and brother-in-law's house tonight. I'm thinking of scheduling a few showings later in the week if you're interested."

When Joel stared at him, stupefied, Isabella almost burst out laughing. "He's *joking*, Joel."

"Oh, right." Joel gave Sidney a fairly hard slap on the back. Sidney didn't budge. "Good one. You had me going for a minute there."

"I'm sure he'll be happy to show you the car sometime." Isabella gave Sidney a sweet smile. "Maybe even take you for a spin around town."

"Be happy to." Sidney winked at her or else a bug might have flown into his eye. At this time of the year, it was certainly possible.

When Isabella crumpled the used, damp paper towel in her hand, Joel took it from her, aimed, and tossed it in the nearest trash can—narrowly missing Hannah Martin as she passed by on the sidewalk. When he called out an apology, she waved and told him not to worry.

Joel turned back to Sidney. "So, how long are you staying in Evergreen?" What an eager puppy. Tommy and Joel should start an Aventador fan club.

"I'm not sure yet. I'm taking some time off work and enjoying the scenery here in Maine."

Isabella tensed at Sidney's words and avoided looking at him. Surely there was no underlying meaning to that statement, although with Sidney, anything was possible.

"Well, I'll be on my way now. I didn't mean to interrupt your date. Enjoy the rest of your evening." If Sidney had a hat, he would have tipped it.

"Nice guy." Joel watched as Sidney continued walking down the street, and Isabella couldn't help but look, too. A few of the townspeople called out greetings and shook his hand.

"Joel, why didn't you tell him we're not on a date?"

He shrugged. "I don't know. I guess I didn't think to say anything. Should I have said something?"

"Never mind. It doesn't matter." Isabella patted the bench beside her. "Time to tell me about Miss Nelson. Start with her first name."

"Oh, right. It's Cathy." For the next few minutes, Joel told her about the pretty sales rep he'd met in the Thai foods aisle at the new international market over in Bethel. Blonde, tall, willowy. His description of her highlighted the fact that Isabella shared no physical characteristics whatsoever with the woman.

Well, no wonder Joel only wanted to be *just friends* with her. That needled her even more since Tristan seemed to prefer the same type. She could easily envision Sidney with a gorgeous blonde on his arm. Is that what *every* man wanted? The dream of physical perfection?

"I can tell you like her," Isabella said as he finished. "You wouldn't step foot in a Thai foods aisle for the culinary delights alone."

Standing, he held out one hand. "I'll walk you home."

Joel was quiet for the four-block stroll. Normally he'd tell her something funny one of his co-workers or a customer in the bank had said or done.

"Are you thinking about your first date with Cathy on Tuesday night?" Isabella said to break the ongoing silence.

"No." He sounded preoccupied.

Joel didn't need to tell her. She *knew*. He'd been thinking about that dumb car again.

Men!

Chapter 7

Sidney's mind was on a conversation he'd shared with Bryce late the night before as he bounded down the steps and rounded the corner into the kitchen on Thursday morning. Caroline was sitting at the table with Ellie, a blanket draped over one shoulder and covering the front of her. Ah yes, feeding time.

"Morning." He headed for the refrigerator and grabbed the bottle of milk.

"Morning. I didn't expect to see you up this early." She sounded tired and sipped what looked like cranberry juice. "Did you sleep well?"

"Like a baby. Best sleep I've had in months. Maybe years. Is that an honest-to-goodness featherbed?"

"Sure is. Seth discovered them during his travels and hasn't slept on anything since."

"I haven't slept on one since our trip to Germany with the family years ago. Ellie get you up in the night?" Retrieving a glass from an upper cabinet, Sidney poured the milk and then returned the bottle to the refrigerator.

"No. She's been sleeping through the night for a while now. I couldn't sleep, so I got up and worked on a new sketch."

"Maybe you were thinking of the bum who unexpectedly showed up on your doorstep yesterday? Wondering what to do with him?" He took a drink of his milk and then chuckled. "Or how to get rid of him."

Caroline smiled through her yawn. "Don't flatter yourself. I'm not your event planner, Sidney. My only rule is that if you make a mess, you're the one who cleans it up."

"Sounds fair. I've heard some artistic types say they're most creative in the middle of the night. Is that how it is with you?" After setting the glass of milk on the table, Sidney pulled out silverware from the second drawer he opened. Give him a few more days and he'd probably navigate the kitchen as well as he knew his kitchen back in Boston, although that wasn't saying much. Ordering take-out in the office and sharing meetings over lunch and dinner in downtown restaurants had become his *modus operandi*. Meals at his place were quick breakfasts-on-the-fly and late-night snacks.

"Depends. I get spurts of energy and creativity at different times during the day. I made scrambled eggs and sausage. There's a plate for you in the microwave."

"I thought I smelled something good. Appreciate it. Seth already gone?"

She nodded. "He had errands to run over in Bethel, and then he's going by the university to take care of some year-end administrative things."

Lounging against the kitchen counter, Sidney crossed his arms and tried to ignore the sucking noises coming from beneath the blanket. "I never would have guessed you'd grow up to marry a mineral-loving adventurer who's also a part-time professor. From what I gather, Seth enjoys teaching almost as much as the Indiana Jones stuff, doesn't he?"

"Yes, he loves it, especially the interaction with the students," Caroline said. "You know how it is when you're together with others who share the same passion. He'll probably transition into full-time teaching once he works the wanderlust out of his system."

Sidney grinned. "Does Seth know you call it that?"

"Of course. He's the one who coined the term. The cache of amethysts his team discovered in Stow and the tourmaline they found on Plumbago Mountain built this house, after all."

"That's great, but I wouldn't exactly call your jewelry designs a little hobby to make pocket change." He'd heard from Bryce that Caroline's clientele was growing in New England and branching across the country. All it took was some well-placed advertising.

"I know you've helped spread the word and given me some referrals, Sid. Thank you."

"Welcome. Your talent speaks for itself. But, if you don't mind, I've decided I kind of hate the nickname Sid." He lifted his shoulders. "Maybe I'm growing up, I don't know."

Caroline's glance was curious. "Okay. I'm sure you'll remind me if I slip."

Sidney punched the buttons on the microwave to warm the food. "Don't tell Seth, but a part of me is jealous. I think every little boy wants to be an explorer when he grows up. Climb mountains, back to nature, the adventure of it all. Just like most little girls want to be a ballerina or a princess." He winked. "Except you."

When the microwave dinged, he pulled open the door and then removed the plastic wrap. He touched the eggs. Satisfied they were warmed through to his satisfaction, Sidney removed the plate from the microwave. Carrying it to the table, he sat in the chair opposite Caroline.

"I'm sure Seth will always have a hand in planning expeditions in one way or another," she said. "The best part is that most of them take place here in New England now, so it keeps him close to home."

"Yep," Sidney agreed. "Home is where the heart is." He caught Caroline's lifted brow. "Sorry for the cliché. Don't know what's come over me. Anyway, Bryce told me a while back that the Oxford Hills area has the highest concentration of natural gemstones of any region its size in the world. I'm sure that was another plus in Evergreen's favor that figured into your decision to move here."

Picking up his fork, he dug into the scrambled eggs. They smelled and looked great. He'd ask for hot sauce, but he'd been trying to lay off the stuff lately.

"Didn't hurt." Caroline peeked beneath the blanket and cooed an endearment.

"Why does watching you with Ellie make me want to sing 'You Make Me Feel Like a Natural Woman'? If I could carry a tune, I might try it."

Caroline studied him for a moment as he continued to eat. "I think running away from home is already doing wonders for your sense of humor. Among other things."

"You think so? I'll take that as a compliment."

"I meant it as one." She sipped her juice and then nibbled on a bite of blueberry muffin.

Should he have said a prayer first? That seemed important in this house. Seth prayed for their meal last night. He didn't mind and had bowed in respect for the tradition as much as deference to a higher being.

"Guess you think I'm a heathen since I didn't pray."

"Sidney, you're not a heathen. You're also not used to praying. I think that's one of the reasons you've come to Evergreen."

"What's that mean?" he said around a bite of sausage. "To learn to pray? To find Jesus?" Grabbing the pepper shaker, he sprinkled it over what remained of his eggs.

"Perhaps. You're obviously searching for something."

"That statement also implies I'm lost."

"Aren't you? We're all lost about something." Her green eyes leveled on him.

"You're also too philosophical this early in the morning. I've always known you'd make one…" He swallowed a curse. "Sorry. Old habits die hard. What I'm trying to say is that you would have made a fantastic lawyer, Caroline. I admire you. For standing up to Mom and Dad, for following your passion to design jewelry, for moving up here to Maine. It's the trifecta of rebellion to find ultimate happiness." He shrugged and took another bite. "You've even become a great cook. This breakfast is terrific. Kudos." He took a long drink of his milk.

She laughed quietly. "Don't sound so surprised."

"You grew up in the same home I did." He'd never known his mother to cook anything.

"Nanny Regina taught me a few things."

"That's good. All she did was catch me in everything I did wrong. So, in the long run, I guess she did me a favor." Sidney took another bite. "Why is it everything here tastes so much better?"

"We use organic and locally grown fruits and vegetables. Less additives and preservatives."

"Okay, but other than learning to cook on the sly"—he grinned again—"you did everything expected of you when you were younger. You studied hard, made stellar grades, joined all the social organizations, excelled at Wellesley, went to Harvard Law that first year—"

"Your point?" Her voice held humor even though she'd cut him off.

He lifted his glass in a salute. "To Caroline. Who followed her dreams and found them." Sidney lowered his gaze while she made an adjustment and then pulled the blanket away from Ellie.

Finished with his food, Sidney pushed his plate aside. His heart jumped when he spied the baby's flushed cheeks and pouty lips. "You and Seth are blessed. She's a beautiful child."

Caroline smiled as she burped Ellie. "I don't think I've ever heard you use the word *blessed*."

"That's because I don't think I ever have." Why *had* he said it? Maybe because the truth of that word had hit him hard in recent months. One of the female associates at the firm had lost a baby. A partner's eight-year-old grandson was killed near a school crosswalk in a freak accident. Those things made him think even more about how fragile life could be, how he couldn't control everything, and how easily life itself could slip from his grasp.

Ellie let out a surprisingly loud burp. Wow, that baby had some powerful lungs.

Caroline kissed Ellie's cheek. "Did you hear what Uncle Sidney said about you? He said you're beautiful. And you are. You're Mommy and Daddy's precious girl." She nuzzled her daughter's cheek.

"She's also a star-worthy burper."

"Yes, she is," Caroline said. "She takes after you in that respect. I remember those contests between you and Bryce." Her voice had taken on a faraway quality. "Sometimes it's hard to believe we were ever kids, you know?"

He nodded. "We were expected to act like miniature adults from the time we could walk and talk." Taking a last drink of milk, he drained the glass.

"Do you ever wonder what our lives would have been like if Mom had been…" Caroline hugged Ellie close again.

"She was a lot more approachable toward the end," he said. "Started me thinking that Evergreen is some kind of magical place where people find whatever it is they're seeking."

The change in their mother had been remarkable. After her trip to Evergreen to see Caroline a few years ago, she'd come home to Boston a changed person. Happier. More giving of her time. She revealed things about her life prior to marrying Dad they'd never known. Aspects of her life that perhaps could have made a difference in all their lives if only…

Let it go, Sidney. He didn't blame Mom. He didn't then, and he didn't now, but neither did he live by the *if only* aspects of life. He liked absolutes and certainties.

"Evergreen isn't magical," Caroline said. "The way I see it, coming here was part of God's plan for me and then for Mom in her own way. It's quieter here, and it's a good place to search your soul. Would you like more eggs or anything else to eat?"

"I'm all set, thank you."

Her brows lifted. "Seems you've also rediscovered your manners."

He grunted. "I've always had them. They got pushed by the wayside, I'm afraid. I'm working on that, too." After wiping his mouth with a napkin, Sidney sat back in the chair and crossed his arms. "When you defied the parents and moved up here to Maine, that's when I first began to notice changes in Mom and Dad, some subtle, some more pronounced."

"I'm listening," she said. The baby stirred and made funny little sucking noises. In her sleep, no less. Caroline gently rocked her daughter in her arms, a lovely image of motherhood and domesticity. He didn't remember Mom ever rocking him, holding him close, whispering sweet sentiments, kissing his cheek.

"You showed Mom and Dad they couldn't control you, Caroline. That was a valuable lesson for them to learn. It meant more coming from you than it would have from anyone else."

"Why coming from me?"

"You're the youngest, the girl, the child who could do no wrong."

"I highly doubt that." She didn't seem especially pleased by that sentiment. "You were the first, the smartest, the one held up as the epitome of the perfect son."

"Right." He snorted. "Perfect son. That's an undeserved title. I only did what I'd been groomed to do my entire life."

"You also *wanted* to be a lawyer," she said. "I didn't."

"That's true," Sidney acknowledged. "In your case, the *parental units*, as Bryce is fond of saying, had to adjust to the idea that you weren't defying them so much as you were following your heart. They finally came around, and I know they were both proud of you. We all are."

His own statement hit him hard. "I hate to refer to Dad in past tense."

"I understand. I do the same thing." Shifting her position, Caroline kissed the baby's cheek again. He loved how the nurturing instinct came so naturally for her. Easy to see why. Ellie had worked her way into his own jaded heart in record time. Having her with them before and immediately after Mom's death had brought a welcome reaffirmation of life in its own way.

"I'm thankful you and Bryce are in place at the firm to keep the Prescott name as a strong presence," she said.

His heart swelled. "A part of me wishes you were there beside us. Then I see you here in Maine…so happy and content. Fulfilled. The woman you've become is an amazing person."

"Thank you." Caroline's eyes misted. "I've never heard so many compliments from you."

They'd also come naturally. "I meant every one of them."

"A small part of me would like to be there in the firm, too, Sidney. You realize I might not—probably *would* not—have become the woman I am now if I hadn't struck out on my own."

"I know," Sidney said quietly. "Before she died, Mom asked me to promise to look over you and Bryce. Because of Dad's dementia, she knew I'd be the head of the family now. Funny thing about that." His eyes grew damp. He blinked hard and focused on a photo of a pretty blonde with two young children on the refrigerator door. "The list of my personal failings is longer than I'd like to admit. I don't feel qualified or worthy of assuming Dad's place as the head of the Prescott family."

Reaching across the table, Caroline covered his hand with hers, her expression serious. "Does this mean you're abdicating the throne?"

He laughed, thankful for the release. "Yes, I think I am. You and Bryce can fight it out. As far as I'm concerned, we're all equals, and we make any decisions together that need to be made."

"I agree."

Letting go of her hand, Sidney fiddled with the napkin on the table, bunching it in his fingers and wadding it into a small ball. "Here's the thing. With Mom's passing, and Dad a shell of his former self"—he winced at his own words—"I've finally awakened to the fact that I'm 33 years old and have nothing to show for my life other than a good pedigree, a great education, and a solid track record in the courtroom. Other than that, there's a void. Not a wasteland, mind you. But a definite void."

Caroline studied him for a long moment. "You're saying you haven't found your dreams."

"That makes me sound like a girl, but…yes. I'd say there's an element of truth in that statement." Sidney nodded slowly, the full impact of that admission weighing him down.

"You have plenty of time. In those 33 years, look at all you've accomplished, Sidney. You've built an amazing career. I'm sure a lot of people around you are getting married and starting their families. That's bound to make you look at things—"

"Did you know that Isabella paints?" He hadn't meant to cut her off and wasn't sure why he'd blurted out *that* question.

Caroline gave him a curious smile. "I know Toby—my partner in the jewelry business—is giving Isabella watercolor lessons. He's one of the area's most well-known landscape artists. What made you think of that now?"

He'd bypass that question. For one thing, why admit to a fascination he couldn't explain? Caroline's address book had been sitting on the desk in the study, and he'd quickly thumbed through it last night until he'd located Isabella—last name *Caccavale*. Armed with that information, he'd conducted a little research on his laptop.

As Isabella had told him, she'd been born in California. What he also learned was that she'd graduated with her undergraduate and MBA degrees from UCLA before living and working in Connecticut. She'd co-founded a marketing firm in Hartford that seemed to be thriving. She had online accounts with Twitter, Linked In, Pinterest, and other social media websites plus Facebook, although the first two had been inactive since she'd moved to Evergreen.

He'd discovered precious little about her personal life, only her educational stats and professional accomplishments. Others would only know what *she* wanted them to know. Smart woman.

"I looked up the website for Mahoney's General Store, and it's terrific," he told Caroline. "Isabella's background in marketing showed in every inch of that site. She's very talented."

"Yes, she's a sharp cookie. As you learned yesterday, she's also funny, caring, and very pretty." Caroline smoothed wisps of blonde hair away from her daughter's forehead.

"I know Isabella had a thriving career in Connecticut, so why did she pick up everything and move here to Evergreen? People seem to like doing that." Sidney frowned. "Don't misunderstand. Evergreen seems like a perfectly lovely place. I'm just trying to understand. Have it make sense." Burning in the back of his mind was Isabella's statement about the preservation of her soul.

"In Isabella's case, you should ask her about it sometime."

"Maybe I will." What *would* make Isabella give up a promising career in marketing? That was definitely a story he'd like to hear. Chances were she'd either burned out or else she'd suffered some type of devastating personal loss. He'd try to figure out a way to ask his questions without offending her or making Isabella feel like she was testifying on the witness stand.

"You're intrigued by her." Caroline's gaze settled on him.

"Meaning?" He hoped she wouldn't pursue the idea. Yes, he was fascinated by Isabella, but it couldn't amount to anything, so why bother entertaining the idea?

"Meaning she's had a successful professional career, but then she made some big life changes. It's only fair to tell you that I cautioned Isabella about you."

"What about me?" Sidney tried to keep the defensiveness from his voice.

"To be blunt, that you're not the type of man she needs in her life." Caroline's gaze met his.

"Why would you say that?" He wasn't mad, but he'd like to hear his sister's reasoning.

"Come on, Sidney. I saw the looks you two gave one another yesterday, the body language, the playful teasing, the flirting, the tension. Isabella tried to deny it, but I would have been blind not to see it."

He swallowed. "Any reason we can't be friends?"

"No, but I'm sensing it might be difficult to draw the dividing line," Caroline said. "I can tell you that part of Isabella's journey involved acknowledging she's not the one in control."

"You're talking about God again, aren't you?" So, Isabella was one of *them*. A born-again believer. He'd been guilty of poking fun of Christians. Nothing cruel or targeted, but he'd made some barbed jokes, said some unkind things, even about Seth and indirectly about his sister.

Ashamed, Sidney hung his head, unable to look Caroline in the eye.

"Once I gave my life to Christ, He gave me the strength to make those changes in my life." Caroline's tone was soothing, gentle.

"There's a verse of Scripture from the Book of Philippians that says, 'I can do all things through Him who strengthens me.'" She started to say something else but then closed her mouth.

"Contrary to what you might think, I'm not adverse to the things of God, Caroline." Sidney sat back in his chair. "Please continue."

"I had a good talk with Beverly Landon during my first visit to Evergreen. She's the former owner of the bed and breakfast, and my friend Liesel's mom. We talked a bit about my plans for the future, and she could tell I was conflicted about law school. In the course of our conversation, she asked me a question that made me think hard about my life."

When she paused, Sidney understood that was his cue. "I'll bite. What was the question?"

"She asked if I had a source of strength and comfort I could turn to in my time of need." A flicker of sadness passed over his sister's face. "I realized I didn't. Not really."

"Other than Bryce, you mean," Sidney said. "I'm thankful Bryce has been there since I've failed you."

Caroline's brow furrowed. "You haven't failed me. You've always done what you know how to do best. Like Dad, you're driven to succeed, and you have a brilliant, focused mind."

"That shouldn't be to the exclusion of family. That's one of the reasons I'm here. To reconnect. I *need* you in my life, Caroline." His gaze fell on six-month-old Ellie. "I want to know the stages of Ellie's life. I don't want to be old Uncle Sidney at her wedding one day and realize I never took the time to get to know my niece." He chuckled to lighten the mood. "I even want to get to know the rock doctor better. I think in time we could be buds."

A small smile played across Caroline's lips. Rising from her chair, she walked around the table with Ellie. "Hold out your arms."

"You want me to hold her?" His pulse raced. He'd never held an infant. Not once. What if he dropped her? Hurt her in some way by not holding her properly?

"Yes, I want you to hold Ellie. No time like the present to start bonding with her."

Sidney held out his arms. "I don't mind admitting that facing a jury is way less intimidating."

"Now *that's* a scary statement," she said. "I have full confidence in you."

"Glad one of us does." He wasn't sure what he was doing, but Sidney cradled Ellie and made sure her head was supported per Caroline's instruction. "Am I doing it right?"

"You're doing fine. She's quite content with her Uncle Sidney."

"How about that, Ellie?" His gaze roamed over the baby's face and he ran one finger lightly over her soft skin. Then he lifted the baby's small, pink hand, and marveled over each perfectly formed finger and tiny nail. His heart felt like it was about to burst out of his chest. Never in his life had he experienced such utter sweetness.

Caroline gathered their dishes and carried them to the sink. After running water over them, she left the kitchen after telling him she'd be back momentarily. Soon after, she dropped into the chair beside him and placed a tattered, black, leather-bound book on top of the table. Even though the gold lettering on the cover was so faded he couldn't read it, Sidney knew it was a Bible.

"This was originally Seth's grandfather's Bible. Seth carried it everywhere." Caroline opened the book while he watched, still holding Ellie. Some of the pages had tears and many of them had folded corners. Every available margin or white space was crammed full of notations in precise lettering.

"Looks like some of my law journals. Someone has studied this book. Loved it."

Caroline's voice was soft when she spoke again. "Seth cared enough about my spiritual condition to give me this Bible even though he didn't expect to ever see me again."

"Be honest, Caroline. If he gave you something that meant so much to him, you have to know he thought he'd see you again. At least he hoped he would."

"No, I *didn't* know. We were at two completely different places in our lives." She heaved a sigh that silently conveyed *you don't understand.* "When Seth found out Dad was involved in the manslaughter case against *his* father, I think he pretty much wrote me off. That was it for him as far as I was concerned. By that time, I'd already left Evergreen and gone back to Boston."

"But look how it all worked out." Even Sidney could admit that comment sounded much too smug.

Caroline blew out a breath. "Seth had been working in California, and he had a longtime girlfriend here in Maine when we saw each other again. He had no idea I'd moved to Evergreen."

"Look, I know how a guy's mind works. Christian or not, Seth and I are the same species. I wouldn't have given Mom's favorite Baccarat crystal vase or her Rolex to some girl I never thought I'd see again."

"Not even in the same ballpark," Caroline said. "Completely different circumstances. We're talking about a sentimental and soul-changing gift from the heart."

"I'm sure some women would consider Baccarat and Rolex to be soul-changing."

Caroline's gaze bore into him. She'd had enough of his sarcasm. "It's not all about money. Please get that through your thick skull."

"I know that. It was my lame attempt at a joke. A really *bad* joke. That's one of the reasons I'm here in Maine. Bottom line? You have something I want, but I don't know what *it* is. I'm not sure if it's the kind of love you have with Seth, or with Ellie, or if somehow God can fill this…void…I feel inside." And now he was back at the *void* talk again?

"Being articulate and commanding in the courtroom is different than the challenges and joys of sharing life with the people you love, Sidney. Admitting you're vulnerable and searching for meaning in your life is an important step." Curling her fist, Caroline moved it over her heart. "I've learned there are certain places in your heart that no amount of worldly success can fill. Another person can't fill that void, either. Only *God* can."

Caroline pointed her finger to the opened pages of the Bible. "This book held answers to the questions I was asking myself when I first came to Evergreen. Questions I didn't even know I *had*. When I went back to Boston, I started to read it. Then I got involved in an off-campus Bible study, and a dear friend named Ana led me to faith in Christ. Even though I was young in my faith, that's what gave me the strength to tell Dad and Mom that I was quitting law school and moving to Maine."

She waited until he met her gaze. "Beverly and Seth recognized that I was seeking something outside of myself. Something bigger. And now you're doing the same thing. Like it or not, coming here to Maine is part of *your* journey. You're at the point where I was when I first came to Evergreen. More than any legal case history, this book gives us the history of the world but also hope for the future. One day, the world as we know it will be gone. I'd like to leave a legacy of faith and evidence of a life well-lived. I'm sure you'd like to do the same."

"A legacy that's not measured by worldly or material success. I get it, Caroline. I really do." He wasn't irritated with her. The changes she'd made in her life were clearly positive. Judging by the inner contentment that radiated from her, Caroline had never been happier.

Happier than you. Not that it was a competition in any sense of the word. Making faith *personal* had obviously changed his sister's life for the better. Sidney glanced down at Ellie, love for her filling his heart. He'd never thought it possible to love a child so unconditionally, and he was only her uncle. How must it feel to have a child of one's own?

"I'll tell you one thing. The opportunity to hold this little angel has been worth the trip in itself." Leaning close, he planted a soft kiss on the baby's cheek. "Uncle Sidney will be here for you, precious Ellie. Always."

Caroline surprised him by planting a quick kiss on his forehead. "I'm proud of you, Sidney. I'm going to pray you'll find some answers while you're here."

"Don't faint with shock, but I welcome your prayers. I guess I need to figure out some things for myself. I suppose you expect me to relinquish my hold on Ellie now?"

Her lips curled. "Yes, unless you plan on nursing her when she wakes up again."

That prompted him into quick action. "Ellie, it's been fun, but it's time to go back to Mama now."

"Have fun today, whatever you do. Be sure and apply the bug spray if you take a walk in the woods." Caroline lifted Ellie from his arms. "The bottle's in the upstairs bathroom cabinet."

"I'll douse myself liberally," he assured her. "Thanks. For everything."

"You're welcome. I'll see you later." With a small smile, Caroline departed the kitchen with her daughter.

Sidney stared at the Bible on the kitchen table. Sure, he might take a peek and do a little reading in it while he was in Evergreen. Why not? It couldn't hurt, and it was the least he could do to humor his little sister.

But not now. He had another errand in mind this morning.

Chapter 8

Isabella glanced at the boxes of candles spread on the floor around her. "Tommy, where did you put the box of Charming Chamomile?"

He reached behind him. "Right here, boss."

"Did you do a count?"

"Yep. All there." Tommy placed the opened box on the shelf next to Honeysuckle Harmony. "Check. Which one's next?"

Isabella checked her list. "Luscious Lavender."

"I don't get why people need candles, anyway," Tommy said. "Hey, maybe they'll come up with one of those 'new car smell' candles. I could go for one of those."

Tommy had just broken up with his latest girlfriend, so of course, he wouldn't consider candles romantic. Give him time. Knowing her young assistant as well as she did, he'd find another female companion by next week.

Not that *she* was thinking of romance, but Isabella loved a gently burning candle, light jazz, dim lighting, a cozy dinner, sweet talk, an unexpected kiss… She hadn't thought about such things since she'd left Hartford.

Sidney's face popped into her mind. Isabella shivered although not from fear. *Lord, take these thoughts from me. Sidney Prescott doesn't know you.* Nothing other than friendship could happen between them.

Show Sidney the way. Start by being his friend.

"You okay, Isabella?" Tommy waved to catch her attention. "You look a little weirded out."

Isabella snapped out of her musing. "I'm thinking when the rep comes to the store next week, you should propose a new scent—Amazing Aventador. It could be marketed as the candle for today's modern, sophisticated man. Red, of course."

Tommy grinned. "Now you're speaking my language."

The bell jingled, and they both leaned forward, peering around the end of the aisle.

"Aunt Clara!" Isabella rose to a standing position. "Hi there."

As usual, her aunt was dressed in a Sunday skirt and blouse accessorized with the same delicate pearl necklace and matching earrings she'd worn as long as Isabella could remember. A gift from Uncle Phil's trip to the Orient, those pearls probably adorned Aunt Clara's neck while she slept. By contrast, Isabella always felt underdressed in her aunt's presence.

"Another beautiful day," Clara said as the door closed behind her.

"Tommy, go ahead and work through the list while I talk with her." Isabella crossed the store to embrace her aunt. "What brings you here today? Always great to see you, but I didn't expect you until early next week."

"I've brought a supply of homemade jams and jellies. They're out in the car. You take whatever you want and put the rest out for sale." Bless her heart, she donated most of what she brought into the store for sale. Uncle Phil's estate left her with enough money to get by without having to work. When she did help in the store, Clara would never accept anything other than lunch.

Perhaps the biggest blessing was that she didn't impose her ideas on Isabella for how to run Mahoney's even though she'd owned and operated this same store for four decades. Aunt Clara understood the boundaries. For that, and many reasons, Isabella loved her aunt dearly.

"God spoke to me again."

"How nice. You have conversations with God all the time." What could it be this time?

"Yes, but this is another revelation about *you*, Isabella." Clara gave her one of the knowing looks she'd perfected. A twinge of sadness pinched Isabella at the reminder of her mother. Although her mom's older sister didn't physically resemble her mother, Lucy, some of Clara's facial expressions and tone of voice were uncannily similar.

Isabella was reminded once again that, if not for the woman standing in front of her now, she'd be all alone in the world. An orphan, a word she truly disliked. As a child of the King, she was never truly alone. Still, the concept sometimes made her nostalgic.

Isabella hooked her arm with Clara's. "Shall we go into the backroom to talk about it?" Even if God *had* spoken to Clara, if it was about her, she didn't especially want anyone coming into the store to overhear the conversation.

"Anybody who wants to know can hear just as well right here in the middle of Mahoney's as anywhere else."

"I didn't hear a thing!" Tommy called from behind the aisle.

"Maybe it'd do you some good if you did." Aunt Clara's eyes sparkled with humor. "How are you doing, young man?"

Isabella's young assistant poked his head around the corner. "Fine, ma'am. Always a pleasure to see you."

"Tommy, could you make sure all the candle boxes are in place and then run out to Clara's car and bring in the jams and jellies she's brought?"

"Door's unlocked, and they're on the backseat," Clara added.

"You got it."

"Even though it's still morning, I sure could use a root beer right about now," Isabella said to Clara. "How about you? We can talk and keep the crates warm until Marty and Hank show up in a bit."

"Splendid idea, especially since you're trying to get me out of the middle of your store. Now that you mention it, I *am* a little parched. I've been up since dawn and had more than enough coffee to float a boat."

After handing Clara an open, chilled bottle of root beer, Isabella grabbed a second one and then perched on a wooden crate beside the checkerboard-covered barrel. She took a quick drink from the bottle. "Would you rather have a chair? And a glass for the root beer?"

Clara took a swig from the bottle. "I always thought it tastes better straight from the bottle. And I'll sit on this crate until a certain part of me starts to fall asleep. Then I'll get up."

Isabella grinned. "That's what you say about sitting on the church pew."

The door jingled, and Isabella checked to make sure it wasn't a customer. Tommy had gone outside and was pulling out the trays of homemade goods from the backseat of Aunt Clara's white Oldsmobile.

"You have to admit Pastor Hawkins has been going on a bit long these days. Seems he got himself one of those Bible commentaries, and now he feels the need to share all his newfound wisdom." Clara fixed her with another look. "So, young lady, I understand there's an interesting new man in Evergreen."

Ah, this must be the root reason for her aunt's visit this morning. With Clara, it was never *I hear*, but *I understand*. Isabella figured she'd hear about Sidney at some point but not the day after his arrival.

The older woman sipped daintily from her bottle. "I also understand he's Caroline's oldest brother from Boston. And you were riding in his fancy red sports car through town. That must have been fun for you."

Isabella gave a noncommittal shrug. "He needed help getting to Seth and Caroline's new house. I didn't close the store while I was with him if that's what you're thinking."

The older woman huffed. "That's not my point. I'm not a bit concerned about that. This store's your baby now. You wouldn't leave it unattended, and you were hospitable to a visitor in our little town. Nothing wrong with that."

"Tommy watched over the store for me, and from all appearances—and based on the fact I didn't hear from Sheriff Watters—everything was quiet during the time I was gone. You know how crazy it would be to try and explain the directions to that area of town. It's next to impossible, and his GPS probably would have exploded. But the house is fabulous and worth finding." Isabella took another quick swig of the rich, amber-colored liquid.

"Speaking of which…"

Oh, no. Based on Clara's smile, Isabella had unwittingly given her aunt the perfect segue. Time to ward off any further speculation. "He roared into town," Isabella said quickly. "He's also rather overbearing and pompous. Throws his money around."

"Handsome, too, I understand."

Isabella almost choked on her sip of root beer. "Why does *that* matter?"

"It doesn't, but you confirmed my suspicions."

Shaking her head, Isabella blew out a sigh. "The man's only here in town temporarily. The town gossips can put any speculation to rest."

"God told me you're going to marry that young man."

Stunned speechless, Isabella's cheeks warmed as a flush of heat raced through her. Just because Clara's big proclamation that she'd sell Mahoney's to her actually happened didn't mean a thing. Maybe her aunt was growing crazier with each passing minute. Or maybe *she* was.

"Aunt Clara…" Isabella hesitated, grasping for words. Drawing in a deep breath, she released it slowly as she searched her mind for a response. Coming up with a counter statement had been easy in business, but not so much when it concerned her personal life.

No reason to be thrown off-kilter.

For her part, Clara took another long, slow drink from her bottle. As usual, the older woman appeared completely calm and unflappable. "What you do is your own business, Isabella, but the way I see it, you can't argue with the Almighty. He's the ultimate authority."

"Yes, but I can argue with *you*, vessel of His word or whatever you may be." Isabella focused on the antique reproduction photo of Uncle Phil, Aunt Clara, and her five cousins in Gold Rush era clothing on the opposite wall. The story her mother used to tell about Clara facing down a rattler must be true since Isabella had never seen her flinch in the face of anything.

Lord, help me know what to say.

Not that Isabella doubted the Lord might have spoken to her aunt. Anything was possible. Clara was a proven prayer warrior of the highest caliber. At the moment, Isabella wished Clara would keep her out of it. She could live her own life, thank you very much, although her aunt meant well and had her best interests at heart. If Isabella could humor the daily phone calls from Hattie, why not do the same with Aunt Clara's messages—or whatever they were—from God?

"I still have a lot to learn about how the Lord works in someone's life," Isabella said slowly. "All I'm asking is that you let me handle my life in my own way. Besides, from all appearances, Mr. Prescott seems to place a higher value on worldly things."

Isabella bit back a sigh and lowered her gaze. What a hypocrite she was. During her years in Hartford, she'd been as materialistic as they come. If the Lord could forgive her many sins, then He could forgive Sidney.

Clara leaned close and lowered her voice. "Even if that's true, you know as well as I do that there's always hope for Sidney Prescott as long as he's walking this earth. God led him to Evergreen for a purpose. Maybe it's so Caroline and Seth can share God's love with him. Or maybe so *you* can share with him." She sat back with an expression of triumph. "God brought him here to the store, and then He put you in that car of his, didn't He? That's no small thing."

Isabella tried not to reveal her frustration. "I'll agree there's a good possibility that God sent Sidney here for a specific reason, but I don't think meeting and marrying me is one of them. Maybe you misinterpreted what He said. Did God literally speak to you, Aunt Clara? As in you actually *heard* His voice? If that's the case, does His voice have more of a Sean Connery richness or a Harrison Ford huskiness?" She didn't mean to sound irreverent, but her aunt's proclamation flabbergasted her.

"My hearing and mind are both sharp, young lady. My heart is open to believing that He sent that young man here to meet you. All right." Her aunt shifted on the wooden crate and sipped her drink. "When I say God spoke to me, I don't mean I heard an actual voice. I prayed specifically for you, but I believe He answered that prayer by the events that took place yesterday afternoon. Or He started the process, anyway."

Her aunt met her gaze. "Take things as they come, Isabella. And pray."

"Of course, I'll pray." She would, but *how* to pray was more the question.

"If Sidney Prescott is the man for you."

Isabella frowned. "Aunt Clara, you know how much I love you, but I have to say, it's intimidating when you make a prediction like that. These are life-changing things, you know. Big things. *Huge!* Besides, as far as I know, God doesn't go around telling people whom to marry."

"God certainly made it clear that Hosea should marry Gomer, and that Joseph should take Mary as his wife."

"Okay, I'll give you those two. But in the case of Mary and Joseph, they were already in love and engaged," Isabella said. "They had a head start."

"Yes, and just look how that story ended up." Clara slapped her hand on the checkerboard. "Changed the world, led to God's plan of redemption, and gave us sinners the opportunity of an eternity in heaven. So, who's to say God *doesn't* reveal His will to others?"

"I'm not refuting that, but I'm also not a theologian. Far from it." Placing her hand over Clara's, Isabella gave her a light squeeze. "I just don't want you to be disappointed when things don't work out the way you expect or hope. If Sidney doesn't know the Lord, then that needs to be the focus of our prayers. If God can use me as His instrument in helping Sidney in his faith journey, then I'm all for it. What I *can* promise you is that I'll keep an open mind about that aspect. Nothing more."

"Dear girl, I've always known that God has a tailor-made plan for you. Maybe you'll remain single"—Clara's expression was skeptical—"and if that's God's ultimate will, then so be it. I'd like you to think about something else." She lowered her voice. "He knows Sidney's had something in his life that's broken him, just as you've suffered losses. Bringing that man here to Evergreen might be God's unique way of bringing two hurting souls together in order to heal."

Isabella shook her head. "Most people don't reach my age without enduring some kind of loss."

"You're too young to be such a skeptic. I know my prayers for you will be answered. I'll tell you something else. God's spoken directly to my heart four times in my life since I became a believer in Christ, and two of them have involved *you*, Isabella."

"What are the two times that *didn't* involve me?"

"The first was that I should marry your Uncle Phil even though he'd had a broken engagement and was still grieving that relationship when we met. The second was that I was pregnant after two miscarriages. Isabella, I know how much you were hurting after Tristan's betrayal. All I know is that I want my darling girl to be happy."

"I *am* happy." Tears stung Isabella's eyes, and she blinked hard. *Content* was more appropriate. Tristan's affair with their co-worker still pierced her heart. Maybe she'd never get over it completely although she'd forgiven him and moved on with her life. At the height of her heartbreak, Isabella had shared a heart-to-heart with Clara. Her aunt knew how deeply she'd loved Tristan but also how far she'd fallen into sin.

And yet, here Clara sat, loving her in spite of her past.

Jumping up from the wooden crate, Isabella enveloped her aunt in a hug. "Thank you for loving me in spite of myself."

"I love you for who you are now, and the person you've always been. So did your mother and father." Clara kissed her cheek. "And so does the Lord, honey. He loves you with a passion we can only imagine. I want you to know something else." A tear slipped down Clara's lightly rouged cheek, and she quickly brushed it away.

"What's that?"

Clara's eyes softened as she rested one hand on the side of Isabella's face. "No one told me that young man's first name. You called him Mr. Prescott, but then I said the name Sidney—I firmly believe God put his name on my tongue—before *you* said his first name to see if I was correct. Then you confirmed it."

Isabella stuttered. "Then what...? How?"

"Isn't it obvious? It's *Who*." Clara patted her cheek. "The name Sidney was clear as a bell when God spoke to me. I don't know how else to explain it, but I knew. Funny thing, though. Normally, I don't even care for the name Sidney. I knew a Sidney once, and he wasn't a very nice man. That kind of sticks with a person."

"If it helps, I don't think Sidney likes his name much, either." The name was growing on Isabella, along with the man.

Clara nodded. "I like him already."

"I do, too, Aunt Clara." Isabella barely knew Sidney, and yet she did.

The older woman finished her root beer. "Now tell me something I don't know."

Chapter 9

"Harley Davidson, is that you over there?"

Harley Davidson? Seriously? Sidney followed the direction of the librarian's glare and spied a pimply faced teenage boy with long, stringy, dishwater blond hair and a backpack slung over one shoulder.

"Yes, ma'am." The kid fake coughed into his fist.

"Sit yourself down and stop making inappropriate phone calls while you're in my library, young man. And none of that sex-texting nonsense."

"I'm not being inappropriate, Maid—I mean, Miss Millicent. I swear I'm not."

"And none of that swearing. You know better than that." Marching up to the kid, hands on her hips, the woman planted herself in front of him.

Sidney couldn't look away if he tried. He wasn't about to leave. This scenario was better than the last three or four movies he'd seen. Of course, two of them were chick flicks he'd been dragged to by blind dates set up by misguided associates.

Maid Millicent was younger than he'd thought and attractive—medium height and weight, brownish-red hair pulled back with a clip, plain clothing, sensible shoes—although she sounded, in terms of attitude, like a much older woman.

"If you'd spend half as much time on your studies as you do romancing Jenny Masters, you'd have your diploma by now. You're already behind, so you've got some studying to do. Now, get!" Millicent gave the kid a swift swat with the oversized book in her hand. Sidney tilted his head. Looked like a children's picture book. Would that work for a kid about six or seven?

Before he knew what was happening, Millicent whirled around and stared him down. "And what might *your* name be?"

He almost saluted. "I might be Sidney Prescott, Miss Millicent."

"Prescott? You another one of Caroline's brothers? Another hotshot lawyer from Boston?"

"I'm afraid so."

She shook her head. "The ornery oldest one, I'm assuming. She's only got two brothers, from what I know. And you've got that whole *pawk the caw in Hawvad yad* thing down pat."

His reputation must have preceded him. Sidney wouldn't comment on Millicent's native Maine accent.

"Unless there's a brother I don't know about, that's correct." Why'd he say that? Because with his dad's track record of mistresses, it might have been possible. Surely they would have come out of the woodwork by now. What a sad commentary. For all of his father's brilliant legal victories, his moral failures and shortcomings were sobering.

"You're the one with that monstrosity of a red car that rolled through town yesterday afternoon, aren't you?"

Word got around fast. "Guilty, but it's not my ca—"

"With that pretty Isabella Carnivale riding beside you? You got big eyes for her, Mr. Prescott?"

Maybe if she'd let him finish a sentence, he could try to reason with her. Why couldn't the townspeople get Isabella's last name right? Shouldn't a librarian be more precise? He'd known Isabella less than 24 hours, yet *he* knew her last name. If he corrected Millicent, it'd make her dislike him more. So, he'd stay silent and continue to be amused by it all.

"Well, *do* you? Speak up. You're a fancy lawyer, and you can't even answer my question?" If he were feeling vindictive, he'd make a comment on why some middle-aged librarians were still single. That'd only make him a heel.

Sidney drew in a quick breath. "Look, the length of my stay in town is indeterminate. I doubt anything could happen between Isabella and me even if I do. Have eyes for her. Which I'm neither confirming nor denying." Give him a feisty woman making accusations and he bumbled like an inarticulate fool. Some of his clients had been easier to deal with than this spitfire. The difference? This time, it was personal, and the townsfolk were already giving off signs they wanted to forge a romantic relationship between him and Isabella.

The librarian stepped closer, hands still on her hips, and stared him straight in the eye.

"I didn't ask how long you're staying in town. I asked if you've got eyes for her. From what I know, you're a big city slicker, but that doesn't give you the right to sass me. Or use big words like indeterminate. And, yes, I *know* what it means."

"You don't happen to write for the local newspaper, do you? Looking for a good story?"

That brought a glimmer of amusement in her light eyes hidden behind thick eyeglasses. "I care about Isabella. Her Aunt Clara is an upstanding woman. She's a good friend of mine."

At least this woman *had* close friends in spite of her blunt personality. He'd lost a few of those somewhere along the way. In terms of personal relationships, he had a long way to go.

When she raised the book again, Sidney figured he was about to get a lick with it. He hadn't been swatted like that since Nanny Regina caught him smoking in his bedroom closet when he was thirteen.

"I assure you, Miss Millicent, as lovely as Miss *Caccavale* is, I did not come to Evergreen in search of a woman. I will not play around with Isabella's affections."

The woman snorted. "Be sure you don't play around with *anything*, mister. Most of all, don't you go and break her heart. You hear me?" She poked him in the chest with one finger. "If you do, you'll answer to me and half the people in this town. You got that?"

"Got it. I don't intend to break her heart." It was gratifying to know Isabella inspired such loyalty.

She harrumphed. "Well, no one *intends* to break someone's heart. At least not on purpose or that's just ten ways to crazy. But I know your type." Millicent eyed him up and down. If he'd done the same to her, he'd be accused of sexual harassment. "You're a strapping, handsome fella like that other boyfriend of hers, and he broke her heart. Isabella deserves better."

Millicent was giving him all sorts of tidbits about Isabella's life that might otherwise have taken a long time to get from Isabella herself. *If* she ever dared to tell him. Had her former boyfriend come to Evergreen to visit her after she'd left Hartford? As great as Isabella was, he didn't doubt for a second that she'd had serious boyfriends, a fiancé, or even a husband along the way. A part of him hoped she hadn't, but that was none of his business.

"Can I ask what book you have in your hand?" Sidney pointed to it and then crossed his arms over his chest. As a self-protective measure, he tucked his hands beneath his arms.

She held it up. "A book about the Underground Railroad."

"What, uh, age group would you say that's for?"

"If the child's an average reader, I'd say about seven. Why? You got a child?"

"No, but I know someone who needs a few books for a boy about that age."

"Someone I know?"

He sighed. "Nothing gets by you, does it Miss Millicent?"

"Not if I can help it. I know all the kids in Evergreen. Come with me to the Young Readers section, and we'll find something."

"That sounds like a plan. Thanks."

Millicent beckoned for him to follow but then stopped abruptly. "Wait. You'll need a library card."

"Can't I just use Caroline or Seth's number?"

"Nope. You're responsible for your own debt, especially if you don't return the books. Keeps people accountable. Not enough of that these days."

"Look, I'll do whatever you want. I'll give you a whopping deposit. Cash. Just let me borrow some books. Please." Sidney pulled his wallet from his back pocket.

"What is it with you fancy city people? You think we can all be bought, is that it? Put your bulging wallet back in your pocket." The woman's eyes narrowed with suspicion. "How long did you say you're in town?"

"I didn't. I don't know yet. Indeterminate, remember?"

She snorted. "My hearing's good, but my short-term memory isn't so great. So, what happened to bring you up here to Maine? Did you get fired?"

"No, of course not." This woman would make a killer prosecutor. "I'm one of the partners in a Boston law firm now that my father's...incapacitated." Did she know how it twisted him in the gut to admit that? Why was he even telling her? "All I want is to help out Ned something or other. I don't know his last name. Can you help me do that?"

The harsh lines of Millicent's face softened, and she nodded. "That'd be Marty Kendrick's boy. Now we're getting somewhere. Little Ned likes The Boxcar Children books. They're advanced for him, but his mama's been in here asking for them so they can read them together."

"Do you have any books he might be able to read by himself? That might be better."

"To keep him occupied while his dad plays checkers at Mahoney's every afternoon?"

"You know about that?"

Millicent waved her hand. "Honey, everybody in town knows that. You'll learn soon enough that people in Evergreen know your business whether you want them to or not. Why do you think that sister of yours and Seth built their house on the outskirts of town?"

"Because Caroline is extremely smart." Millicent probably didn't even realize she'd called him *honey*. He didn't hear that endearment often, and it sounded kind of nice.

"Yes, she is. Follow me, and let's go find young Ned some books. I think you might be okay for a city slicker," Millicent said over one shoulder.

"Don't let it get around town. Might spoil my reputation."

"You still need to open your own library account."

Sidney grinned. "I wouldn't expect anything less, Miss Millicent."

Chapter 10

With the short stack of library books for Ned tucked under his arm, Sidney stepped into Mahoney's. The door was propped open this time so the annoying bell didn't jingle to announce his arrival.

Isabella was nowhere in sight as Sidney strolled up and down a couple of aisles. After grabbing a can of shaving cream and a bottle of shampoo, he stopped to look over the selection of men's vitamins since he'd forgotten those, too. Maybe it was psychological, but he needed to take a vitamin every morning, even if it was an over-the-counter brand instead of the insanely expensive kind a partner's wife had coerced him into buying.

As Sidney carried his selections to the counter, he wondered what Isabella's threshold was for using a credit card since he only had fifty and hundred dollar bills. Stopping in at Evergreen Bank seemed advisable.

"Clive, stay away from me! Stop right there. I'm warning you. Don't take another step."

Sidney halted at the sound of Isabella's voice. What on earth? Sounded like it came from the backroom. Was that Clyde or Clive? Wasn't Clyde the name of one of her employees? Surely it wasn't him.

"Come on, baby. You know you want me. You've been coming on to me ever since I hit town." That voice was deep and low, the words nothing less than…..*smarmy*.

"That's a lie, Clive! I feel nothing for you. You hear me? Nothing!"

Somehow, Sidney found this conversation unbelievable if not improbable. Not to mention Isabella didn't sound convincing. Straining to hear anything else, he lowered the can of shaving cream and the other items to the counter one at a time.

Silence ensued. Sidney carefully stepped around the end of the counter, trying to be as quiet as possible. The floorboards creaked, betraying him. Stopping, he held his breath. No sounds emerged from the backroom but neither did anyone come to the front counter to check. Where was Tommy?

If Isabella was in danger, he needed to help her. At least Evergreen must not have many shoplifters. Still, Sidney would think Isabella would keep a closer eye on the store. He darted a glance around the upper perimeter but didn't see any security cameras. That didn't surprise him. She could stand to clean around the ceiling fans. An old store like this must get a lot of dust.

The man was speaking again, but his voice was so low that Sidney couldn't make out the words. *Smack!* What was going on here? Sounded like Isabella slapping the guy's face. What if the man was manhandling her, forcing himself on her?

"Ouch! What was that for? I oughta teach you a lesson you'll never forget," the man snarled.

Foolish move or not, Sidney needed to take action. If something happened to Isabella, and he'd overheard and done nothing about it, he'd never forgive himself.

"Okay, that does it, buddy! No one treats a woman like that." Sidney barreled around the corner. Barging into the backroom, he stopped short. Isabella sat at a small table with a man sitting beside her who looked about fifty—balding, average-looking, chewing on something. Papers were strewn across the table. They both looked up at him with curious expressions.

"Hey, Sid." Isabella lifted a brow with a small smile. With her hair in a high ponytail and a light blue UCLA T-shirt, she looked casual, comfortable. Adorably appealing.

Sidney stared at her like a simpleton. "Izzy." Something inside him shifted.

"What's up?" She pushed a plate across the table. "Sweet roll?"

"No, thanks." Moving his hands to his hips, Sidney shook his head. Talk about feeling like a colossal fool. "I, um, thought you might be in some kind of trouble. I heard... Never mind. My mistake, apparently." He shifted his gaze to the man. "Clive, I take it?"

"Gerald Watkins." He shrugged and continued chewing.

"I'm sorry," Isabella said. "Forgive my lack of manners. Gerry, this is Sidney Prescott. He's Caroline's oldest brother." Was it his imagination or did her voice hold a bit of respect?

Sidney managed a somewhat curt nod. "Nice to meet you, Gerry."

"Same here, Sid. My wife has some of your sister's jewelry. She does real good work."

"Yes, she does, thanks."

"It's expensive but worth it."

Sidney swallowed a not-so-gracious comeback. "I'll be sure and give her your regards." Walking farther into the room, Sidney lowered the stack of library books on the table with a definitive thud. "For Ned." He darted a glance at the painting on the easel. Judging by the gazebo, she was painting Evergreen Park. The painting was lovely.

"Oh, that's so nice of you! I hadn't had a chance to get over to see Millicent yet." Isabella's surprise was clear as she shuffled through the books. Her smile was full of clear gratitude. "Thank you, Sidney. I really appreciate it."

"Welcome. I figured I might as well try and make myself useful. By the way, I'm now the proud owner of a lifetime membership at the Evergreen Public Library."

Isabella's brown eyes sparkled. "Then I'm sure you're Millicent's hero. Do you need to buy something? Tommy ran an order across to the sporting goods store and should be right back any minute, but I can come out if you're ready to—"

"Nothing that can't wait until later. I'll see you around."

Sidney left the backroom and headed straight for the open front door. In this case, he almost wished that stupid bell would ring to announce his departure. After all, his exit would be more dramatic that way, and Isabella seemed to like drama.

Liesel handed Isabella a glass of lemonade. Settling into a white wicker chair, she carefully lowered her steaming mug of hot tea to the small table between them. "Are you sure you don't want a sandwich or something to eat? It's no trouble. I made cookies for the guests."

"No, thanks. I need a listening ear more than anything else." Isabella glanced over the expansive yard. "Ah, the view from the front porch at Landon's. Such a great place to be in the summer. Did Caroline tell you she chatted with Seth about the birds and the bees right here on this porch?"

"I heard something about it, but it was more about the birds than the bees from what I understand. Let me guess. You want to chat about Caroline's brother."

Isabella sighed. "Is there anyone in town who *hasn't* heard about Sidney?"

"Driving a car like that? I doubt it. He couldn't fade into the town landscape if he tried." Liesel tucked a long strand of blonde hair behind one ear and gave Isabella a weary smile before taking a sip of the tea.

"The baby still suffering from colic?"

"Yes, but I'm hoping it'll get better soon," Liesel said. "I talked to Mom last week, and she told me I was the same way. I never knew that before, and I did some research this morning. The two most common causes of colic are reflux and food or formula allergies. He's still so young, and I'm only breastfeeding him at this point. It's possible he has an allergy to something in *my* diet."

"Hard to believe a baby could have allergies already."

"Wheat and dairy are two of the most common offenders. You know Paul's had issues with dairy, so I suppose it's possible…" Liesel waved her hand. "There are so many variables, and I'm too tired to try and figure it out. I'm praying he grows out of it sooner than later."

"Tell you what," Isabella said. "I'm going to come over one afternoon whenever you say, and I'll take the baby and Bella to the park and then bring them back here. You and Paul can take a drive and treat yourselves to a long lunch. Just make sure to leave a bottle of breast milk."

Liesel's eyes grew wide, and she looked as though she'd burst into tears any second. "I don't know what to say. You'd really do that? That's so unselfish, and the sweetest offer I've had in weeks. Months, maybe." She knew how much Liesel missed her mother. If it weren't for her father's health, Isabella figured they'd probably never have moved away from Maine. At least Beverly was able to fly back quite often for visits.

"Well, you don't have to cry about it." Reaching into her purse, Isabella pulled out a tissue and handed it to her friend. "Here, take this."

"Don't pay any attention to me." Liesel dabbed beneath her eyes. "You know how I am. I don't operate well when I don't get at least five hours of sleep. I'm sure that has something to do with it. We're heading into the tourist season, and there's a lot to do around here besides taking care of the kids." She smiled through watery eyes. "Don't tell on me, but it's really nice to sit and share a few minutes of girl talk. I've missed this lately. You and Caroline are like my oasis in the desert. I don't know what I'd do without either one of you."

Isabella reached for Liesel's free hand and squeezed. "Love you, my friend."

"You, too." Liesel checked her watch. "I have about twenty minutes until the kids wake up."

"I need to get back to the store by then, anyway," Isabella said. "Have you hired a few of the local girls to help you out this summer?"

Liesel nodded. "All taken care of, thank the Lord. Now, tell me what's on your mind."

"Here's the thing, Liesel. I'm not sure what to make of Sidney. I'll admit at first I thought he was pompous, arrogant, and borderline chauvinistic."

"I hear a *but* in there somewhere." Liesel smiled from behind her mug as she took a drink of her tea. "Ah, it's the perfect temperature now."

"Ned Kendrick almost succeeded in toppling the pickle jar yesterday. Sidney rushed into the store and saved the day—well, at least the jar. He also made a suggestion to borrow library books to keep Ned occupied and out of trouble."

"That's a good idea," Liesel said. "I'm surprised you haven't moved that jar before now. I've always said it's an accident waiting to happen. I remember Clara chasing a few pranksters out to the front sidewalk through the years. She'd threaten them with her broom. From what Mom told me, Marty Kendrick was one of the worst culprits when he was a kid. As they say, the apple must not fall far from the tree."

Isabella enjoyed a long drink of her lemonade. "Why doesn't that surprise me?"

"So, tell me more about Sidney." Liesel shifted in the chair and sipped more of her tea.

Isabella briefly filled her in on the ice cream incident at Barron's the night before and how Sidney made an appearance. "Then he shows up in the store this morning with a big stack of books he borrowed from the library for Ned," she told Liesel. "You have to give credit to a man who braved a verbal smackdown from Millicent. I found his gesture very considerate. Noble, even. Great follow-through, too, because you know how guys can be selectively forgetful."

"I call it selective hearing, but the concept's the same." Liesel said.

"Gerry was in the backroom with me earlier today, and we were running over lines from the play he's in at the Bethel Playhouse next month. We were going over a scene that's confrontational and intense. Don't let it get around, but it's not that well-written and riddled with clichés. Anyway, Sidney overheard, misunderstood, and he—"

"Get out!" Liesel slapped one hand on her leg. "Don't tell me Sidney seriously thought it was *real?*"

"Yep. He sure did. Sidney barreled straight into the backroom to defend my *honor* real."

"Oh, Isabella, that's priceless," Liesel said once she stopped laughing. "I think I'm going to like this guy. I've heard how he roared into town, and all the guys are swooning over that sports car—not to mention half the women are swooning over the *man* in the car—but Sidney sounds like a decent guy at heart. Besides, he's Caroline's brother. That alone gives him a definite advantage, don't you think?"

"I suppose so." Isabella shifted to face Liesel, tucking one leg beneath her. "Sidney told me he's running away from home."

Liesel's brows lifted. "That's odd. I mean, what high-powered lawyer does something like that? Was he joking?"

Isabella shrugged. "I don't know. Maybe?"

"How long is he staying in town?"

"Two or three weeks, or so he says. I haven't talked with Caroline since yesterday after I showed him how to get out to the house. You heard about that, too, I'm guessing?"

Liesel nodded. "Of course. I have reliable sources."

"I kind of gave him a hard time and made him prove who he was, but I felt like I had to protect Caroline, you know?"

"I'd have done the same thing," Liesel agreed. "From the photos I've seen, Sidney doesn't look like either Caroline or Bryce."

"He doesn't. As far as running away, Sidney's one of the senior partners at the law firm, so I guess he can do whatever he wants,"

Isabella said. "He told me he's handed over his cases to Bryce and his other trusted associates. According to Caroline, Sidney never takes time off. As you can imagine, she was shocked when he showed up on her doorstep out of the blue."

Isabella and Liesel both waved to a few residents driving by in their cars.

"If Sidney took the time to make sure his cases were handled, and announced his plans to leave, that's not running away," Liesel observed. "That's taking a leave of absence."

"Maybe he meant it more like running away in another sense."

"Like what? Emotionally?" Liesel quirked her brows as she took another sip of her tea.

"I have no idea." Isabella checked her watch. "I only have a few minutes, but there's more. Aunt Clara marched into the store this morning with another one of her proclamations. This time, she announced that God told her I was going to marry Sidney."

Isabella thought Liesel would sputter her tea. Instead, she lowered her mug to the table, the essence of calm. "Your dear sweet aunt. I wouldn't worry too much about it."

"I'm not worried." Isabella frowned. "I know Aunt Clara has my best interests at heart but doesn't she realize the pressure she's putting on me by saying something like that?"

"It's only pressure because you're *allowing* it to pressure you, Isabella. Your aunt says lots of things. She's lovable, she's eccentric, but she's also lonely since Phil died. She doesn't mean any harm, but my take is that she's matchmaking again. She says things to plant the idea in someone's mind to oh, I don't know, try and help them see a situation or another person differently."

"Are you saying Aunt Clara made predictions about you and Paul?"

"Oh, yes." Liesel nodded, and a slow-moving smile creased her face. "Suffice it to say that I didn't like Paul early on. But Clara challenged both of us to dig deeper and get to know the person beneath the surface."

"I can't believe you didn't like Paul. You two are so perfect for each other. So, did Aunt Clara predict you'd marry him?"

Liesel waved her hand and smiled. "Dating, marriage, kids, the whole thing. And we're not the only ones. I understand she predicted

Caroline and Seth would get together from the first time Caroline was here in Evergreen."

"From what I know, they made a strong connection even though they didn't get together for a year or two later."

"Kind of like the strong first connection you've made with Sidney?"

"The truth, Liesel? Sidney scares me."

"Why's that? He doesn't sound scary."

"You know what I mean. If I take the time to dig deeper and get to know him, I have a good feeling I'll like him a whole lot better than I should." She tapped her curled fist over her heart.

"That's a problem?"

Isabella rose from the chair. "I suppose you'd say it's only a problem if I allow it to become one. I need to focus on being his friend. But, at the same time, it might be best if I keep my distance. I guess the question in my mind is how to be his friend without being attracted to him. How and where do you draw the line?"

"You're good friends with Joel, and he's an attractive man."

"Yes, but Joel doesn't make my palms sweat and my breath catch in my throat whenever I see him. But none of this even matters since Sidney's not a Christian, and he's going back to Boston. A one-two punch. Make that a three-punch since Caroline more or less told me he's not the kind of man who will settle for one woman."

Isabella raised both hands in the air. "There you have it! Case closed."

"Seems to me like the case is wide open, my friend." Liesel smiled. "My advice, if you want it, is to relax and allow God to work. After all, look how He worked for Paul and me, and Caroline and Seth. Remember, Caroline wasn't a Christian when she first came to Evergreen. As her story proves, anything can happen."

"That's true." Isabella forced a smile. "Just say a prayer for me, please. And pray for Sidney. Thanks for the chat and the lemonade."

"Anytime. And don't think I won't take you up on the offer to watch the kids."

Isabella turned and walked backwards across the expansive front yard. "Name it and claim it, my friend!" Lost in thought, she turned around as she reached the pavement.

Bam! Straight into a man jogging on the sidewalk.

Chapter 11

"I'm so sorry…" Isabella jumped back and gasped as the man put a gentle hand on her arm.

"Whoa. Steady there. Are you okay?"

Sidney. She should have known. That firm chest and those taut muscles couldn't belong to a full-time resident. Were his ears burning? "You again? Are you stalking me?" Evergreen was small, but she'd never run into a tourist this many times in such a short span of time.

She could stand to be a little more polite to the man, but he flustered her. In ways she decidedly wished *not* to be flustered.

He really had the grizzled look happening this afternoon since he hadn't shaved. She wondered if Sidney would come back into town to pick up the shaving cream he'd left on the front counter at Mahoney's earlier in the day. Avoiding his gaze, Isabella glanced across the street and tried to ignore the stares from a few ladies.

Move on, ladies. She might as well give it up. As the oldest single female in town, she and the big city lawyer were the hottest topic in town. Might as well set up lawn chairs and have a parade.

"Hello to you, too. How'd you know it was me? You weren't paying attention, and you didn't even look up before you asked if I was"—he grunted—"stalking you."

"Sorry for being rude, Sidney. I was just startled, that's all." Isabella nodded to his right hand. "That ring of yours is quite distinctive. I'm guessing it's your Harvard Law ring?"

"Yes." Twisting it around his finger, Sidney glanced at the ring with its large ruby stone in the center. "Too much?"

"Not if you like your brass knuckles Ivy League. You earned the right to wear that ring, after all. It looks heavy. I'm surprised you're not walking around lopsided."

He grinned. "Tell you what. How about I put the ring on a chain, and you can wear it around your neck for a few hours? That way, you can feel how heavy it is. Are you game?"

Isabella slid one hand to her hip. "Have you developed a fever? Are you bored? Why would you suggest such a thing?"

"I guess having an intriguing woman bump into me in broad daylight in the center of town makes me a little stupid. Let's agree we've got a mutual stalking thing happening between us and call it day."

Sidney removed his sunglasses. She'd broken a sweat wrestling with a pickle jar and yet nary a drop dampened his running shirt. The man barely seemed winded. Impressive, but what was halfway fair about that? Isabella made a mental note to ramp up her exercise regimen. Make that *start* one. Genetics were on her side, but once she hit 30, all bets were off.

His appreciative gaze flickered over her, taking in her high ponytail, T-shirt, and lived-in jeans. All the way down to her tennis shoes. Sidney's lips curved. "You look adorably fetching today, by the way."

"I'll agree that bumping into you has exposed your flirting gene." Shaking her head, Isabella moved past him. "Stalking each other sounds a little...weird and inappropriate."

"I call them as I see them." Taking her by the arm, Sidney gave her a swift tug and pulled her to the edge of the sidewalk.

"Hey! Now wait just a red-hot min—"

Seconds later, a teenage boy zoomed past them on a bicycle.

Sidney raised his hand in the air. "Hey, Harley." The kid waved and kept on going.

Isabella righted her cockeyed T-shirt after Sidney released her arm. "You've been in town a day, and you've already met Harley?"

"You're welcome. Yes, we met this morning. Harley's also a card-carrying member of the library. Interesting name."

"Yes, isn't it? His parents are Charlie and Marley. They thought naming him that might open doors for their son. *What* doors, I have no idea. In any case, thank you for ensuring I wasn't splattered all over the sidewalk by a...well, by a Harley Davidson."

Catching his amused chuckle, Isabella averted her gaze. She glanced at the front porch of Landon's where Liesel raised her mug in a silent salute.

"Is that Liesel?" Sidney waved and Liesel responded in kind before she headed inside. Who knew the man could be so neighborly?

"Yes. If you continue to stalk me, I'm sure you'll meet her soon enough."

"I'll meet her on Saturday night if not before. Caroline invited them to the house for dinner."

"Well, there you go."

"Up until now, I've referred to Liesel as Refrigerator Lady."

Isabella had started walking but she stopped. "And why is that?"

"Her photo's on Caroline's refrigerator. I assumed she was a missionary for the church."

"Sidney, your thought process truly fascinates me, but if you'll excuse me, I should get back to the store."

"Then I might as well tag along since I left a few things on the counter this morning."

"Yes, before you stalked out," she teased. "I put them under the counter. I figured you'd be back at some point." She waved him on ahead. "Don't let me slow you down."

He fell into step beside her. "I ran all the way into town, so I'm good."

"Show off. You must run regularly. Do you run up and down Beacon Hill?"

"No, I go to a club near the office."

"Of course, you do."

"Isabella, you know what you need?"

She could think of a few things, but she wasn't about to tell *him*. "A dill pickle?"

"That's an idea. Might help your disposition."

Isabella frowned as she stopped at the crosswalk. "You are such a sweet talker."

"I'm teasing, but you could stand to be a little less defensive."

"Add it to my list of faults. As long as we're chatting, please don't call me Izzy."

"Deal. As long as you don't call me Sid."

"Deal." She rolled her eyes when he jogged in place. Would the light never change? She'd consider jaywalking, but as soon as she did that, Hamilton Watters would choose that moment to turn onto Elm Street for his afternoon break.

"So, are you dating Lover Boy?"

"How long did you say you're sticking around town?" Isabella said as she jogged across the street. Sidney raced past her, crossed his arms, and lounged against a trash can. Why was he asking about Joel? He still hadn't told her about the challenge, wager, or whatever it was with Tommy.

Turning left, Isabella started toward Mahoney's when she heard a commotion behind her. She stopped and brought a hand over her mouth not to burst out laughing. Seemed Sidney had almost toppled the trash can, and a few residents had come to assist him and make sure he'd survive.

Within seconds, he'd already caught up with her.

Isabella couldn't help her grin. "You're already causing trouble."

"At least I'm not a bad actor."

Her grin faded. She wouldn't give him the satisfaction of a response. Was he talking about her or Gerry? Didn't matter. They were both bad actors. Unlike Gerry, at least she knew better than to try and act on the *stage*. On the other hand, it showed remarkable courage to stand up in front of a live audience.

Jogging ahead of her, Sidney opened the front door of the store and motioned her inside.

"Chivalrous or not, you have a bad habit of dropping conversation bombs." She stalked past him.

"Conversation bombs?" Sidney came inside the store so close on her heels that Isabella felt his warm breath on her neck. Shivers ran down her spine.

Turning, she ran into his chest. Again. "Owww." She rubbed her nose. "I'm having a déjà vu." This was silly. And ridiculous. They were both acting Harley's age.

Not wanting anyone to overhear their conversation, Isabella tugged on Sidney's shirt, pulling him back outside. Okay, so he *was* a bit sweaty. Small comfort.

After nodding to a few passersby, she faced him. "You say things to get me curious or all riled-up, and then you don't follow-up. Tell me, why do you do it, Sidney? Do you get some kind of weird thrill from teasing me?"

"I got the library books. Don't know about you, but I'd call that follow-up."

"That's true. I even told Liesel about that act of kindness." She chewed on her lower lip. "That was a very nice thing to do, actually."

His brows lifted. "Talking about me with the locals already, are you? I'm flattered, Miss Caccavale."

Isabella's eyes widened. "How'd you know my last name? I mean, no one else in town ever gets it right." She wasn't sure what to think, but she couldn't help but be flattered.

Sidney leaned almost nose-to-nose with her. "At least I got it right. Someone should. Not bad for a guy who hasn't been in town but a day, don't you think? I have no idea what you're talking about with the conversation bombs. Here's a novel idea. Why don't you ask me a straightforward question? If you do, I might just give you an honest answer."

"You're not forgetful either," she huffed. "I'm sure if you think about it hard enough, you'll remember."

Chapter 12

What was Isabella talking about now? The Lover Boy question? The bad acting comment? Maybe his brain was on a minibreak. For now, Sidney was content watching her. She was correct in that he loved to make her squirm. She was even more attractive when riled. He liked sparring with her. He followed her as she disappeared inside the store again.

"Clyde, I'm back! I appreciate your minding the store. Everything go okay?"

An older gentleman with graying hair and wire-rimmed glasses limped into view.

"No problems. How was your chat with Liesel? Little Paul still got the croup?"

"Colic, and yes, he does. Liesel's fine except for a lack of decent sleep."

"Is that city slicker I heard about staying over at Landon's?"

Isabella's cheeks colored a shade of pink.

Stepping forward, Sidney offered his hand to the other man. "Hello, Clyde. I don't want to presume anything, but I might be the aforementioned city slicker. Sidney Prescott."

The older gentleman shook his hand and laughed heartily. "Yep, using a word like *aforementioned*, you must be the one. I heard you're from Boston, young fella, and that you blew into town driving that fancy red Italian sports car everybody's talking about. Prescott, you say?" Clyde scratched his chin. "Any relation to Caroline and Bryce?"

"Yes, sir. They're my younger sister and brother. I'm more the black sheep of the family. They're the ones who do the family proud. And the sports car is only a loaner."

"Welcome to Evergreen all the same."

"Thanks." Sidney darted a glance at Isabella. "It's been very interesting so far."

Isabella had moved behind the counter and seemed to be searching for something. "Clyde, did you see a can of shaving cream and a couple of other things? Mr. Prescott left them here this morning, and I put them on the shelf below Cash. I don't see them now."

"Oh, sorry. I reshelved them since I didn't see a note telling me to hold them."

"No, that's fine. We can just pull them again."

"Don't bother. I'll get them." Sidney darted around the aisles, gathering the items while Isabella continued to chat with Clyde.

"Could you prop open the door on your way out?" Isabella called to the older man as he prepared to leave.

"You got it," Clyde said. "Nice to meet you, Sidney."

Sidney walked to the end of the aisle. "Same to you, sir."

"Hope we'll be seeing you around town. You here long?"

"That's the question of the hour. I'm thinking at least a couple of weeks."

"Glad to hear it. I think you'll find our little town hospitable." With a polite nod, Clyde began whistling an unfamiliar tune and headed out the door. He forgot the door, so Sidney lodged a wooden wedge beneath it.

Meow.

A black cat lazed in the sunshine outside, at the base of the park bench by the front window. "Well, hello there." Crouching, Sidney started to scoop the black cat in his arms before he thought better of it. Maybe that wasn't the best idea. He stroked the cat's head, and the feline leaned into it, closing his green eyes.

Isabella came to the doorway. "This is Humphrey. You can pet him. He's friendly. He belongs to a family down the street, but this is his regular hangout."

"How old is Humphrey?"

"From what Aunt Clara told me, I think he's about seven. He started coming around when he was a kitten. He's considered one of our regulars."

The cat warmed right up to him. Tucking Humphrey under one arm, Sidney dropped onto the bench. He patted the space beside him and gave Isabella what he hoped was an inviting smile. "Sit with me?"

"Why, Top Dog, are you playing nice?"

"I think I am. Not sure how long it'll last, so you'd better take advantage of my better side while you can. You don't have a back entrance for customers, do you? You'll be able to see if anyone comes in?"

"True, but I'm not used to sitting still," she said. "Evergreen might be considered a sleepy town, but I don't like being lazy."

Beneath Sidney's fingers, a rumble of pleasure came from the cat's belly. He'd never had a pet, so he was surprised Humphrey seemed to like him. "Somehow I don't think anyone could ever accuse you of being lazy."

"Call it downtime then. Like I was having with Gerry this morning, by the way. He's a local actor and asked me to run lines with him." Isabella lowered to the bench beside him.

"I figured as much," he said with a quick grin. "Not without first feeling like an idiot for storming into your backroom like some misguided hero." Sidney nudged her arm. "For what it's worth, I'm thankful that scene wasn't real."

"I found your concern very sweet. And I'm not dating Joel. We've always been"—she raised her fingers in the air to indicate quote marks—"just friends."

Isabella watched as he continued to stroke the cat. "Besides, I got 'friend dumped' last night. Joel's found someone else he wants to date. So, it looks like it's just me and Humphrey for a while."

When she also stroked the cat, Sidney enjoyed the brief touch of her hand next to his. This was nice, sitting on the bench together, talking. When was the last time he'd enjoyed quiet conversation with a woman? No expectations, just conversation?

"Confession time," he said. "I could have borrowed shaving cream and those other things from Seth."

"I know, but I'm glad you came by. Do you have a cat in Boston?"

"No. Never had one. Never had a dog either. Animals, marble floors, and priceless works of art aren't a good mix."

"Well, then, you've missed out on one of most satisfying things of life. Did you ever *want* a pet?"

Sidney considered the question. "I didn't feel like I missed out if that's what you're asking." He shrugged. "You can't miss what you don't have, right?"

"True." Sitting back on the bench, Isabella made a clucking noise. "You poor rich boy. You've been so deprived."

"Now who's being smug?" In a playful move, Sidney pushed Isabella's hand aside and then ran his fingers down the middle of Humphrey's back. "I'm only home to sleep, so that wouldn't be fair to a pet. It would be pointless to hire someone to walk my own dog."

"So then you get a cat. They're very self-sufficient. You don't even have to walk them."

"But you have to clean out a litter box," he protested.

"Nothing like cleaning a litter box to keep a man humble." Tilting her head, Isabella's smile teased the corners of her lips.

He could get used to that smile, those lips. "Are you suggesting I find a companion?"

"A companion might bring out your softer side." In a return move, Isabella pushed his hand away so she could pet Humphrey. Her cheeks flushed pink again. He liked making her blush. For the moment, he needed to change the subject.

"Tell me, what do you do in your spare time? Hone your painting skills?"

She laughed. "You and your honing talk. If it's cold outside, I like to make tea or hot chocolate and curl up on the sofa with a good book." Isabella clasped her hands on her lap and swung her legs back and forth, reminding him of a kid. In her jeans and T-shirt, her hair scooped back in a high ponytail, she could pass for a college student. Pretty. Spunky. Fresh-faced. Isabella didn't wear much makeup compared to the other women he knew, except for Caroline.

When he realized she was waiting for him to say something, Sidney forced his thoughts back on-track. "And in the warm weather?"

"I hike, or swim, or take my easel outside and work on those honing skills." She tossed him a grin. "I'm on the church beautification team, and we plant flowers, trim brushes and trees, paint, things like that. Whatever needs to be done."

"I haven't had many opportunities to work with my hands," Sidney mused.

"You've never done community work in Boston? Stuff that's good for the image?" She snapped her fingers. "Community service to pay off all those speeding tickets?"

"The short answer is no. You won't see me in a neon orange vest picking up trash by the side of the highway."

Isabella's smile sobered. "I think volunteering our time and talents is like anything else. If we're not exposed to it early on, it's more of a learned behavior. Have you and Caroline been close through the years?"

Sidney considered the question. "Not really. I hope that doesn't make me sound like a bad big brother. A bad...person."

"Of course not. You're what, five or six years older than Caroline?"

"Seven. I'm 33, same age as Seth."

She nodded. "That's a fairly significant age difference, especially when you're in school. And I wouldn't consider you a bad person by any stretch of the imagination. Bad would be if you'd kicked Humphrey to the curb. But look at you making all nice with him." Isabella gave the cat an affectionate rub on the head and then tweaked his ears. "Since you work with Bryce at the law firm, would you say you're closer to him?"

"In some ways, yes. He's three years younger than me, and he's tight with Caroline, as you probably know. I hear a lot about what's happening with her through what Bryce tells me." Sidney shifted his position on the bench. "How about you? I know you grew up in California. How many brothers and sisters do you have?"

A wave of sadness clouded Isabella's expression.

"I'm sorry, Isabella. I didn't mean to overstep any boundaries."

"No, it's okay. I grew up in southern California with wonderful parents. I was an only child. My parents wanted more kids, but it never happened. My grandparents all passed away either before I was born or by the time I was in high school. The only family I have left is Aunt Clara, my mom's older sister, and Clara's five children and their offspring."

"Your mom and dad are gone?" He hated to ask the question.

Isabella nodded. "They died in a car accident in California when I was in my junior year at UCLA. Head-on collision. They were killed instantly and didn't suffer. My dad, especially, would have hated being kept alive artificially, and mom would never have recovered if Dad had been taken and she'd been left behind. Their love was rare—based on friendship and a deep faith. They'd been each other's sweetheart from the time they were in grade school. I don't think either one of them would have wanted to go on without the other."

Sidney reached for her hand. "I'm very sorry, Isabella. I had no idea."

She sniffled, her dark lashes damp with her unshed tears. "We deal with things as they come, but the loss devastated me. I walked around campus with this perpetual ache in my heart. Went through the motions of living. My grades faltered, and I let relationships go. Instead of drawing comfort from friends, I pushed them out of my life."

Releasing her hand, Sidney gently shifted Humphrey to her lap. "Here. I think you might need Humphrey more than I do right now."

She sniffled and hugged the cat, burying her face in his fur for a long moment. "Humphrey's seen me shed a few tears, haven't you, sweet kitty?" She glanced over at him. "Don't go thinking I'm a crybaby."

"Not for a minute." Her tears were beautiful, a part of her, although Sidney hated the reason for them. She'd been through so much, and he'd had no idea. His natural instinct was to pull Isabella into his arms and hold her, comfort her, but he knew he shouldn't.

"I finally snapped out of my melancholy and understood I needed to immerse myself in living again. I knew it was the only way to heal. Aunt Clara flew out to California to see me. I considered transferring to a New England college, but by that time, I was anchored in the UC—University of California—system."

"Did your faith in God falter after your parents' deaths?" Sidney wasn't sure what possessed him to ask such a personal question, especially one about God, but he knew Isabella wouldn't answer if it made her uncomfortable. She was one of the most giving, generous, and open people he'd ever met.

"I was mad at Him for a while, but I wouldn't say my faith faltered," she said. "It's like being furious with someone you love. Your love for them doesn't go away."

"That makes sense." Sidney had the example of his parents' relationship through the years as a prime example. "You can respect someone yet still hate things that have happened, hate the things they've done."

"Right." She lifted her gaze to his. "Sidney, have you ever been introduced to Jesus?"

"If I say no, does that mean you can't associate with me now?"

Humphrey jumped off his lap. Now even the cat was rejecting him. "I'm sorry. Please know I'm not ridiculing your faith, Isabella. If anything, I'm trying to understand it. Of course, I've heard about Jesus, but no, I've never really known much about Him. Caroline told me this morning she believes that's one of the reasons I'm here in Evergreen—to explore my faith." Sidney blew out a sigh. "I think she's right. She gave me an old Bible that belonged to Seth's grandfather, and she encouraged me to read it."

"That's wonderful. I hope you'll take the opportunity." The way her eyes lit made Sidney want to go back to the house and immerse himself in that Bible. That wouldn't be the proper motivation, perhaps, but he had to start somewhere. She was right in saying she hoped he'd *take* the opportunity. That was a conscious choice on his part to make…or not.

Isabella appeared deep in thought. "What I like to do is live my faith as honestly as I can. I fail all the time. I'm not the poster girl for living a sinless life, but since I moved to Maine, I've tried to be more in tune with God's will."

"I wasn't raised in the church, so I never thought much about God," he admitted. "He was someone we prayed to on the holidays, but it's not like He sat beside me at the dinner table. Other than that, I had no idea what any of it meant other than being the means to the end."

"The means to an end?"

"I couldn't eat until the prayer was said, as shallow as that sounds. We were the classic holiday churchgoers. We'd go to a late Christmas Eve service and then go home and open our gifts. So I'd associate prayer as being the forerunner to something else I wanted more. My dad never had a belief system other than doing what was best for Duncan Prescott." Sidney sighed and stretched out his legs in front of him. He should have done his cool down exercises. After flexing his calf muscles, he reached down and lightly massaged his right calf. Isabella waited patiently.

"And then you have my mother who apparently became a Christian a long time ago, but she never told any of us until after Caroline moved here to Maine," he said. "I always thought that if you loved God, you'd care enough to share your faith, especially with your family. She kept it private, not that I could fault her. Mom had it rough for a lot of years."

"Did you ever ask your mom why she never said anything about her faith or why she never took you to church on a regular basis?"

Sidney's eyes grew damp and the dull ache in his heart surfaced. "I was pretty close to her in the end, and she shared some things with me." He ran his hand over his face and sucked in a quick breath. "Because of circumstances in the marriage, my mom had closed up emotionally. I don't know if you're aware that Caroline was in a car accident during the time our parents came up here for a visit. That was when she and Seth had just started dating, but they were solid and headed toward marriage."

"I didn't know about the accident. Was she hurt?"

"Banged up a bit but nothing major. Caroline's accident prompted my mom to talk about the circumstances of her marriage to dad. That's convoluted and another story for another day. I suppose you could say that's when Mom came back to her faith."

"Does it give you comfort knowing your mom's in heaven?"

"More than I ever thought it would, but I'm not exactly sure why." Sidney appreciated how he could share private thoughts about his family with Isabella knowing she wouldn't judge him. He'd never discussed religion with anyone other than his mom, Caroline, and Bryce. Most of his associates at the firm were Catholic, Buddhist, atheist, or outright rejected any form of organized religion.

"Jesus instructed His followers to share their faith, and it's what we're called to do as believers in Christ, but everyone's journey is different." Isabella's voice was quiet. "I'd grown up in the church. I loved hearing stories about Jesus and His miracles. How he loved children and even His enemies. My story's not anything dramatic. My mom led me to faith in Christ when I was twelve. We knelt by the side of my bed and prayed the same as we always did, but one night, I confessed that I was a sinner and asked Jesus to come and live in my heart."

"It's special because it's *your* story, Isabella. Thanks for taking the time to listen to my story, especially since I know you need to get back to work."

"I think God knew you needed this time, Sidney. I think I did, too." Squeezing his arm, Isabella leaned against him for a moment, her lovely smile back in place. "For once, I'm thankful I didn't have any customers." She rose from the bench. "I'd better get back inside."

"I'll come in long enough to pay for the things I forgot this morning, and then I promise to stop stalking you." Sidney stood up beside her. "If I don't shave soon, I'm going to look like a mountain man."

"I like your company. Stop in anytime." Isabella tilted her head and studied him. "I kind of like the scruffy look on you."

"You do?" He ran his hand over his grizzled chin. "Think I should keep it?"

She shrugged. "Your choice."

"Isabella?" He hesitated, unsure whether he should voice his next thought.

"Yes?" She paused with one foot over the threshold.

"Thanks for not trying to push anything down my throat."

"It's not my job to preach. It's my job to love you quietly and show you by example." She rolled her eyes and dipped her head as that lovely flush of color crept up her neck and into her cheeks. "I hope you know what I mean."

"I'm not sure, but I'll take it," he said. "It's not every day a beautiful woman—a beautiful *person*—tells me it's her job to love me, quietly or not. I'm honored."

She nodded. "For what it's worth, Sidney, thank you for pulling me out of harm's way today. You were quite gallant. Now, are you coming inside or what?"

"Or what." Sidney smiled and followed her into the store.

Chapter 13

Seth sat at the breakfast table when Sidney walked into the kitchen on Friday morning. His brother-in-law was already dressed for the day in jeans, a short-sleeved red polo, and a casual jacket draped over the back of his chair.

"Morning," Sidney mumbled. By contrast, he was still in his sleep pants and T-shirt. At home, he was usually up, dressed, and out the door before seven.

"Morning. Sleep well?" Seth said as Sidney poured a bowl of cereal and added a little milk. He liked his cereal crunchy, not soggy.

"Sure did. I'm going to order a featherbed when I get back to Boston." He carried his bowl to the table and sat opposite Seth.

"Nothing like them. It's a good thing Caroline likes them, too."

That made Sidney chuckle. "I think that's a given."

Seth grinned. "Your sister doesn't mince words if she doesn't like something. Good thing we agree on most things."

Sidney figured he might as well get to the heart of the matter. "Look, Seth. I know you don't like *me* much."

"That's not true." Seth raised his coffee mug and took a tentative sip. "I don't know you well enough to not like you, Sidney. We can remedy that if you're sticking around. I can tell you one thing."

"What's that?"

"I like a man who gets straight to the point."

"Hazard of the job." He grinned. "I admire you, Seth. From what I can see, you've got it all."

"And you don't?"

That question surprised him. "I've achieved what I always *thought* I wanted." Sidney took a bite of the cereal and tapped his fingers on the table. "Bottom line? I'm learning that it's not enough."

Seth lowered his mug and took a bite of blueberry muffin, chewing slowly. "Here, have one." He pushed the plate across the table. "They're hot out of the oven and made with wild blueberries grown locally."

"Don't mind if I do." Selecting one of the muffins from the plate, Sidney took a bite. "Oh, man." He savored the warmth and rich succulence of the fresh berries. The muffin was loaded with them. "You're right. This is one of the best things I've ever tasted. No lie."

"Thanks. I made them fresh this morning."

Sidney almost choked on his second bite. "*You* made these? I mean…more power to you, buddy." He gave Seth a thumbs-up sign.

Seth chuckled. "My friend Beverly Landon taught me how to make them a few years ago. Bev's like a second mom, and she's a fantastic cook. I stayed at Landon's whenever I'd come into town, and I was usually the first one in the kitchen for breakfast. One morning, she lined up the ingredients on the counter and basically told me to get busy."

"No wonder Caroline married you." Sidney pushed the last of the delicious muffin in his mouth. "*I'd* marry you for one of these babies." He'd need to keep up the jogging routine to work off the muffin, but it was worth the calories.

Seth grinned. "As long as we're sharing truths, what exactly is it about your life in Boston that's not enough?" He took another drink of his coffee.

"I love the research and the preparation involved for a trial. I love case law. I love when the legal system triumphs. But I'm only as good as my last courtroom victory. Most people tend to have a short-term memory."

"That's true enough in general, don't you think?"

If nothing else, Sidney knew the man sitting across from him was fair. The history between his family and Seth's was ugly. His father had tried to destroy Seth's father in a Boston manslaughter trial years ago. Yet their two fathers had made peace with one another. Even Seth and Duncan had grown closer than Sidney could ever have expected before his dad's decline.

If Seth possessed any lingering anger, he was man enough—*Christian* enough—not to direct that anger at Sidney. The Christian part of the equation had to be the key. Seth was a good man to the core. Caroline had chosen well.

"I had a client who got off because of a mistrial fourteen months ago. Blatant jury tampering, open and shut case. But he was guilty." Sidney took a few bites of his cereal.

"Do you have proof?" Seth lowered his mug to the table.

"Not definitive proof, no, but I felt it in my gut. I'd bank my career on it. That's how sure I am. The client swore up and down he didn't do it, but he was guilty."

Seth met his gaze. "What was the charge?"

"Embezzlement. Fortune 500 company." Seth appeared confused, prompting him to explain. "I handle high-profile, white-collar criminal defense now—wire fraud, forgery, embezzlement."

"You're no longer handling the other cases?"

"No. I wanted to be able to look at myself in the mirror with a modicum of respect. I switched over to the new caseload a little more than two years ago. I'd like to live to see my fiftieth birthday."

Was it his imagination or did Seth appear pleased? "I see."

"I guess Bryce never told Caroline. I should have told her. Sorry."

"How much was your client accused of embezzling?"

"A half million, give or take. CFO of the company."

Seth whistled under his breath. "That's a boatload of money."

"Tell me about it."

"After the trial was finally over, did you ask him again if he did it?"

Sidney shook his head. "I couldn't. I didn't want to hear it if the man confirmed my suspicions. In some ways, I don't like the man I've become, Seth. I can't *respect* the man I've become. Above all, I want to be a man of integrity."

He couldn't believe he'd admitted that much to a man he barely knew. Yet Sidney knew in his gut that he could trust Seth with the truth. This man was married to his sister. He was *family*.

"From what I know, that's not in question."

"It's not, but I know the truth. Lawyers get a bad reputation because people feel they distort reality and, more often than not, protect the guilty. That's not what I signed on for when I took the oath to uphold the justice system and the laws of the Commonwealth of Massachusetts. I swore before the judge—and ultimately before God—to not willingly or wittingly commit any falsehoods."

Seth nodded. "You're having an attack of conscience?"

"In a manner of speaking yes. I have clients who are innocent, but let's face it, the majority of them wouldn't be on trial if their lives were lily white, so to speak."

After finishing his cereal, Sidney sat back in the chair.

"In the case of that particular client, if there was blatant jury tampering, then a mistrial was the proper verdict in spite of the circumstances," Seth said. "I know it's a tough one, but other than recuse yourself, you did your job."

"The reason to recuse myself is a conflict of interest or impartiality. I said nothing, and so the victory was hollow. I've had more than my share of those in the past few years. If the client fee is high enough, I'm expected to take the case, and toss aside my personal convictions of guilt or innocence." Sidney heaved a deep sigh. "Because I'm the almighty Duncan Prescott's son, and he was The Shark. Also called The Snake. Take your pick. He went for blood, and he got it."

Resting his elbows on the table, Sidney rubbed the heels of his hands over his eyes. "I don't mean any disrespect to my dad."

"Even more than Bryce, as the eldest son, you have high expectations placed on your shoulders to carry on the Prescott legacy," Seth said. "Caroline understands that, and so do I."

Sidney raked a hand through his hair. "Bryce was smarter than me in pursuing a different type of law. I used to think I was cut out for the cutthroat cases. Now, I'm not so sure. Caroline always thought I'd make a good prosecutor. There are times I wish I'd taken that route. I guess I'm more drawn to the underdog. The challenge is in trying to get an acquittal or a verdict of innocence. But, what good is it if I wake up in the middle of the night soaked in sweat? If I constantly suffer from heartburn and have to pop antacids all the time? That's why I work out so much." He had a secret fear he'd keel over from a massive heart attack within the next decade if he didn't do something to alleviate the heavy stress.

Seth's blue eyes narrowed. "From what you're saying, maybe it's time for a change. Switch to something more gratifying and rewarding that doesn't create so much inner conflict and turmoil for you."

"That's where my thinking's been headed lately," Sidney said. "I've already switched to a different practice, and I'd hate to be perceived as wishy-washy. Neither do I want to leave the firm."

"I don't know why you'd necessarily need to leave. Maybe you could take your practice in a different direction. Don't worry about what anyone else thinks. They know you well enough to know you're solid, and I'd hope they'd support your decision. You know Bryce will. You're not the only criminal defense attorney at the firm, are you?"

"No." Sidney laughed, but it lacked humor. "Bryce told me he thinks the partners might call an emergency meeting to discuss whether I'm going through a crisis of some sort. Caroline asked the same thing when I showed up on your doorstep." He shook his head and marched his fingers on the top of the table again. "In all honesty, I can't blame them."

"Only because it was sudden and out of character for you. I know Caroline understands, and I feel safe in saying Bryce does, too. Your personal losses in the past six months alone have been a lot for anyone to absorb. Whether you realize it or not, I'm sure that has something to do with this reevaluation of your practice. Not that you asked, but I'd say this trip is good for you to step away, catch your breath and regroup. Everyone needs time away, Sidney."

Bryce suffered the same losses and yet he'd adjusted well. Ditto Caroline. Then again, his brother and sister had supportive spouses. Who did *he* have? Not even a pet.

Sidney forced a smile. "I hope you're right. You're a good guy, Seth. Thanks for the talk."

"Anytime. Would you mind if I said a prayer for you?"

"Um, no. I guess not." A part of him found the idea of prayer comforting. "We don't have to hold hands, do we?"

Seth grinned. "Not unless you want to."

"Good. I don't like your baking *that* much. And this might sound stupid, but thanks for loving my sister. For making her happy."

"That's my honor. Caroline makes it easy."

Following Seth's lead, Sidney bowed his head. Unlike the other man, he didn't close his eyes but stared at the woodgrain of the sturdy kitchen table instead.

"Father, you know the burdens Sidney has on his shoulders at the firm," Seth prayed. "We lay those burdens at your feet. We ask that you work in these circumstances to reveal your perfect will for him, and to bring him closer to a saving knowledge of you. We ask these things in the name of your Son, Jesus. Amen."

"Amen." Short and simple, the way Sidney preferred his prayers. "People talk about legalese, but you Jesus people have your own language."

A frown creased Seth's brow.

"I didn't mean that in a bad way," Sidney assured him.

"Basically, we present our prayers to God through Jesus."

"Because you believe He died for you."

"That's right. He shed His blood so that we might have eternal life with Him in heaven." Seth's gaze settled on him. "If you'd like to sit down one night while you're here, I'm more than happy to answer your questions."

"I'll let you know." Planting his hands on the table, Sidney lifted out of the chair and gathered their dirty dishes. "I'll take care of these. I'm sure you need to go and study rocks or something."

Although Seth smiled, Sidney could tell he was preoccupied. "I've got a couple of meetings over in Oxford Hills today." He retrieved his jacket and shrugged into it.

"Caroline told me she got a tee time for us early on Monday morning," Sidney said. "You okay with that?"

Seth nodded. "I'll look forward to it. I'm headed into town tomorrow morning about nine. The annual Twilight Dance is held on the second Saturday in June every year. Some of the guys are meeting at the park to put the dance floor together, string the lights in the trees, that kind of thing. If you're interested, you're welcome to come and help out if you'd like. Depending on how many show up, it'll take a few hours tops. Liesel will provide lunch."

"Sure." Sidney set the dishes in the sink. "Count me in."

"Great. How are you at wielding a hammer?"

"I haven't a clue." Sidney ran a hand over his chin and tried not to feel too foolish with that admission. He'd rarely held a hammer, but he was coordinated. "I suppose there's no better time to start than tomorrow morning."

"You look capable, and we can always use the help. It'll be a good time to meet some of the other guys. Paul will be there."

"I'm hoping this Twilight Dance has nothing to with vampires."

Seth chuckled. "Not at all. A small band plays in the gazebo, and it's a fun evening of dancing under the stars."

"So, Caroline's going to stuff us full of good food at dinner tomorrow night, and then we're expected to work it off on the dance floor?"

"We don't get too crazy," Seth said. "Some of the kids might have a dance-off. They usually do. And some of the adults might challenge them to prove they can still dance."

Sidney grinned. "Sounds like fun." He opened the dishwasher.

"You were wrong about one thing, you know."

"What's that?" Sidney turned to see Seth standing in the doorway, his briefcase in hand.

"I've always liked you, Sidney. I haven't always agreed with everything you've done, but Caroline and I know how closely you watched over your mother before she died. How you took care of the details and made sure she was as comfortable as possible. We're aware you spent time with her to the exclusion of other things in your life."

Sidney swallowed. "I did what anyone would have done."

"Still, that was an uncommon sacrifice, and we appreciate you," Seth said. "You weren't in the frame of mind to hear it during the memorial service, but thank you. I'm glad you're here now. Families need each other."

If the man didn't leave, Sidney might just cry. "Yeah, they do." His voice sounded like he had gravel in his mouth.

"Call my cell if you need anything today." His brother-in-law tapped the doorjamb. "You're welcome to stay with us as long as you need."

"Thanks." Sidney stared after Seth as he departed. "I might just do that."

Chapter 14

Sidney spent the rest of the morning making the acquaintance of shopkeepers up and down Elm Street, Evergreen's version of Main Street. Why, he had no idea. He'd never been so sociable in all his life. Other than when he'd been on vacation at Martha's Vineyard or in Newport, Rhode Island, he'd never taken the time to leisurely stroll up and down a street and poke in and out of stores. He'd pretty much hated it in the past, and he'd only been interested for the food since many of the restaurants had an outdoor patio, which he enjoyed, and the opportunity to appreciate a decent live jazz band was always a good thing.

The owner of the sporting goods store, Roger Meecham, went on for at least a half hour telling him about his six grandkids. Sidney knew their names and which sport they played. Even the four-year-old girl, Jillian, was on some kind of team—T-bone? No, T-ball, whatever that was. Roger proudly pointed out the photos lined up on the wall behind the register. Sidney had to admit, those kids were awfully cute. If *he* had any hope of having kids someday, let alone grandkids, he'd better make some major life changes soon. He didn't stand a chance of procreating if he spent the majority of his free time at the firm or in the gym.

First you find love, Sidney. That's how it was supposed to be done. Did he want to get married? Did he want to try and raise one child or more in this crazy, mixed-up world?

Yes.

He'd never admitted it to himself, much less to anyone else, but he wanted those things. Like everything else in his life, he didn't want to do it halfway. Is this what people called cleansing their aura? Caroline, Seth, Isabella, and the members of their church would probably call it following God's will or plan for his life.

His parents more or less had an arranged marriage and look how that had worked out. Not great. Caroline's marriage was solid, and now Bryce was a giddy newlywed. Sidney couldn't miss the goofy grin on his brother's face, a clear indicator of what he'd been up to at home, when he arrived at the firm some mornings. He'd give Bryce a slap on the back or a knowing wink like guys did when they didn't know what else to do or say. But he was genuinely happy for his younger brother. Bryce was as sharp as ever with clients and maintained more than his share of the caseload. At least the man was happily married, and his after-hours activities didn't interfere with his work for the firm.

Wow. This kind of thinking was why he was single.

Leaving Meecham's Sporting Goods, Sidney paused on the front sidewalk. When he pulled his sunglasses from the pocket of his jogging pants, a half roll of antacids fell onto the ground. He scooped it off the sidewalk and tucked it back in his pocket before positioning his sunglasses. The sun was warm, the sky was clear. Another beautiful day in Evergreen, Maine.

Sidney glanced down the street at the open door of Mahoney's. He figured he was exercising uncommon restraint in not hanging out on the bench. Nothing like being obvious. Humphrey occupied his usual spot by the front door, making him smile.

He walked in the direction of the general store. Close enough to hear the sound of Isabella's laughter. He liked her laugh. Liked her voice. Moving closer, he caught a glimpse of the lovely store owner. She wore khaki shorts today with a pink top. She embodied everything he liked and admired in a woman. Strong in body and character. Feminine. Sexy. Intelligent. Compassionate. Confident with a hidden vulnerability. A great sense of humor. Adorable when she was embarrassed. A smile that nearly knocked him down the last few times he'd glimpsed it. Curves that made him want to rest his arm around her small waist and draw her near. Lips that made him want. . .

Something stirred inside, the desire for a woman Sidney hadn't allowed himself to feel in a very long time. He'd felt the beginnings of those same stirrings yesterday while sitting with Isabella on the park bench. This was more than infatuation. Any number of women could catch his attention, but few had been able to hold it. Now, every time he thought of Isabella, every time he anticipated seeing her, he found himself smiling.

This can't go anywhere. He didn't know how to stop these thoughts, but he couldn't dwell on them. He respected Isabella. He'd never known a woman with the kind of faith she'd shared with him. Isabella *lived* her faith, and to his surprise, he liked that.

Sidney sidestepped an older woman walking two poodles—those tiny toy dogs, one black, one white—and moved closer to the curb where he could better see Isabella. Her long, dark hair was pulled back in her customary high ponytail. Must be easier for her to wear it that way when she worked in the store. He liked it this way, but he loved seeing her hair down—lush, full, and tumbling around her shoulders—the way she'd worn it the first day he'd met her.

"Sir, I think we need to untangle you."

"What?" Sidney reluctantly jerked his gaze away from Isabella. He glanced down when he felt something tug on his right ankle. One of the woman's poodles—the white one—had managed to wrap its leash around his foot. How had he missed that? This situation was ironic if not somewhat Freudian.

"I'm so sorry for the trouble," the woman said. "Bessie saw a piece of candy on the ground beneath your shoe, and she went after it."

Candy? A quick glance at the sidewalk confirmed his suspicions. An antacid had broken loose and was half-lodged beneath his foot. Bessie was sniffing and pawing at the pastel-colored tablet, trying to get at it. The older woman made an attempt to retrieve the leash and sighed with frustration when her efforts proved unsuccessful.

Sidney grabbed the antacid from under his shoe and tossed it in the trash can.

"Wonderful aim! You must be a basketball player," the woman observed. "My Henry played basketball back in the day. I used to love watching him play." A hint of sadness tinged her words.

"I was on swim teams and ran track when I was younger. I play an occasional game of pick-up basketball, but apparently it takes more than a law degree to figure out how to help Bessie. If I could have the leash, I should be able to free her." Both dogs were well-behaved as he tried to unwrap the leash from his ankle. Yappy little dogs irritated him, and he avoided them at all costs.

After his efforts failed, Sidney frowned before fresh inspiration struck. "Tell you what. Here, you take hold of the leash while I try something else." When the woman took the leash from him, Sidney dropped to one knee and quickly untied the lace on his right running shoe. Then he stood up and pushed off his right shoe. "Success!"

The older woman laughed and clapped with delight. "Bravo! Let me guess. You must be Sidney Prescott."

"That would be me." How did she pick him out from among all the other visitors in town? Plenty of people strolled up and down the streets, tourists judging by their leisurely pace and gift bags in their hands or over their arms. Sidney smiled when he spied a few Mahoney's bags. Judging by the increased traffic on Elm Street, the weekend would be a busy one.

"I'm Hattie Nelson. I hope we'll be seeing more of you here in Evergreen. We sure could use an experienced attorney here in town if you'd ever think of moving here like your sister did."

Sidney briefly took the older woman's hand. "It's my honor to meet you, Miss Hattie. There's not a law office in town?"

"No, and it's a real shame. Not since Crawford Banks retired," she said with a sigh. "There are a few small firms over in Bethel and some in Oxford Hills. Most of the young lawyers want to go to the bigger cities. That's understandable, but they're also wet behind the ears and the ink is barely dry on their diplomas."

"Yes, ma'am. May I ask how you know that I'm Sidney?" As far as a family resemblance, Bryce looked more like Dad with each passing year. Caroline was more a combination of their parents. Sidney was his own man and had always been told he resembled his maternal grandfather.

Hattie brightened. "I should have explained. Caroline and Seth had a holiday party this past Christmas. It was a few months after they moved into their new home, and as you might be aware, you're in her family photos. Plus there's that proper Boston accent, and you mentioned a law degree. Sidney, I was very sorry to hear of the loss of your mother. I met her when she was visiting once." Hattie's voice was filled with nostalgia. "I also lost my Henry in the past year." Her blue eyes—similar in color to his mother's—were filled with compassion. "We were married a few months shy of fifty years."

"My condolences to you, as well." Removing his sunglasses, Sidney met her gaze. "I'm thankful you were able to enjoy many happy years with your husband." The love shining in her eyes was undeniable.

"The blessing of family is something that should never be taken for granted, young man. Through the times of both hardship and great joy, those are the people who are there for you. Loving you, supporting you."

"Miss Hattie, I'm learning the wisdom of those sentiments more every day."

The woman eyed him with a warm smile. "We finally have a new medical office with three doctors. If I may say, Evergreen is a perfect place for a young couple to raise a family. We might not have all that Boston can offer, but we have family values and hardworking people here. You can always go into the city for the weekend."

Sidney grinned. "As lawyers are prone to saying, I'll take it under advisement."

"You do that. Well, I'd better be on my way. I'm very glad to have met you. I hope to see you again." Hattie tugged on the leashes for the dogs. "Come now, Bessie. Frankie, you too."

Sidney purposely walked in the opposite direction from Mahoney's and darted across the street, being careful not to jaywalk in case Sheriff Watters happened to be on his reported morning donut and coffee run. No sense in tempting the man into issuing him a pedestrian violation.

After sampling five flavors of the delicious ice cream at Barron's, Sidney decided strawberry cheesecake was his favorite. He'd shied away from the boutiques although the ladies in one of them tried to lure him inside by offering him homemade cookies and milk.

"Just keep walking," he'd said under his breath. Waving to them, he'd hastened his pace.

Manelli's Grill sounded like a good restaurant for lunch. A few of the servers and patrons gave him odd looks as he was escorted to a table for one and waited for his meal. He wanted to challenge them and say, *Stop staring. You've never seen a guy eat solo before?* How many times had he dined on his own in Boston? Countless times. If he wasn't with clients, partners, associates, or potential recruits, he *preferred* eating by himself.

Lost in thought, Sidney started when a middle-aged woman leaned too close for comfort. "Young man, would you like to join us for lunch?"

A meek-looking gentleman—presumably her husband—stood behind her. One look at that poor guy and Sidney could tell he was henpecked.

"Thanks for the kind offer, but I need to eat and run today." Not exactly a lie although it was stretching the truth a bit.

"You must be the man from Boston I've heard so much about. Caroline's brother."

"That's right." Sidney forced a smile. Pushing back his chair, he rose to his feet. "Sidney Prescott. Nice to meet you...?"

"I'm Barbara Olander, and this is my husband, Darren." The woman waved her hand at Darren in a dismissive fashion, an action that didn't seem to bother Darren as much as it did Sidney. Reaching around Barbara, Sidney offered his hand to the other man in a barely disguised gesture of sympathy.

Darren shook his hand with a polite smile but said nothing. Small wonder.

"How long will you be gracing us with your presence in town, Mr. Prescott?" This woman seemed in no hurry to move along. She sure was laying it on thick, same as the perfume she must have bathed in.

"A couple of weeks at this point. I'm playing it by ear."

"Playing the field, you say? Would you like for me to set you up with a—"

"Playing it by *ear*, Barbara." Ah, Darren *could* speak.

"I see. Well, that's more like it," she said. "I hear you've taken a liking to that pretty Isabella Cockamamie. She's one of our sweetest unmarried gals in town." She eyed him up and down like Millicent had done. These small-town Maine women could be fairly brazen. "She's about your age, I'd say."

Sidney tamped down the quick rise of irritation mixed with the urge to laugh. "Yes, I'm friends with Isabella *Cac-ca-va-le*." He made sure to pronounce it correctly and enunciate. Maybe he was being a jerk, but he couldn't help it. Last names weren't a big deal here, he supposed. That was one explanation for why so few people seemed to get Isabella's last name right.

"Oh well, my mistake," the woman huffed. "As you might have guessed, I have a little bit of a hearing issue." This woman had an agenda. He'd seen her type many times. She was a busybody and a gossip. On the other hand, she seemed to hold genuine affection for Isabella, so she couldn't be all bad. Perhaps he'd be better off not to jump to hasty conclusions. He'd learned not to do it in his professional life, so the same principle should apply in his personal life. Funny how he'd had more of a personal life since coming to Evergreen than the past few years combined in Boston.

"Come, Barbara," Darren said. "We need to leave Mr. Prescott alone and go to our table now. The server is waiting."

Barbara gave Sidney an exaggerated wink. "I told Isabella to bring you round to my shop sometime. Jams & Jellies. We're over on Oak Street if you'd like to come by one day while you're out and about. I'll give you a free jar of my world famous blackberry jam on the house."

World famous? Yes, this woman was prone to exaggeration. "Thanks. Nice to meet you both." He watched as Darren took his wife by the elbow and guided her to a table on the other side of the restaurant.

"Cockamamie, my…" Sidney closed his mouth. For as long as he'd remembered, he'd cursed, but only under his breath. In private. Not in the courtroom, not to anyone else, and not in his personal conversations on the phone or in person. That didn't make it any better. Matter of fact, he'd almost let one slip in his conversation with Caroline the other morning.

He wasn't perfect, and he wasn't above a word or two slipping out when he was severely provoked. Thankfully, he'd learned to control his temper, and keep his anger in check, so it didn't happen often. His father had cursed like a sailor until the last few years. Bryce never did. Then again, his brother was a better man in many respects.

Sidney had looked at that Bible—the old one that had belonged to Seth's grandfather—earlier in the morning before leaving the house. He'd gone into Seth's study and read some random chapters. Done that dumb thing where he closed his eyes, opened the book, and pointed to a passage of Scripture. If God was really watching over him, he figured the Almighty would give him the words He wanted Sidney Jefferson Prescott to hear.

Interestingly enough, he'd landed in the Book of Proverbs 2:6-9. Talked about how it was the Lord who was the source of all wisdom, and how God was a shield for those who walked in integrity, and how He'd guard the paths of justice, preserving the way for those who followed Him.

Considering how he'd discussed the issue of integrity with Seth that very morning, the words struck Sidney as being intended for *him* to read. Is that how God worked? If so, who was he to refute it? Stranger things could happen, stranger things *had* happened.

The server, a pretty blonde teenager with a nametag that read KAITLYN, brought his order of grilled trout with lemon butter. As he prepared to eat his meal, Sidney did something he'd never done in his life, in private or in public.

Bowing his head, he began to pray. Not because it was expected, not because he was in church or sitting around a dinner table, not because anyone watched. Simply because he felt the need and genuinely wanted to pray.

Sidney suspected God could see him and maybe, just maybe, He was smiling.

Chapter 15

After lunch, Sidney sprinted down to Mahoney's. He couldn't wait to tell Isabella that he'd prayed. Who knew he could be so excited about saying a prayer? Some of the partners at the law firm would probably be struck dumb if they could see him now. This jaunt to Maine to find himself, run away, or whatever it could be called, had been the best decision he'd made in years. He wished he'd done it sooner, but would things have worked out this way at any other time in his life?

Along the way, several of the townspeople waved, smiled, and called to him by name. Some he'd met personally, some he hadn't, but it seemed a lot of people recognized him, a strange but wonderful occurrence. Some New England towns had reputations for unfriendly citizens, but he'd never know it judging by the people in Evergreen.

Sidney entered the general store with a bright smile. He found Isabella in COSMETICS, thankfully alone. Wrapping his arms around her waist, he lifted her from the floor, and swung her in a circle. "Good afternoon, sunshine!"

"Well, hello to you, too," she said. "You're in a great mood. Any particular reason?" She planted her hands on his chest and then slid her hands up to his shoulders.

He lowered her slowly, and it took every ounce of self-control he possessed to resist drawing this woman close and kissing her.

"Sorry," he said.

"I see you shaved."

Sidney caught her hand with his and resisted the urge to lace their fingers together. "Isabella, this probably isn't anything I should boast about, and I'm not, but I want you to know that I prayed for my meal. I feel like a kid in school who's received the highest grade from his favorite teacher. I've had court victories that left me feeling hollow inside, but the simple act of saying a prayer made me feel like I've won a hard-fought case today." He raised his arms to the side and gave her a brilliant smile. "Who knew?"

He must be nuts. Dreaming. Something.

A gorgeous smile spread across Isabella's face. "You did?"

He nodded with enthusiasm. "Indeed, I did. I don't know if God heard it, and—if you don't think He did—it's probably best if you don't even tell me. That way, I can remain forever happy in my ignorance."

"That's a very big step, Sidney. I think God hears the prayers of those who are seeking Him. I can't tell you how thrilled I am, and I appreciate your telling me."

A man burst into song from somewhere at the back of the store. Isabella laughed at his befuddled expression. Sidney cocked his head to one side. "Just so we're clear, that's not *God* singing back there, is it?"

Isabella giggled. "No. I'd like to hear God sing, as a matter of fact. That's Hank Jergens. He's a regular and plays checkers with Marty for a few hours each afternoon. Ned had a doctor's appointment today, so that's why Marty's not here. Hank will probably sing until one of the other guys comes in, or a tourist, so he can start another game. Normally, he only sings along with Randy Travis and George Strait, but it sounds like he's expanding his repertoire today. The one playing now is a Conway Twitty song called 'That's my Job.'"

"That's the actual name of the song?"

"Yes," she said. "My dad loved that one. It's a sentimental song about a father-son relationship. From what I remember, it's about a caring dad who called parenthood his favorite job. This is the time of year you hear it most often since it's almost Father's Day."

That thought sobered him to a point, but Sidney refused to allow thoughts of his own father spoil his positive attitude this afternoon. "It's nice to know there might be men in the world who actually feel that way about fatherhood. My dad was a huge influence on my life, but there were things I wish he'd done differently." *Or never done at all.* "I'm sure he could say the same about me."

"I'm sorry about your dad, especially now that he's…" Isabella's voice trailed. Sidney understood her awkwardness. It was hard for anyone to know what to say, but he appreciated her compassion.

"Thanks. I've never listened to much country music. You?"

"I have to be in the mood, but I'm nostalgic for the old classics," she said. "The older country legends my dad used to like—Loretta

Lynn, Johnny Cash, Patsy Cline. He called their songs 'true country' as opposed to the more modern country pop stars. I switch the playlist around for the store. Aunt Clara used to only play gospel music and old hymns, but I try to give the customers a mix."

Sidney followed her to the front counter. "Which begs me to ask which musical styles *won't* you play?"

"Heavy metal, grunge, rap." Isabella pretended to shudder. "Now what's *really* fun? The sing-alongs."

He crossed his arms on the counter with a wide grin. "Let me guess. Musicals?"

"You know it, counselor. Later in the summer, they show musicals on the big screen at Evergreen Park and everyone sings along. Guaranteed, it's the most clean fun you can have north of Boston."

When Isabella started to sing the song from *The Sound of Music* about the lonely goatherd and then started yodeling, his laughter nearly drowned out the sound of the bell.

If he didn't know it before, Sidney knew it now. He was falling in love with Isabella Caccavale. Maybe he was already there. When had that happened? As though in a stupor, he stood rooted to the floor, marveling over this newfound revelation.

Stopping her singing, Isabella shot him a look as she greeted her customer. "Good afternoon, Letitia. How are you today?"

"Hi, Isabella. I'm fine, but Larry's got a nasty head cold."

"Oh, I'm sorry to hear that. Do you need help finding anything?"

"I just need a box of tissues and maybe some cough drops. You know how the cough comes at the end of a cold, and those middle-of-the-night hacking spells can be the worst."

"Check the COLD/ALLERGY aisle," Isabella advised. "Tissues are on the endcap."

Sidney called to the customer. "Mrs. Baldwin, have you tried mashed potatoes?"

Isabella widened her eyes and her giggles bubbled over. Letitia darted a glance at her and then at him. Clearly the woman thought he was crazy. Maybe he was. He'd said a prayer and realized he was falling in love. What more could a guy ask from a Friday afternoon in small-town Maine?

"As a matter of fact, mashed potatoes can't cure this. You must be Caroline's brother. Stanley, is it?"

"It's Sidney." He stretched out his hand.

"Well, it's wonderful to meet you. I heard you've been in town. I'm guessing you must have already met my Larry." She shook his hand.

"Only by reputation. I tried to buy out Isabella's full stock of bagged potatoes the other day, but she insisted on keeping some for you since she expected you to come into the store. She told me how much your husband loves his mashed potatoes. I can't blame him. They're a personal favorite of mine, too."

"I see." Letitia obviously *didn't* see, but hopefully she wouldn't fault Isabella or take her business elsewhere. The woman turned to go. "Enjoy your stay, and I hope to see you again."

"I can't believe that entire conversation," Isabella whispered, still giggling, when Letitia moved out of earshot.

"It's a gift, what can I say?" Sidney tapped her nose. "Listen, I'll stop loitering, but I have a question before I go."

"What's that?" Crossing her arms on the counter, Isabella faced him. Oh, she was lovely. He needed to keep talking or he might break his resolve and kiss her.

Patience. It's too soon.

"Speaking of a job, does Hank have one? For that matter, does Marty have a job, other than being a father?"

Isabella visibly swallowed, her laughter gone. "Hank lost his right leg in a work-related accident, and he's on permanent disability. He does handyman jobs to make ends meet. He's not married. Marty makes furniture in his garage and does fairly well."

Guilt rushed through him. "I'm sorry if my questions came across as unkind. I had no idea about Hank, but I shouldn't have made assumptions."

"No harm done." Her voice was kind, so gentle. "You couldn't have known. You'll be happy to know Ned loves the library books you brought in. As far as I know, he hasn't tried to sneak behind the counter to touch the pickle jar."

"It was the least I could do. Glad the plan worked," he said. "I'm sure you understand my underlying motivation in borrowing the books wasn't exactly altruistic."

Her lips curved. "You mean you weren't trying to promote the whole reading is fundamental concept?"

"Only insofar as books are a good alternative to Ned pulling pranks on the gorgeous owner of Mahoney's General Store. I guess I wanted to do something to help a friend. I envy the close friendships you share with Caroline and Liesel. The friendship Seth shares with Paul."

"Surely you have friends."

He met her gaze. "Not close ones, no. I'm going to work on that when I go back to Boston."

"I'm sure Seth and Paul will be happy to be your friends. And then you have…well, me." Was it his imagination or did Isabella seem somewhat sad when he'd mentioned leaving?

Leaning across the counter, Sidney kissed her cheek. "Thank you for being my friend. And now, in Marty's absence, I'm going to the back and challenge Hank in a rousing game of checkers."

Chapter 16

Early Saturday morning, Isabella cranked up the music on her iPod and plugged in her earbuds as she bounced outside the store to the beat of Mandisa's "Overcomer," one of her Top Ten all-time favorite contemporary Christian songs. How could anyone hear that tune without wanting to sing and dance? Light and energizing, it was a song of empowerment. A song of hope. A song that reminded Isabella that no matter what hardships and challenges may come into her life, she could face them with the power of God inside her.

"Yes! It's all about grace!" Isabella pumped her fist in the air as a young couple jogged by with their two kids in one of those side-by-side infant strollers. She'd never seen them before, so they must be visiting the area. "Morning! Gorgeous day, isn't it?" They probably thought she was nutty, or full of energy, or both. She refused to be embarrassed or intimidated. What good was an infectious faith if it didn't spill over and flow out of her?

In a way, "Overcomer" could be her personal theme song. Life and others had tried to knock her down, but she'd survived and ultimately emerged as a more content, fulfilled woman. In some ways, Tristan's betrayal had strengthened her. Not that she'd ever want to go through that experience again.

She was different than she'd been fourteen months ago. Maybe she'd come to Evergreen to lick her wounds after the breakup, but she'd prayed about the decision and followed the leading of the Lord. She'd made some bad decisions morally, but after confessing those sins, she'd been wrapped in the kind of warmth, mercy, and forgiveness she didn't deserve.

Still bouncing to the music, singing along, Isabella moved around the corner of the store and unlocked the small outdoor storage area. Hauling out the green garden hose, she tugged it to the front sidewalk. After closing the front door, she ran back and turned the knob—grunting since it liked to stick—and cranked on the water.

A few moments later, she aimed the hose at the front window. Isabella sprayed the window, the bench, and the sidewalk. She stepped closer and inspected a dark spot on the ground. Someone must have dropped chocolate ice cream at the base of the park bench. She concentrated on the spot by training the hose on it, but it proved stubborn. Grabbing her bottle of cleaner from her hip belt, she sprayed the ground liberally. "Take that! And that!" She cackled like a crazy person. "And that should take care of *you!*"

A dark flash in the corner of her eye caught her attention. "Well, hello there, Humphrey. How are you this fine day?" The cat blinked lazily and then darted off when she continued her work. "Come back and see me again later!"

Next she worked on another area closer to the curb while she waited for the biodegradable solution to soak into the chocolate stain. Lifting her face to the morning sun, Isabella smiled. Thank goodness the rain would hold off until sometime tomorrow in order to give them a perfect evening for the Twilight Dance.

The guys normally hosed down the building and sidewalk each morning, but she enjoyed the physical exertion on occasion. She'd given Clyde the day off since Aunt Clara had tipped her off that he always spent the entire day of the Twilight Dance pampering Ginny, his wife of forty plus years. He made it almost like an anniversary—lunch at a favorite restaurant, followed by either a relaxing massage or a leisurely hike, dinner, and then dancing the night away. Clyde loved to dance, and didn't allow his limp—an old sports injury—to slow him down.

Isabella sighed at the pure romance of it all.

She couldn't imagine being married to someone for forty years. One thing was for sure—she'd need to like them as a person. Be friends with them. That was a large part of the problem in her relationship with Tristan. They'd jumped right into being more than friends in the physical sense. Even now, her cheeks flushed with shame at the thought. She'd been in love and disregarded everything she'd been taught. She'd been a "good girl" until she met him during her undergraduate days at UCLA. Tristan's intelligence and quick wit had drawn her to him. Charismatic and gregarious, he was nice looking without being drop-dead gorgeous, but she wasn't the glamour girl type he usually dated. A lot of girls—tanned, blonde, stereotypical California girls—wanted Tristan. The fact that he flirted with them should have been her first clue the odds were against the man being faithful to one woman for an extended period.

As she continued her work, Isabella's thoughts transitioned to Sidney. She loved seeing him working alongside Seth, Paul, and a few of the other local men to construct the dance floor when she'd walked past Evergreen Park. At the time, she'd been listening to her music. The spontaneous way Sidney threw his hand in the air accompanied by a smile aimed straight for her, *only* for her, made Isabella's heart skip a few beats. She liked the way the breeze sifted through his hair, lifting it, and tossing it about with abandon.

My, oh my, the man was handsome. After only a few days, Sidney looked like he *fit* in Evergreen, something she'd never have thought possible. In his jeans, a maroon Harvard T-shirt, and a tool belt slung low on his hips, he looked good. *Really* good for a guy who was reportedly a powerhouse in the courtroom and more accustomed to wearing suits and an air of intimidation. No, *authority*. That sounded less threatening.

Although Sidney possessed qualities similar to Tristan, Isabella had glimpsed an inherent kindness in the man from Boston. She'd jumped to conclusions about Sidney when they'd first met, but the differences in the personalities of the two men were now much clearer. Tristan must have had ADD because he couldn't sit still long enough to have a conversation like she'd shared with Sidney yesterday, sitting on the bench outside the store. Tristan rarely asked deep questions, and he'd never seemed to truly *listen* to her.

Matter of fact, Sidney had shown more compassion for the loss of her parents than Tristan ever had although he'd been by her side for their joint memorial service and burial. Tristan had squirmed on the church pew and tugged at his collar as if he couldn't wait to escape, his behavior similar to that of an antsy small boy. Then he'd had the gall to express gratitude she "only had to go through this once" because her parents had died together. Even now, the thought sickened her. No sooner had she placed the white roses on their side-by-side caskets than he was itching to leave and said, "Cemeteries creep me out. Let's get out of here." That should have been another clue.

Isabella had been so fully immersed in her grief that she'd mistaken their physical relationship as confirmation that someone loved her, and that her life would somehow move forward. When she left UCLA for a semester and traveled, he communicated with her several times a day, claiming he was pining away for her.

"Fat chance you were pining away," Isabella muttered. Tristan had probably *pined away* with several women, one a so-called good friend at the time. For good measure, she pulled out her bottle of cleaner and sprayed it wildly into the air. "Take that, you idiot!"

"Hey! Watch it!" A woman jogging by the store must have gotten the downwind of that spray. Waving her hand in front of her face, she shot Isabella an angry glare.

"Oh, I'm so sorry! Totally a mistake! Come inside for something on the house." Isabella clamped one hand over her mouth, embarrassed, as the woman kept moving. How awful was she to be thankful the woman was only visiting Evergreen?

Not a great start to the day.

She checked her watch. *Yikes!* Fifteen minutes until opening. Of course, her thoughts wandered back to Tristan again as she finished her work. Might as well ride the old memory train to the end of the railroad station or these thoughts would continue. Her former boyfriend's lack of faith *should* have been the first clue to run screaming in the opposite direction. Isabella had tried to tell him about Jesus and foolishly believed he'd listen. For all he had cared, she might as well have been talking about worshipping a praying mantis.

After he'd betrayed her with one of their account executives while on a business trip, Isabella rededicated her life to the Lord. She vowed never again to date a man who wasn't a Christian. Not that Christians were perfect, but at least she might stand a better chance for a lasting relationship that could lead to marriage.

Enough serious thinking. Time to go back inside and prepare to open for what she expected would be one of her busiest days so far this year.

Isabella hauled the hose back around the side of the building and drained the excess water. Then she piled the hose back into the storage unit. Her cell phone rang as she returned the bottle of cleaning solution to the shelf in the backroom. She checked the display. *Caroline Barnes.*

"Hi, Caroline! How are you?"

"Terrific. Listen, I know you're probably busy this morning, but I wanted to invite you to dinner tonight at the house. I apologize for the late notice. I think my hormones are still out-of-whack or I would have called you earlier in the week. Paul and Liesel are coming at six and bringing the kids. After dinner, we're all going to the Twilight Dance. We'd love it if you could join us."

"I, um…" Under normal circumstances, she'd jump at the invitation. Sidney would be at this dinner. Would going be a wise move or walking straight into temptation?

"Do you already have plans tonight?"

"No, not exactly. Well…no."

"Isabella, I think my comments about Sidney the other day were premature. Since he's been here in town, Seth and I have already seen some changes for the better in my brother."

"Sounds like getting out of Boston is a good thing for the Prescotts." That sounded more flippant than she'd intended. "I mean…"

"I know what you mean, and you're right," Caroline said. "It's been good to have Sidney here. He's opening up and being honest about personal matters in a way I've never seen before."

Isabella smiled. "You might be interested to know your brother came to see me yesterday afternoon, and he told me he'd prayed for his meal."

"He didn't mention it, but that's pretty awesome, isn't it?"

"Yes, and then this morning—this has nothing to do with anything, really—Sidney was wearing a tool belt and wielding a hammer. He was with Seth and some of the men over at the park putting together the dance floor." What a silly thing to say, but it was all Isabella could think of to deflect the course of the conversation.

"Oh, Sidney's downtown? I thought he was still sleeping. Wearing a tool belt, huh?" Her friend laughed quietly. "That's something I'd like to see. Did you get a photo?"

Isabella's smile sobered, and she ran a hand over her hair. "Caroline, I'll be honest. I like Sidney a lot more than I should. I'm not sure if that's good or bad. I'm not even sure I can explain it except to say that, even though I know God's working in his life, Sidney's not a believer. After all I went through with Tristan, I can't go down that road again. I just…can't. And then you have the fact that Sidney's going back to Boston, and he's reportedly a workaholic…"

And now you're running down the list of reasons why you're not *falling in love with the man even though you are.*

"Calm down, sweetie. I'm not inviting you to dinner to be Sidney's date. I'm inviting you because you're our good friend."

Leaning against the counter, Isabella said a silent prayer. *Lord, what do I do?*

"How late are you working today?"

"Until four. Clyde has the day off, and Tommy's coming in to close for me." If everything went according to plan, the scheduling should work. She should have time to run home, shower, and change, and get to Caroline and Seth's house by six o'clock. *If* she decided to go.

"You're planning on going to the Twilight Dance, right?"

"I thought I'd at least stop by," Isabella said. "Marijane's Twilight Punch is one of my new favorite things in life. And yes, I realize what a sad commentary that is." She chewed on a fingernail before frowning and tucking her hand in her pocket.

"Whatever you decide, I completely understand," Caroline said. "I'll leave it as an open-ended invitation. Just know we'll be here if you'd like to join us. And if you don't come for dinner, then I hope we'll see you at the dance."

"I think you're a great friend, Caroline. Thanks for understanding." More than anything, she wanted to go to the dinner, but that's what scared her. Why put herself in a position to be hurt by a man who was only passing through town?

Isabella's gaze fell on an open magazine lying on the back counter. Funny, she hadn't noticed the magazine last night when she'd closed the store. She flipped the magazine over and glanced at the cover. *Automobili Lamborghini S.p.A.*

A Lamborghini magazine? Opening it, she quickly flipped through the pages. Some of the articles and ads were in English, but other sections were in Italian and German. How did this get here? Thumbing through a few more pages, she laughed when she read that the magazine was characterized by the three Lamborghini brand attributes—extreme, uncompromising, and Italian. Well, that was fitting.

Had Sidney brought this magazine to the store for Tommy to see? She noted it was from a few years ago. "Very mysterious," she murmured.

Lost in thought, she started when the bell jingled.

"Sorry, boss. Didn't mean to scare you. I forgot something…" Tommy smiled as he spied the magazine on the counter. "That's where I left it!"

No wonder Sidney's borrowed car held such a fascination for Tommy. The Lamborghini represented more than a passing fancy.

Isabella closed the magazine and then handed it to him. "May I ask where you got this magazine?"

He scratched the side of his blond head and gave her his appealing lopsided smile. "If I tell you, you've gotta swear not to tell a soul."

She lifted a brow. "Promise me this doesn't involve anything illegal or contraband."

"I don't think so. Okay, here's the thing." He lowered his voice to a whisper.

"Tommy, just tell me. The store's not open yet, so we're the only two people here. No one else will hear you."

"Oh, right. See, Miss Millicent orders them special for me through the library. She lets me keep them, but she won't let me reimburse her. Believe you me, this baby ain't cheap."

"Of course not. It's extreme, uncompromising, and Italian. And generous of Millicent."

Tommy laughed. "Right. I'd better scoot. I've got places to go, people to see." He slapped the magazine against his forearm. "See? The library's name and address are right here on the label."

How silly that she hadn't noticed. "So it does. Don't forget you're coming in at four today, and you'll close the store for me, right?"

"Thanks for the reminder. I'll be here, boss." He grinned. "Wish me luck. I'm gonna ask Casey Martin to come to the dance with me tonight."

"Nothing like waiting until the last minute."

"She just broke up with Carl Rogers last week. I had to give her some space, you know? You going to the dance with Sidney?"

"No," she said slowly. "Why do you ask?"

Tommy shrugged. "Just heard you two have been, um, friendly around town, that's all."

Her cheeks flamed. "Friendly?" It's not like they'd been at the kissing booth. Well, that wasn't the best thing to think about, either.

People in this town needed to get a life and stop speculating about hers. Unkind or not, it was the truth.

"I'll see you tonight, Isabella. Save me a dance."

"See you then." She moved over to Cash. Time to prepare for the busy day ahead.

Five minutes later, she opened the front door and propped it with the wooden wedge. The wonderful aromas of the Java Joe coffees from Barron's wafted down the street.

Isabella breathed in deeply. "Good morning, world! We're open for business."

Chapter 17

Isabella noticed the customers seemed more upbeat than usual. The gorgeous weather and the festive mood in anticipation of the Twilight Dance must have a lot to do with their excitement. The locals were enthusiastic about the town event, and that seemed to translate to the tourists, which in turn meant increased business. A win-win for all.

Many shoppers who came into Mahoney's carried bags from the other stores. A weekend with great weather was always profitable, and several of the main merchants ran specials to cross-promote one another. A few of the shopkeepers had tried to convince Isabella to open Mahoney's on Sundays, but she'd remained steadfast in not bowing to the pressure, preferring to stay true to Aunt Clara and Uncle Phil's tradition.

Isabella glanced at the big clock on the side wall. Close to one o'clock. She still hadn't made a decision although she was leaning toward accepting Caroline's dinner invitation. Was she overthinking everything? As the relationship with Joel proved, she *could* be "just friends" with a man. She was also beginning to really dislike that term, description, expression, or whatever it was.

"Miss, are you Isabella…Cannelloni?"

Isabella bit her lower lip not to laugh. "I'll answer to that name." What did it matter, anyway? "How may I help you?"

"Splendid. I hear you have some lovely scented candles." The woman appeared well-to-do in her chic casual wear—a straight, khaki skirt with embroidered blue whales, a sleeveless white blouse with matching whales on the collar, and a scarf expertly knotted around her shoulders—and spoke with a distinctly southern drawl. "Joan at the Evergreen Boutique suggested that I come and pay you a visit."

"That was very nice of her. If you'll follow me, I'll be happy to show you the candles." For the next five minutes, Isabella helped the woman decide between the various scents. Robust Rose and Lovely Lily won out, and the customer wanted an entire box of each.

As she kept an eye on other customers in the store, Isabella's mind wandered a bit until she heard the woman mention her summer home on the Cape. An idea popped into her mind. "Would you be interested in seeing our quilts? They're exquisite and handmade. One of a kind, and they'd be perfect for a guest bedroom."

"That sounds like a fabulous idea. Lead the way."

Hearing the bell, Isabella glanced at the front door as Seth and Paul entered the store. "Hey, guys. All ready for tonight?"

"Hi, Isabella. Almost there." Seth gave her a polite nod. "We're taking a break to get a cold drink, and then we're headed back over to string the lights."

"Help yourself. Earl and Clyde restocked the cooler this morning."

"Yes, ma'am," Paul said with his customary smile. A quiet man, he was such a great husband to Liesel, and he'd been one of Seth's best friends for years. The two men headed to the back where Hank was engaged in a rousing game with a tourist.

The bell sounded again a couple of minutes later.

Sidney. He whipped off his sunglasses and glanced around the store. Was he looking for her? Was she still in high school? *Goodness, Isabella.* She needed to get a firm grip on reality.

Isabella's gaze moved to his feet…steel-toed safety boots. Who knew? *Be still, my heart.* With that tool belt, the man was rocking the whole construction worker look. He had everything but the hardhat and plastic goggles. The whole *alpha male* image. In the *many looks of Sidney* department, this one ranked near the top. Who knew?

"I'll be back in a moment," Isabella told the woman.

"Take your time, and you're right. These handmade quilts are beautifully done."

Isabella's steps slowed as she approached Sidney. "Are you lost again? Need more toiletry items?" She couldn't seem to stop teasing this man.

He pushed a stray lock of dark hair off his forehead. In just a few days, his hair had grown longer. "I wanted to see you, so I'm not lost."

"Oh." Momentarily flustered, she smiled. "Your cohorts are already here getting a cold drink."

"I know. I'll join them in a minute. How are you, Isabella?"

"Good, thanks. Business has been brisk, the way I like it. The gorgeous weather always brings in customers for the weekend, and I'm thankful."

Sidney didn't say anything else but neither did he make a move to leave.

Isabella touched one hand to her cheek. "Do I have something on my face? You're staring."

"Sorry, no. Maybe I've, uh, been in the sun too long." His T-shirt was damp with sweat, unlike when she'd run into him while jogging. He'd clearly exerted himself and worked those muscles.

Stop that. You're staring as much as he is.

Her gaze momentarily dropped to the ground. Again. "Nice boots."

"Thanks. I borrowed them from Seth. We wear the same size."

"That's convenient. I know the guys must be thankful for your help. Sidney, have you tried Moxie yet?"

"Excuse me? Moxie?" He grinned and slid his hands down to his hips. "Can't say that I have. Sounds intriguing. Is that the sister drink of Mojo?"

"I wouldn't doubt it." Laughing, Isabella shook her head. "Are you sure you're not a closet marketing rep? Moxie is the official soft drink of Mainers. Since 2005. I have no idea why I remember random things like that."

"You like history," he said. "And Mainers would be…?"

"Citizens of—"

"Maine. Right. I'm a little slow today. Which way?"

Lost in his bluer-than-ever eyes, she couldn't think straight. "I'm sorry. What?"

"The Moxie? My cohorts?" His grin grew wider. "Which way?"

"Oh, right." Isabella angled her head toward the back of the store. "They're in a cooler at the back." She tried not to roll her eyes. "The drinks, not the guys. Follow the laughter, and you'll find them both. If you'll excuse me, I need to get back to my customer."

He nodded. "I'll see you in a bit."

"Yes. Until then." They were acting like two infatuated high school kids. She resisted fanning her face, but it had suddenly grown very warm inside the store.

Isabella felt Sidney's gaze on her as she returned to assist the woman with her selections. Based on their frequent laughter, the men were enjoying their drinks while talking with Hank and his competitor. From what she could tell, they were debating the odds for the Red Sox making it to the World Series this year. Sidney had gotten along well with Hank yesterday, and they'd played at least four or five rounds of checkers.

Not long after, she heard a man cough and sputter. Ah, yes, that must be Sidney. The Moxie must be taking effect.

Isabella rang up the sale for not one, but two, queen-size quilts for her customer. The woman was staying at The Evergreen Inn until Tuesday, so Isabella offered to gift wrap the quilts and have them delivered on Monday afternoon.

"You're such a dear," the woman said. "Do you have a website where I can leave a review?"

"We sure do. I'd appreciate that, and feel free to mention the quilts. I've also recently commissioned baby quilts and lap quilts for seniors if you might be interested. I'll post photos on the website soon. You can always send me a message if you have any questions." Isabella plucked out one of her business cards from the holder on the counter and handed it to her. "Thank you again for coming in today. I hope you'll tell your friends about us."

"I sure will. Your little town is absolutely charming." With a smile and a wave, her satisfied customer departed.

Isabella pulled out her clipboard. *Call Francie on Monday and order more quilts. Check on the progress of the baby quilts and lap quilts for seniors.*

Seth and Paul strolled over to the counter, and Seth handed her money for their drinks. "I hope you can come to the house for dinner tonight."

Isabella glanced up in surprise. "Thanks. I'm considering it."

Seth dropped his change into the small container for contributions to the Youth Services Center where Paul worked as a counselor. "If nothing else, take pity on us and get my brother-in-law out of our hair for a few hours at the dance. I'm sure you can handle him."

"Oh, I don't know about that. Is he a bad houseguest?" Isabella could see the top of Sidney's head as he slowly made his way to the front. He must be checking out some of the merchandise on the way. Probably taking notes for more suggestions.

Seth grinned. "He's a blueberry muffin hound. Other than that, he's not too bad."

"Hope to see you later, Isabella. See you in a few minutes, Sidney!" Paul called over his shoulder before following Seth out the front door.

"I'll be there." Sidney rounded the end of the aisle. Sauntering toward her with a serious expression, he lowered his empty bottle on the counter with a definitive thud. "You could have warned me."

Isabella batted her eyes. "I have no idea what you're talking about."

"Give me the truth. What's in this stuff? Do you dislike me *that* much?"

"First, let me give you an explanation of what just happened to your taste buds."

He leaned one elbow on the counter, his hand fisted beneath his chin. "This I can't wait to hear."

"I imagine it rolled over your tongue easily and tasted like Coke or root beer. But when you kept drinking it, well, then it tasted more like—"

"Medicine."

"Exactly." Isabella grinned. "Wintergreen and bitters, to be specific. It's made from gentian root, an herb found in the pastures of the Alps and the Himalayas. How's the aftertaste?"

"I'm sure you know how it is. Bitter as anything."

"It's said that the dry, bitter aftertaste is like vermouth. And even though it's a shock at first, it's not all that unpleasant once you get used to it."

"If you say so, Isabella. By the way, I'm not a big drinker. Never had vermouth."

"I didn't think you were. A drinker."

"Oh. It's just that after the comment Caroline made at the house when I first arrived in town..." His cheeks colored. "Never mind. Tell me more."

Sidney was extremely cute when he stumbled over his words, but the big city lawyer wouldn't appreciate it if she pointed that out. As it was, Isabella suffered from a tendency to ramble when in the presence of a highly attractive man.

Moving on.

"It's one of the oldest, mass-produced soft drinks in the country but started out as a patent medicine," she said. "The guy who created it was born in Maine, but it was first made in your home state of

Massachusetts, as a matter of fact. And now it's made in Bedford, New Hampshire."

"Absolutely…scintillating." Sidney seemed to be half-listening by this point. He was getting that glazed-over look she recognized whenever she spouted too many random facts. That reaction wasn't exclusive to this man.

"Not impressed by any of that? Try *this* on for size: the Mainers like it because it's manly."

Sidney straightened and pulled at the collar of his T-shirt, glancing down at his chest. "Now that you mention it, I see a new hair sprouting down there that wasn't there a few minutes ago."

She grinned. "See? Moxie has its benefits."

"Answer a question. Have *you* ever tried this stuff?"

"Um, no. I don't need hair on my chest."

He burst out laughing. "You are the most spontaneous woman I've ever met."

"I'm not sure that's a good thing. Go get another drink. My treat. To make up for this one."

"Nope." He winked. "I'm all fortified now. And manly." Pulling out his wallet, he handed her a ten. "Keep the change."

"You've got to stop throwing your money around. People will talk."

"This is the smallest bill I have. Tell you what. Put the change in the donation jar for the kids at the Youth Services Center."

"All right, when you put it that way." Ringing up the sale, Isabella made a big show of dropping single dollar bills and spare change into the jar. "The kids thank you."

"Now, I need you to do something for me." Sidney waited until she met his gaze.

"Depends. What is it?"

"Come to the house for dinner tonight. The way I see it, you owe me."

She couldn't stop her smile. "How do you figure that?"

"After that drink"—Sidney nodded at the empty Moxie bottle—"you owe me some sweetness."

"Huh. That's a line I've never heard before. Corny, but also fairly original."

"See you later, Moxie." Sidney turned and strutted out the front door. In *very* manly fashion.

Chapter 18

Isabella stepped into the front foyer as Seth held the door. "What smells so divine?"

"Caroline's lobster lasagna. New recipe. I sampled it earlier, and you're in for a treat." Seth took the two bottles of sparkling grape cider she handed to him. "Thanks. This will be the perfect accompaniment."

Caroline swept around the corner from the kitchen and gave Isabella a side hug. "I'm so happy you decided to come." Her long blonde hair was pulled back into a chic chignon, and she wore an elegant, retro-looking green dress with fabric that crisscrossed on the bodice. It was a given that her emerald necklace and matching earrings were her own designs. For a woman who preferred jeans and sweatshirts, Mrs. Barnes cleaned up extremely well.

"Aren't you at your Grace Kelly-ish best tonight?" Isabella said with a bright smile. "You look spectacular. Sorry, I was running a little behind schedule. Tommy showed up late at the store, so I had to rush. How do you manage to look so put together all the time?"

"Thanks, but I guess I fooled you." In spite of her words, Isabella could tell the evening's hostess was pleased by her compliments. "You should have seen me twenty minutes ago. I was running around upstairs, half-dressed with wild hair."

"You didn't hear me complaining." Seth kissed his wife's cheek.

"Off with you, sir." Caroline gave Seth an exaggerated wink and a mock push toward the family room. That must be where the men had gathered.

"Isabella!" Bella scampered into the front hallway and wrapped her arms around her knees. "You brought bubbles!"

Laughing at Bella's word for sparkling cider, Isabella leaned over to tap the child's cute button nose. "I sure did. Try not to drink it too fast or else it'll tickle your nose like it did at Christmas. Remember?"

"Uh huh. It felt funny." The little girl rubbed her nose and darted off again.

"Bella, no running in the house!" Paul called from the door leading into the family room. "And don't go in the nursery again. Ellie and Paul need to sleep." Paul waved. "Hi, Isabella. Glad you could join us."

Sidney poked his head around the corner and then stepped into the doorway. "Good evening. Thanks for coming."

Isabella smiled. "Hi there." They stared at one another for a few seconds. What was she doing? Well, he'd started it. In his dark slacks and V-neck, lightweight blue sweater, the man looked devastating. All clean-shaven and GQ-ish tonight. If she ever saw him in a tux, she might just faint. She'd dealt with a ton of male models at the marketing firm, but not one of them had done a thing for her like this man did.

He's forbidden fruit. "Oh, be quiet," Isabella muttered under her breath. She hurried after Caroline and into the kitchen. "Put me to work. What can I do to help?"

"We're finishing up everything now, and we should be ready to eat in a few minutes."

"Isabella! Aren't you beautiful tonight?" In a lovely pale yellow cotton dress, Liesel skirted around her with a tray of fresh bread. After lowering the tray on the granite-topped island in the middle of the room, she tugged off the oven mitts. "Turn around and give us the full view of this scrumptious pink confection. Is this new?"

"No, I've had it since Hartford. I just haven't had the opportunity to wear it here."

"You look like you're ready to twirl under the stars tonight." Caroline's tone sounded wistful.

"The men will fall all over themselves to be the first to dance with you," Liesel said with a sweet smile.

"Thank you. This is really fun to get all gussied up for a change."

Isabella had changed her dress six times before turning to the mirror and declaring, "No more!" More than any other, this pink dress made her feel soft, feminine, and *womanly*. The sleeveless dress was simple, elegant, nipped slightly below her natural waistline, and highlighted her toned upper arms and calves. The skirt was her favorite feature, made from an underlying layer of tulle with chiffon that swished about her knees with every movement. Whether or not she did any serious twirling tonight remained to be seen. Her silver sandals with a modest heel were the perfect complement to showcase the dress to its best advantage.

"I need to run upstairs and check on Ellie. I'll be right back." Caroline darted out of the kitchen.

Isabella's stomach growled. Loudly. Embarrassed, she moved her hand over her belly. "I guess I didn't realize I was so hungry. Everything smells fantastic in here. What's in that bread?"

"It's herb bread with rosemary and basil. There's also a sourdough loaf." Liesel removed the second loaf from the smaller oven. "I heard the stores were crazy busy today. Did you take time for lunch?"

Come to think of it, she *hadn't* eaten anything since her bowl of whole grain cereal and poached egg for breakfast. "It was one of the busiest days I've had in a long time. I took a tuna sandwich, but I guess I never sat down to eat it."

Caroline swooped back into the kitchen. "Here, Isabella. Try on this pink amethyst necklace for me." In her hand, she held a delicate silver necklace with a pink stone pendant. "Turn around, please."

"It's beautiful. One of your new designs?" Isabella lifted her hair off her neck so Caroline could fasten the clasp. Sometimes she asked Isabella to wear one of her jewelry creations to get a feel for it—how heavy it was, how people reacted—and then report back to her. Liesel used to do the honors, but with a small child and an infant, wearing a delicate necklace was a thing of the past, at least for now.

"Yes, it is. Okay, there we go." Putting both hands on her shoulders, Caroline turned her around to face Liesel. "What do you think?"

Liesel nodded. "I think it's a definite keeper. Brings out your eyes, your hair, and the bloom in your cheeks."

"Oh, no! I can't keep the necklace," Isabella protested. "This is too valuable."

"I know pink amethyst is your favorite, and I won't take no for an answer," Caroline said.

"Then you have to allow me to babysit Ellie until she's a teenager as a proper thank you."

Caroline laughed. "Better yet, I'll let you toss the salad." In less than a minute, she'd collected everything from the large steel refrigerator and stacked them on the island.

"You're too good to me, but I've got it covered. One tossed salad coming up." After opening the utensil drawer, Isabella stopped when someone came alongside her. One whiff of the subtle masculine cologne, and she knew it was Sidney.

After nudging her hand away from the drawer, he pulled out a long-handled fork and spoon. "Will these work?"

"They should do nicely. Thank you." She started to take them, but he resisted, making her work for them. Finally, he released his hold.

"Welcome. You're beautiful, Isabella." He turned and addressed his sister. "Caroline, give me a job."

Sidney was already flirting. This couldn't be good.

Isabella poured the raspberry vinaigrette dressing over the fresh garden salad with tomatoes, cucumbers, and all manner of vegetables. Lost in thought, she gave up after counting five different kinds of vegetables. Hoping no one noticed the flush in her cheeks, she wondered how Sidney could hold such power over her emotions.

He's just a friend, Isabella.

Right. And she was…Queen Isabella. She almost laughed out loud. Opening the bottles of sparkling cider on the counter, Sidney glanced over at her with an expression of curious amusement. Ah, skip it. The man already knew she was nutty.

Seth and Paul came into the kitchen, and the three men worked together to fill their glasses.

Finished preparing the salad, Isabella carried it to the dining room. Caroline knew how to set an elegant, inviting table—lit candles, off-white linen tablecloth, fine crystal, her best china. Lush, blooming red roses from Seth's flower garden sat in a cut crystal vase in the middle of the table. The man nurtured and grew the best roses in the county, maybe the entire state.

Isabella smiled. "Just a simple get-together with friends." Her gaze landed on place cards. She had to take a peek. Sidney was at one end and Seth on the other. Caroline would be seated to Seth's right, and she would sit on Sidney's right. Bella would sit next to her—the little girl's booster seat and Disney princess plate and cup were already in place—while Paul and Liesel would sit opposite them. The seating arrangement made perfect sense.

Isabella hoped Sidney wouldn't try to play footsie with her beneath the table. He wouldn't, would he? She wouldn't put it past him. Then again, did she *want* him to flirt? This was getting more dangerous by the minute. Her good sense told her to cut her losses, make her excuses, jump in her SUV, and leave. But no. She'd never been a woman to call upon her common sense when the signs were there that she *should*. Why start now?

You are completely hopeless.

Standing in a circle in the dining room a few minutes later, they all held hands for prayer. Sidney stood beside Isabella, Liesel on the other. Sidney slipped his hand over hers so naturally, as if he'd been doing it for years, making it difficult for her to concentrate on Seth's words.

"Thank you, Father, for our friends and family gathered with us tonight. We give you the honor and glory for the love, and for the strong bonds of family, faith, and friendship represented here. We ask that you bless the hands that have prepared the food, may we partake in good health, and we pray that our conversations will be pleasing in your sight. We ask these things in the name of Jesus."

"Amen!" Bella clapped her hands. "Eat!"

Sidney gave Isabella's hand a light squeeze.

The conversation flowed freely around the table. Seth told them about his next planned exploratory trip. Paul updated them on new programs at the Youth Services Center. For his part, Sidney seemed content to eat his meal and listen to the conversations around him. Other than complimenting Caroline on the out-of-this-world lobster lasagna—layered with baby spinach, mozzarella, parmesan, white cheddar, and Alfredo sauce—he remained quiet except for playing peek-a-boo with Bella. When he let down his guard, Sidney seemed much more relaxed and content. Nothing grabbed Isabella's attention faster than a man who related well to children.

At one point, she was surprised to find an extra piece of herb bread on the side of her plate. Giggling, Bella pointed to Sidney. When she glanced at him, he shrugged and put one finger over his lips before taking a bite of the sourdough bread.

Sidney helped Isabella clear the table, and they worked together to carry the dishes back into the kitchen. She began to rinse and load them into the dishwasher, and Caroline made the coffee. Paul scooped Barron's homemade vanilla ice cream into bowls while Liesel and Seth set out a variety of toppings—fresh strawberries, blueberries, as well as chocolate and butterscotch sauces. Bella's job was to sprinkle chocolate shavings and add a maraschino cherry on top for those who requested them.

Judging by Bella's giggles, Sidney had apparently taken it upon himself to "assist" her. Isabella smiled as she listened to their lively chatter and darted a glance over her shoulder. He'd perched the little girl on a tall chair at the island and teased her with a cherry, dangling it by its stem and acting like he was going to eat it.

"Uncle Sidney! Stop that!"

Uncle Sidney? Bella barely knew Sidney. When had she started calling him that? None of the adults corrected the child. Huh? When did *this* happen? Even she wasn't *Aunt* Isabella. Not that she was jealous. Okay, maybe a little bit.

"I want Ellie and Paul to get big so I can play with them now," Bella whined as she left the kitchen a couple of minutes later.

"Think of all you're learning now that you can teach them later." Liesel followed her daughter from the kitchen, bowls of ice cream in her hands. From the times Isabella had babysat Bella, she knew the little girl loved playing teacher.

Isabella turned back to the dishes.

"You're not having ice cream?"

Her pulse raced at the sound of Sidney's voice. The kitchen had emptied of everyone but the two of them. Isabella wouldn't be a bit surprised if that was planned.

"I couldn't possibly eat another bite. The meal was delicious, wasn't it?" From her position at the sink, Isabella glanced over her shoulder again. Leaning against the island in the middle of the kitchen, Sidney spooned a bite of the fresh mixed berries into his mouth, watching her with a thoughtful expression.

"Caroline's turned into an excellent cook," he said. "I found out since I've been here that Nanny Regina taught her a few things on the sly. I feel a little cheated. And I figure these berries have to make the ice cream healthier. What with the antioxidants and vitamins. Right?" Sidney spooned another bite of the ice cream into his mouth.

Isabella turned back to her work. "That's what I hear."

"Are you planning on going to the dance tonight?"

"Yes." Isabella continued rinsing the dishes, her heart pounding. "Are you?"

"I was thinking about it. After all, that's what the challenge with Tommy was about." Before she could react, Sidney was beside her. "Aren't you going to ask? I know you've been curious."

She swallowed. "I'm not sure I *should* ask."

Lord, what's happening here?

She knew better than to play with fire, but the more she was around this man, the closer she came to that very thing. The temptation was great, and she was already in deep emotionally.

"Why not?" His manner was playful, his voice teased. When she didn't answer and picked up another plate, Sidney put his hand on her arm. "Isabella, stop doing the dishes and talk to me."

Wiping her hands on the dishtowel, she turned toward him, fully aware Caroline or someone else could come in the kitchen at any moment.

"Isabella, I'm very attracted to you." His voice was quietly earnest. "Am I wrong in believing you feel something for me, too?"

"No," she whispered as moisture dampened her eyes. Turning back to the sink, she gripped the edge with both hands. "You're not wrong. That's why I'm afraid."

"Hey, are you crying?" He set the dish on the counter, and the spoon clanged in the almost empty dish. Moving one hand to the side of her face, Sidney caressed the line of her cheek, her jaw, his touch soft as his gaze sought hers. "Why the tears? I didn't mean to make you cry. Tell me."

She inhaled a quick breath. "Sidney, I made the mistake of falling for a man named Tristan in California." When Isabella turned her head, he withdrew his hands. How did he expect her to think when he touched her? When he looked at her with such tenderness?

"I met him in undergrad at UCLA. We went through grad school together, and we were friends. *Good* friends. The relationship quickly blossomed into a full-blown affair that went on for several years. I ignored everything I'd ever been taught, broke my vow to God, and to myself. He was a brilliant, charismatic man, and I gave myself to him in every possible way."

Blinking hard, Isabella knew she had to keep going, no matter Sidney's reaction. "We became business partners in a marketing firm in Hartford. Tristan took everything I had to give in every sense of the word, and then—once he tired of me—he threw it all away for another woman who offered more than I could." A tear slipped down her cheek. "I can't even believe I just told you all that." She gasped a little and moved one hand over her middle.

"It's okay. I'm glad you did. Come here." When Sidney reached for her, Isabella summoned every ounce of strength within her to resist him.

"I can't." Planting her hands on his chest, she stepped back.

Caroline breezed into the kitchen, coffee pot in hand. Seeing them, she stopped and stared. "Oh. I'm sorry to interrupt. I'll just be leaving now." Quickly setting the coffee carafe on the nearest countertop, she hurried from the kitchen.

Isabella groaned. She'd been foolish for coming tonight and should have known better.

"Let me go talk to her." Sidney dipped his head to catch her eye. "Are you okay?"

Isabella nodded, her emotions jumbled, feeling somewhat numb. "Go talk to Caroline. That's more important right now."

His jaw tightened, but he didn't sound angry. "Fine, but this conversation isn't over." Sidney headed out of the kitchen after his sister. "Caroline, wait!"

Not knowing what else to do, Isabella plunged her hands back into the dishwater. This might be a good time to say a prayer.

Chapter 19

Following Caroline across the hallway, Sidney caught the curious stares of the others in the family room. Small wonder since his sister had flown out of the kitchen and he'd been in hot pursuit, calling her name. Going inside the small study, he quietly closed the door.

Crossing her arms over her middle, Caroline paced the floor behind Seth's desk. Purposeful or not, it put a barrier between them, an invisible wall that bothered him.

Sidney approached the other side of the desk and raised both hands. "Before you say anything, nothing happened between Isabella and me. Don't read anything into what you saw. We were only talking."

Caroline stopped pacing and stared at him. "I was beginning to believe you've changed, Sidney, even in the past few days. Now, I'm not so sure. Nothing might have happened yet, but the way you looked at her during dinner wasn't platonic. I didn't want to discourage a friendship between the two of you, but I also warned her about you. She's my friend, but I can't stand by and watch while you hurt her. If that's your intent, then you can pack your bags and leave now."

He'd try not to take offense at her cutting remarks, but Sidney felt sucker-punched. "And I'm your brother. I guess I can see where your loyalties lie." He rested his forearms on the back of a wing chair, leaning on it, gathering his thoughts. "Isabella was just telling me about Tristan when you came into the kitchen. That guy was a user. I'm not. What makes you think I'd ever hurt her?"

"She was devastated by that man's betrayal," Caroline murmured. "Sidney, you date a woman a few times, probably long enough for her to form an emotional attachment. Then you drop her, walk away, and never look back. You don't want a woman so much as a career. Isabella's not the type of woman to have a one-night stand or an affair. She's learned her lessons, she's recommitted her life to the Lord, and she's one of the best friends I have in the world.

Neither is Isabella the type of woman to take a backseat to your career. She deserves so much more than that."

His heart dropped along with his jaw. Wow. His sister had an even lower opinion of him than he'd thought. Swallowing hard, Sidney tried to grasp the reality that Caroline held his character in such low esteem. "I hope you'll believe me when I tell you I'm not the cad you clearly believe I am. I don't date women for sport, sleep with them, and then dump them."

"What about Kat?" Her tone and expression reflected her disbelief.

"Your actress friend, Kat?" Sidney blew out a sigh. He'd tried his best to push that memory from his mind. "We had some drinks and danced at a club a couple of years ago when she was in Boston with a press junket for that independent film she did." She'd been one of Caroline's best friends from Wellesley, even come to Evergreen with his sister on her first trip. Kat was a gorgeous tease who'd manipulated and used him for the purpose of generating publicity.

"We exchanged a few flirty emails and phone calls, and Kat invited me to the Hamptons for a weekend. I was exhausted after a long trial, and like a fool, I mistakenly thought it'd be a good way to wind down, get away, and have a little fun. Kat clung to me from the minute I arrived. When the flashbulbs started popping, I should have turned around and gone straight back to Boston. I put her off for two days—*nothing* happened that shouldn't have, not that I owe anyone an explanation—and then went home, but the damage had already been done. Photos of us surfaced in some of those tabloid magazines."

Shaking his head, Sidney ran his hand through his hair. "I felt used, and the publicity wasn't good for my professional reputation or the firm. Kat's not known for being truthful. That's why she's such a successful actress. If I *were* the lowlife scum you seem to think I am, then I would have had a no-holds-barred, wild weekend with her. Give me some credit. I've tried to be a decent man in that regard. If not for moral reasons, I try to uphold the family name and keep my professional reputation intact."

Caroline stared at him for a long moment. "Forgive me for bringing it up, but as long as we're getting everything out in the open, I should ask what happened with the girl in your first year of law school."

Sidney groaned and ran his hand over his brow. "Caroline, that was a trumped-up accusation by some girl I met at a bar in Cambridge. Sorry to be blunt, but she wanted to stick it to the rich guy. Nothing happened, the truth came out, and the judge exonerated me. Dad didn't buy me off, and justice prevailed. You can choose to believe me or not, but the truth is that I've dated very few women since Olivia, and not one of them more than a handful of times. Yes, I go to bars sometimes, but I go home alone."

Seemed he'd surprised her with that revelation. "Olivia from prep school and undergrad? That Olivia?"

"Yes, *that* Olivia. For a long time, the end of that relationship soured me on getting involved with anyone else."

Caroline's eyes narrowed. "Why do you think that is?"

"We were young and stupid, full of dreams. Not that I'm blaming her for anything. I loved Olivia in the way I haven't loved another woman since—physically, emotionally, *every* way. I was in it for the distance, but Olivia decided she didn't want to play second fiddle to my career path. Looking back, I can't say that I blame her."

Sidney cleared his throat. "I haven't allowed myself to get close to another woman since for the simple reason that I haven't taken the time. To reach my professional goals, I concentrated on my studies and establishing my career. I had a focused, one-track mindset where everything else took a backseat, including my personal life. So you're right in that regard. Until now, I've pushed aside any other serious relationships, but I never allow them to get to the point where anyone gets hurt."

"Olivia broke your heart," Caroline murmured. "I never realized that." She dropped into the chair behind the desk.

He stared at his hands. "It's part of growing up, I suppose. I know I haven't always been a very nice person, Caroline. I'm working on trying to be a better man, and I think that's another part of the reason I'm here."

His sister's eyes were bright with emotion. "I hope you can forgive me, Sidney. I've assumed things about your character that aren't true. We haven't really known one another for years, have we?"

Sidney slumped into the chair. "That's because the Prescotts of Boston have always kept everything hidden deep inside where no one on the outside could see our dysfunction. We rarely discussed the important things."

There wasn't a family on the planet that didn't have their secrets and issues, but his parents seemed to have had more than their fair share. To a certain degree, the three Prescott children were left to deal with the fallout. At least his younger siblings seemed to have fared better in the personal arena than Sidney had.

He swallowed hard. "I saw how Dad's affairs devastated Mom." He stared at his hands on his lap. "I made a vow a long time ago that I'd never do that to a woman if I ever *found* one to share my life."

Caroline slowly shook her head. "After all these years, you're afraid of being hurt again."

Resting one elbow on the chair, Sidney's chuckle held no humor. "Mom sent me to a psychologist in Cambridge for a couple of years after the breakup. As much as anything, she didn't want me to lose my focus. I was what, all of twenty years old?" He'd been furious she'd insisted he go to those sessions. "It's like a Prescott wasn't allowed to have a broken heart without getting therapy."

Sidney waited for Caroline to look at him. "I never want to hurt Isabella. You have my word on that. I'm attracted to her, yes, and I'd like more. Above all, I want her to be happy, and I'd like to be her friend."

In truth, he was getting in deeper by the minute whenever he spent time in Isabella's presence. He hadn't felt this way about any woman since Olivia, but at this point, saying that to his sister would only create more tension between them.

Caroline's shoulders heaved with her sigh. "When I first came to Evergreen and met Seth, he was a strong Christian. I'd only begun to understand that I needed the Lord in my life." Taking the paperweight he'd given her, his sister cradled it in her hands. "At the time, I knew God brought Seth into my life for a reason. In a lot of ways, the friendship you and Isabella share mirrors what Seth and I shared in the beginning of our relationship."

"I agree," Sidney said. "There are definite parallels. Are you aware that Mom talked with me about her faith?"

Caroline blinked hard and stared at him. "No. You never mentioned that before."

"Part of me didn't accept what she said. It was the last time she was truly coherent, three days before she died. Considering how weak she was at the time, Mom grabbed my hand in a surprisingly tight grip. Then she ordered me to be quiet and listen for once in my life."

"Sounds like her." Caroline smiled through watery eyes.

"Mom told me her biggest regret was that she didn't live out her faith in front of us. Then she cried and said"—he sniffed and rubbed his hand over his jaw—"'Sidney, when you came into the world squalling at the top of your lungs, I knew you'd be the stubborn one.' She could barely rasp out the words, but then Mom told me she hoped that I'd meet Jesus one day and give Him a place in my heart."

Overcome with emotion, Sidney averted his gaze and focused on a framed photo of their family on the wall. He'd been about twelve at the time, the good son standing behind his mother, one hand on the chair where she sat, wearing an appropriately solemn expression. He remembered the session photographer advising them to think about something sad. Ironically, he didn't want them to look happy or carefree. As though wealthy Boston families listed in the Social Register couldn't laugh or have fun. How absurd.

He had a family portrait hanging in his penthouse. Painted by some famous Italian artist, he'd been sixteen then and complained because he'd missed a swim meet in order to be there for the last portrait sitting. That portrait had hung in his parents' bedroom until his mother's death, and she'd specifically bequeathed the heirloom to Sidney in her will.

Now, he was imminently thankful he'd missed that swim meet, and he'd give anything to have that time together with his parents again. Perhaps that's why building stronger relationships with Bryce and Caroline meant more to him now.

"I didn't tell her, Caroline. I couldn't tell Mom what she wanted to hear." A tear slipped down his face and onto the carpet, but Sidney let it go. He wasn't ashamed to cry like he'd once been. "I look at Dad now and see the man who was my hero reduced to a shell of the man he once was. For all his brilliance, what does he have left? A lasting legal legacy without question. But what else?"

"I like to believe he will leave behind a legacy in his three children." Caroline gave him a sad smile. "We're not perfect, but we have each other. I happen to think that's something very special."

He pushed himself up straighter in the chair. "I've had an epiphany in recent days, Caroline. I want what you have with Seth. I want what Bryce has with Tiffany. I want a wife, marriage, children, family. At the end of my life, I want to say I experienced *love*."

Raising his hands, Sidney gave her a helpless look. "There! I said it. This is a personal breakthrough."

Lifting from the chair, her eyes never leaving his, Caroline walked around the desk and stood beside him. "Stand up."

"You sound a lot like Mom right now. I have to say, it's a little scary."

When he rose to his feet, she wrapped her arms around him and rested her head on his shoulder. "Mom wouldn't have wanted you to lie to her, Sidney. I had one good talk with her toward the end, too. She didn't expect you to change overnight, or to grant her dying wish before she died, but she wanted you to know about Jesus, and she planted the seed in your mind. Everyone comes to Jesus in their own way, in their own time. And now you're here, asking questions, and reading Scripture." Pulling back, his sister's green eyes softened. "He's preparing your heart."

Caroline lowered her head briefly before looking back up at him again. "Forgive me for misjudging you. I know Isabella's confused. I know you're confused. *I'm* confused. She doesn't want to be hurt, you don't want to hurt her, and I don't want either one of you to be hurt. I love you both dearly, and you haven't known each other long at all."

"Admit something to me, Caroline. Did you fall in love with Seth when you first came to Evergreen? That hiking trip when you met him?"

"I fell in love with the *idea* of a man like Seth, yes."

Sidney gave her a look worthy of one he'd given countless jurors.

"Yes, a part of me fell in love with Seth that first weekend here in Evergreen."

"A big part," he said.

She smiled. "A pretty significant part. Are you happy now?"

"Yeah, I kind of am because you, of all people, understand how it's possible to form a lasting connection with someone in a very short period of time. Maybe there *is* something here in this magical town." Sidney chuckled. "In the water, the trees, the people, everything."

"No, Sidney." Caroline put both hands on either side of his face. "It's not nature. It's not the people. It's *God*. You may not have taken that step of faith to invite Him into your heart, but He sees all, He knows all, and God *knows* you're searching. My prayer for you is that you stop long enough to hear His voice and seek His will in regard to your feelings for Isabella and your future direction at the firm. Work on *you* and get straight with Him, and then, I promise you, everything else will fall into place."

"I know you're right." Sidney laughed a little. "See? Admitting my little sister might be right. That's something that would have been completely anathema a few months ago."

"Here's one last thing you might want to know." Caroline dropped her hands to her sides.

"What's that?"

"I know Mom asked you to watch over Bryce and me, and how she told you that you'd be in charge of the family. That's true, and I'm not disputing that. But she also asked me to watch over *you*, Sidney. Mom encouraged me to invite you to the house, spend time with you, make sure you get to know Seth, and Ellie, as well as any other children we might have."

"She asked you to watch over my *heart*, in other words," Sidney said. "I have to give you credit. Based on this talk tonight, you're on the case. You're also watching out for Isabella, and I can't fault you for that. You're a great sister, and you're a terrific friend. Loyal almost to a fault."

"I'm glad we've had this discussion." Caroline kissed his cheek.

"Me too, Caroline."

Chapter 20

Isabella breathed in deeply of the fresh, crisp evening air. She lifted her face to the stars. The vast expanse of a night sky always made her feel closer to her parents.

"I hope you're dancing tonight." Wisps of her hair brushed across her face in the light breeze, making her smile. Maybe it was silly, but Isabella liked to believe it was a kiss from her mother.

Evergreen Park was enchanting with thousands of miniature white lights twinkling in the trees. What a gorgeous evening. They couldn't have ordered better weather for the Twilight Dance. The temperature hovered in the low 60s, and she'd brought her sweater if she needed it. Liesel had taken it from her and tucked it beneath the stroller. As it was, she wouldn't have come if Liesel hadn't practically dragged her out of Caroline and Seth's house and stuffed her in the back of the minivan with Paul, Jr. and Bella. Liesel could be bossy, but Isabella loved her for it.

When she'd left the house, Caroline and Sidney were still in the study, hashing it out, talking, or whatever they were doing. That situation had been the elephant in the family room, but they'd all tiptoed around the subject with grace. That was the beauty of close friendships—even in their awkwardness, they could still be comfortable with one another.

The scent of roses wafted to her, carried by the breeze.

"You'd better go ask that handsome Sidney from Boston to dance before some of the other girls do." Barbara came to stand beside her. Thankfully, she'd lowered her voice.

"I don't have any claims on him," Isabella said. "Sidney is free to dance with whomever he'd like." For the past thirty minutes, she'd been all too aware of the glances aimed at Sidney from hopeful females.

"Don't be so magnanimous, sweetie." Barbara arched a perfectly manicured brow. "It's true what they say, you know. All's fair in love and war. Sometimes we need to fight for our man."

"Come on, Barbara. Let's leave Isabella alone." Darren tugged on his wife's hand. He gave Isabella a polite nod. "Have fun tonight."

"Thank you," Isabella murmured.

In a way, it's like Sidney was the popular boy in school, and all the girls wanted to be his girlfriend. That made Isabella's thoughts drift back to her freshman year in high school. She'd never been a popular kid. A little pudgy and a self-professed bookworm, she wasn't considered attractive. She didn't wear the trendy clothes, she wore no makeup. A few of the popular girls had pulled her into the bathroom during lunch and promised to make her look pretty so Matt Taylor would ask her to the football homecoming dance. He wasn't the football captain, but Matt was cute and smart, and Isabella had harbored a crush on him for years.

Why had she ever trusted those girls? They'd pulled out scissors and whacked away on her hair. What she ended up with was a hideous chop job with very short, ugly bangs. The barbs had been biting and cruel. She'd spent the night of the dance holed up in her room crying, and she vowed no one would ever make a fool of Isabella Caccavale again. If only that were true.

Tightening her arms around her, Isabella recalled her mother's words, imprinted on her heart. "Those kids want to undermine you because they're jealous of something you have that they don't, Isabella. You have more intelligence and compassion than anyone I know."

Her mother's voice had been quiet and kind as she'd smoothed those hideous bangs to one side and sweetly kissed her forehead. "Because of your sensitive nature, you'll unfortunately suffer fools. You'll feel their attempts to belittle you more than others, but you can't allow anyone to glimpse your pain. Rise above it, and go about your life. Lean on Jesus to give you the strength you need. He'll always uphold you when others try to tear you down."

She'd never forgotten her mother's words although she'd stepped outside of the Lord's will for a time. The main thing was that she'd found her way home again.

"I miss you, Mom and Dad," she whispered. "Love you."

"Isabella, can you help me?" Clyde's wife, Ginny, sidled over to her. "My honey pie got me this beautiful orchid corsage, but I guess I didn't get it pinned on very well. It keeps flopping around." She demonstrated with a frustrated sigh.

"Let's see if we can't pin it more securely. Hold still for me," Isabella said, grateful for the distraction. "This dim lighting doesn't help." The woman seemed to be holding her breath as Isabella worked. "Okay, there you go. See what you think."

Ginny gave the lovely flower a slight tug to test it. "I'm sure it's fine. You are a love. Have fun, honey, and we'll see you later!" Clyde nodded to Isabella as he walked toward his bride.

Isabella sensed Sidney watching her from across the park. When their gazes locked, he nodded and mouthed *Hi* from where he was engaged in conversation with a number of the men.

Joel approached with an unfamiliar blonde woman by his side. Ah, yes, this must be Cathy Nelson. He handed her a cup. "I brought you some Twilight Punch."

"Thank you." She appreciated his thoughtful gesture. After Joel made the introductions, it became quickly apparent Cathy was assessing whether or not she posed a potential threat for her new boyfriend's affections. If it wouldn't be socially inappropriate, Isabella would assure Cathy she had no reason to worry. She had no designs on Joel other than to hit him up for a small business loan if Mahoney's faltered financially.

From their seats in the gazebo, the band struck the first few notes and then began playing an upbeat Big Band tune. Thankfully, that was the impetus for Joel to excuse them from what had become an increasingly awkward conversation.

Standing to one side, Isabella watched as several couples made their way to the dance floor in front of the gazebo. The sight of the older couples, especially—some married more than fifty years—swaying together to the music, touched her heart. Wrapped in the arms of their respective partners, they exchanged sweet nothings and stole kisses.

That was what love should look like.

This was what life should be.

Liesel and Paul watched from a nearby park bench. Paul, Jr. was cradled in his mother's arms while Bella played with her friend Katie. Caroline and Seth arrived a few minutes later with baby Ellie in the most upscale baby carriage she'd ever seen.

High-pitched, feminine laughter rang out in the night. Isabella recognized that distinctive laugh, part girlish giggle, part sultry seductress. A sinking feeling settled in her stomach. Kayley Harris, the prettiest single girl in Evergreen. Model thin, statuesque, striking features, long auburn hair. At twenty-six, she'd dated most of the eligible guys in the county, but none of them had reportedly measured up to her standards. Heaven only knew what that meant.

When Kayley laughed again, Isabella's gaze zeroed in on her. She wore a mid-thigh dress, ridiculously high heels, and a plunging neckline that left precious little to the imagination. Isabella could only hope the girl didn't bend over or she might spill out the front of that dress or show too much…oh, never mind. Not worth stewing over.

Really, though, how could she be critical of the way Kayley dressed? Could others see the sins of *her* past hidden beneath her smiling exterior and ultra-feminine dress? The townspeople thought she was *sweet Isabella something-or-other.* Guess again.

In her college days, she'd worn clothing every bit as short, clingy, and revealing as Kayley's. Her Tristan days. Reeling from the death of her parents, she'd bought into the misconception that dressing provocatively imparted the image of a strong, confident, successful woman. She'd been misguided in her own clothing choices, so she had absolutely no business faulting anyone else.

A strong breeze made her shiver.

You are forgiven. Lay your fears, your worries, your insecurities, at the foot of the cross.

The dark, ugly stains of her past were gone, erased by the loving Father, cleansed by the shed blood of her Savior. Isabella *knew* that, but at the end of the day, the doubts and insecurities clung to her like prickly burs on a cashmere sweater. Would they never release their possessive hold on her?

"Everything okay?" Caroline laid a gentle hand on her arm. "I'm sorry that I interrupted you and Sidney back at the house. I hope you're not upset with me."

Isabella dipped her head. No one else milled about in the immediate vicinity.

"I'm not upset." She drew in a quick breath. "The park, the lights in the trees, the dancing…romance is all around me. I don't want to leave, but at the same time, I'm thinking I should listen to that inner voice urging me to go home."

"For what it's worth, I hope you stay," Caroline said. "And not just so you can watch the kids so we can dance."

"Of course, I'll do that. You know you don't have to ask. Besides, how could I be mad at you when you gifted me with this?" Isabella lifted the beautiful necklace around her neck. "This is precious to me, and I can't thank you enough."

"Tell you a secret. I thought of you when I designed it, and I knew all along that you were the one I wanted to have it."

They watched the dancers for a few minutes, making observations and talking quietly together. "Caroline," Isabella said finally, "I'm not questioning God's will, but I'm trying to understand why He's brought Sidney into my life. He's the first man I've met since my breakup with Tristan who makes me *feel* again. Who makes me *want* to feel again. I hope that doesn't sound weird. If that makes you uncomfortable, please tell me now. He *is* your brother, after all."

"Not at all. Go on," Caroline encouraged.

"I met your brother on Wednesday afternoon. And here it is, Saturday evening, and I'm already dreading the idea of Sidney leaving town."

Caroline's smile, as always, was kind. "Tell me what makes Sidney different from the other men you've met since moving here."

"He's like this tidal wave that rolled into town, but it's not like I'm being swallowed by it. I'm not drowning. Actually, I'm…coming alive again, as weird as that might sound."

"You're being very poetic tonight."

Isabella lifted her shoulders. "I don't know why I'm thinking these things. Sidney challenges me, and he's fun. We've shared some good talks. But ever since I met him, I wake up every morning wondering, 'Will I see Sidney today?' Then the truth slams into my mind that he doesn't share my faith in the Lord, and his life is in Boston. For all I know, he's out there being charmed by Kayley as we speak."

Isabella's gaze traveled across the park, but there was no sign of Sidney. "How can I possibly compete with a woman like that?"

"Simple answer? You don't," Caroline said. "Isabella, I think what happened in Hartford made you feel somehow less than worthy of God's love, much less a man's love. There's not a single person alive who doesn't have regrets or something in their past that makes them feel ashamed. But look at all you've accomplished since you've come to Evergreen. You've taken over Clara's store, made improvements, and increased the revenue. Your background in marketing shows in that new sign on the outskirts of town, the store's website, and in the way you've run successful store promotions and advertising campaigns."

"I had to use my degree in some way." Isabella appreciated Caroline's compliments more than her friend could know.

"More importantly, you've got Hattie Nelson interested in life again after she lost Henry, and even Millicent takes more time with her appearance. Those are very *good* things."

"I can't take credit for Hattie and Millicent. Those are the benefits of goat's milk soap, a little blush, and lipstick."

"It *is* you, my friend," Caroline insisted, smiling. "No amount of money can buy the self-confidence you've given those two women. You make people want to be around you. You're smart, you're funny, you're optimistic, and—as much as anything—you make them feel good about themselves. That's a special quality not many people have, but *you* do."

"Thank you," Isabella said. "I can't tell you how much your encouragement means."

Caroline breathed in and released it slowly. "Sidney's still hurting after Mom's death. He spent a lot of time with her right before she died. He told me tonight that she'd shared more about her faith with him, including her hope that he'd come to know the Lord. That impacted him. I've given him Seth's grandfather's Bible, the same Bible that Seth gave to me when I first visited Evergreen. That Bible, and Seth's friendship, changed my life. God knew, as He always does. The verse that gives me comfort, the one I go back to over and over again, is Romans 8:28: 'And we know that God causes all things to work together for good—'"

"'To those who love God, to those who are called according to His purpose.'" Isabella smiled. "Thanks for the reminder. That's an appropriate verse."

"As forceful as he can be, you're right. Sidney can be like a tidal wave," Caroline said. "In the last few years, he's changed. Believe it or not, he's not nearly as strong as he used to be. He's always been formidable, but he's softened. He's changed even since he's been here in Maine. Things are beginning to fall into place for him, Isabella. I truly believe that. For now, I think it's best to be gentle with him. If we push too hard, he'll probably run away. But if we model our faith quietly, and love him, that's the best way we can reach him."

"And they'll know we are Christians by our love," Isabella murmured.

Chapter 21

"Mr. Prescott?" An older black gentleman offered his hand. "Toby Daniels. It's nice to make your acquaintance. I've heard a lot about you, young man."

"That might be a dangerous thing." Sidney shook Toby's hand and returned his smile. "I understand you're a great landscape painter, Mr. Daniels. Not only that, but you're also the man who works his special brand of magic with my sister's jewelry designs."

Toby shook his head. "Call me Toby. Your sister has a God-given talent. Isabella's a mighty fine painter in her own right. I understand you have your talents, too."

"I try my best," Sidney said. He wasn't sure if Toby meant in a courtroom, so that was the most politically correct response. Considering he didn't spend his time doing much of anything but practicing law, that was likely his intended meaning. "Are you planning to take your wife for a spin on the dance floor tonight?"

"In a bit. Thelma's talking with the pastor's wife at the moment. Do you have any special plans while you're visiting?"

Sidney took a drink of his punch before answering. "Spending time with my family." His voice caught. *My family*. What a great thing to be able to say. He was getting soft again. Clearing his throat, he continued. "Speaking of the pastor, I was speaking with Isabella the other day and she mentioned a beautification team at the church. Do you happen to attend the same church?"

"I do, as a matter of fact. Evergreen Community Church."

"Do you know of any projects that could use my help? I'm game if you're willing to take on an untrained worker."

Toby chuckled. "If you're offering, I'm sure we could find something to keep you busy. I've heard you big city lawyers can cause trouble if you're not kept busy."

"I suppose that depends on who you're talking to." Sidney raised his cup in a toast.

"Let me see what I can find out in terms of any projects," Toby said. "Should I call Caroline to get a message to you or would you prefer I call you directly?"

"I see Isabella every day. Why don't you tell her? She'll let me know."

"She's a sweet gal."

"Yes, she is."

"Smart, too," Toby observed. "And so are you. I can see straight through that plan, son." Was that a twinkle in the older man's eye?

"I beg your pardon?"

"You don't need a convenient excuse to check in with Isabella every day. That young lady appreciates a straightforward approach."

Sidney chuckled. "You caught me. Isabella's also worked in the corporate world. We understand each other."

Toby's smile faded. "That corporate world nearly destroyed her. Thank the Lord her Aunt Clara had the vision to sell the store to Isabella. The timing was providential."

Vision? So many things in that statement aroused Sidney's curiosity. He wasn't quite sure where to begin. "Providential?"

The older man nodded. "She doesn't suffer fools." Did Toby's words hold a thinly veiled warning?

"If it's a question in your mind, I care about Isabella, Toby. First and foremost, she's my friend. I respect her, and I won't ever lie to her."

Toby moved forward and planted one hand on Sidney's shoulder. "Just make sure you don't lie to yourself either, young man. Be willing to listen and open your mind to the possibilities that God plants right in front of you."

By the time he could formulate a response, Toby was already gone.

Sidney moved his gaze across the expanse of Evergreen Park. Isabella danced with Tommy, and he twirled her beneath his arm. Happy and carefree, she was laughing at something he said. Tonight her hair was curled on the ends, cascading down her back. *Beautiful.* Caroline was right. He'd stolen plenty of glances at Isabella during dinner. She was irresistible with those big brown eyes, long, dark lashes, soft-looking lips, a hint of color in her cheeks. Sidney's gaze traveled the length of her. As cute as she looked in her jeans, T-shirts, and shorts, *this* vision was the enchanting image of Isabella Caccavale he'd remember when he returned to Boston.

You'll miss her when you leave.

Soft sounds interrupted his musing. What was that? Like the mewling of a cat, or the soft whimper of a child. Had Humphrey come to the Twilight Dance? Surveying his immediate surroundings, Sidney searched for the source. Listening. Waiting. There it was again.

And then he saw her. Beneath a large pine tree, half-hidden, was the shadowed outline of a woman. Sidney's first thought was not to intrude. A closer look confirmed she was alone.

His eyes widened, and he stepped closer. "Millicent, is that you?"

"Go away, Sidney. Mind your own business." He heard muffled sniffles.

"You can yell at me all you want, but I'm afraid I can't walk away. Would you like me to take you home?"

"No." When she twisted her hands together, a tissue dropped to the ground. Before Sidney could retrieve it, Millicent snatched it up and stuffed it in the pocket of her dress. The outfit flattered her, and she wore her hair down for a change. The eyeglasses were missing.

"You look very nice."

"Sweet talker."

"Okay then, I take it back. Contrary to what you might have heard, I don't throw compliments around freely."

"You're the funny one, aren't you?"

"Not usually," he admitted. "A courtroom doesn't lend itself to a lot of humor. I inject it here and there when I can, but it's not appropriate in most cases. Pun intended, I suppose."

Feeling awkward, Sidney stuffed his hands in the pockets of his slacks. He *could* walk away but something stopped him. This woman was hurting, and he couldn't leave her crying beneath a towering pine tree.

"He doesn't know I exist."

"May I ask who—?"

"Hank Jergens."

Ah, yes, the country crooner. "I caught the floor show at Mahoney's when he tried out a Conway Twitty song yesterday afternoon. Something about a job, an ode to fatherhood. Since it's close to Father's Day, I guess they play that song on the radio a lot."

"That'd be 'That's My Job.' It's not as controversial as some of Conway's other songs."

Sidney snapped his fingers. "That's the one, and I wouldn't know about controversial."

"Why won't he dance with me?"

"Conway? I'm pretty sure he's dead."

"Hank," she snapped. "Pay attention, Sidney."

"Right. Just checking. You obviously know your country music, Millicent. Look, I don't really know Hank, but I've met him, and he seems like an upstanding kind of guy. I played a few games of checkers with him yesterday since Marty couldn't be there. I know Hank lost a leg on the job. Is it possible he doesn't dance?"

"He's not dead, he's got a prosthesis. He gets around. No reason he can't, well, shake a leg." When he heard more sounds, Sidney thought Millicent was crying again, but this time she was laughing. So much so that her shoulders were shaking. What a strange little bird she was. On the other hand, he found this scenario fascinating.

"Is Hank here tonight? Somewhere?"

She angled her head in the direction of a few tables set up to the back of the gazebo. "He's over there doing what he does best."

"Singing?"

She sighed. "You sure you went to Harvard? Do you *hear* a man singing, Sidney?"

"Then I'm guessing he has a checkerboard game going on tonight?"

"Something like that. The fool thinks no woman will want him, so he spends all the livelong day playing checkers. I got this new dress, and I've been using the goat's milk soap like Isabella told me, and he hasn't said two words to me tonight."

"For what it's worth, Millicent, I have a suggestion. You might want to come out from under the tree. A man can't ask a woman to dance if she's not within his range of vision."

Millicent turned her head in Hank's direction and didn't speak for a long moment. "Dance with me," she said.

"Excuse me?"

"Your hearing's fine, isn't it? I asked you to dance with me."

"Sounded more like you demanded, but why quibble?" She wanted to make Hank jealous? In its own way, that was very sweet. Why not? Sidney hoped it might work. "Miss Millicent, will you do me the honor of dancing with me?" He paused. "What's your last name?"

"Don't ask," she grumbled.

"Fair enough." He crooked his elbow. "Shall we go dance close to the gazebo?"

Stepping out from under the shadow of the tree, Millicent hooked her arm through his. "You *can* dance, right?"

"No worries. My mom made sure I learned to dance. I'll try not to embarrass you with my lack of skill." Sidney patted her hand resting on his arm. "Let me lead, okay?"

Sidney was relieved to see a few couples dancing near the gazebo. They wouldn't be as obvious this way, and it should be interesting. "Hank's a handyman, right?"

"Yes." They began to dance together. Of course, this one had to be a ballad. No problem.

"Here's a thought. Have you considered hiring Hank to repair shelves at the library?"

Millicent was quiet for so long Sidney figured she hadn't heard. "Or, you could invite him to come to your house and…fix something."

"The only thing that needs fixing is his attitude." After she snuggled a bit too close, Sidney took tiny steps back to put a respectable distance between them.

"You can't very well invite him over to fix an attitude. How about an appliance? Anything along those lines? A broken toaster or a malfunctioning oven?"

"Don't think I don't know what you're doing," she said under her breath.

How could he convey to Millicent that a gentle word might go a long way toward capturing Hank's attention? "I'm trying to give you suggestions to spend some time with Hank so he can fall in love with you. Is that wrong? I thought that's what you wanted."

She snorted and then clamped a hand over her mouth. "Do you think he heard that?" The words came out muffled, and Millicent looked up at him with wide eyes.

In response, he threw his head back and laughed. "Millicent"— he elevated his voice slightly—"you just reminded me of that Conway Twitty song I like so much."

"What are you—?" When Sidney gave her a look, a slow smile crossed her face. "It's working. Hank's looking over here." Millicent sounded excited. Her fingers gripped his arm tighter. "Say something else like that."

"What? Talk Twitty to you?"

"Shhhh." She laughed.

"Which country music singer that he impersonates or whatever is your favorite?"

"George Strait."

"Give me the name of a Strait song, Millicent." Wow, that sounded strange enough.

"'Give It All We Got Tonight.'"

"I'm trying here," Sidney said. "Give me some credit."

"It's the name of one of George Strait's songs," she hissed.

"You've gotta love country music." Sidney winked, and then he started to warble although he couldn't sing his way out of a paper bag. Closing one eye, he kept going, and he wouldn't stop unless Millicent tried to shush him. She hadn't stomped on his foot yet. Soon enough, he felt a tap on his shoulder. He sure hoped it was Hank.

"That's not how it's done, city slicker."

Still dancing, Sidney opened both eyes and gave Hank a mock glare. "Not how what's done, Hank? I'm trying my best to dance with lovely Millicent here."

"You shouldn't be singing if you can't do justice to the song."

"Think you can do better?"

"Yes." Hank looked at Millicent. "How about it? You want to dance, Millie?"

Millie? Cute. "You know, Millicent was just telling me—"

"You can move on now, Mr. Prescott," Hank said. "I've got it covered."

In the moonlight, Sidney could see Millicent's blush. "I'll do that. You two kids have fun." With a nod, Sidney backed away. He doubted either one of them even noticed. He spied Isabella a few hundred yards away. Softly clapping, she smiled and mouthed *Bravo!*

Closing the distance between them, Sidney didn't hesitate as he pulled her into his arms. "Thank you. Thank you very much," he said in his best imitation of Elvis. "Shall we dance, Miss Cabaletta?"

"Cabaletta? What's that mean?" she said as he spun her in a half-turn.

"A simple aria with a repetitive rhythm."

Spinning beneath his arm, Isabella laughed. "You made that up. And I'm not sure it's safe to dance with you."

"I did *not* make it up. It was used in 19th-century Italian operas." Sidney tugged her close. "And we're friends. Is there a law in Evergreen that friends can't dance with one another?"

Isabella nodded to where Hank and Millicent danced together. "You did a very good thing over there tonight." She patted his chest, sending warmth searing through him. "Beneath all the bravado, you're a kindhearted man, Mr. Prescott."

"I couldn't leave her standing beneath that tree *pining* away, could I?"

Isabella's laughter filled his soul.

Chapter 22

Isabella observed with more than a little fascination as Sidney bounced Ellie on his knee and sang a song under his breath.

"You're terrific with her, Uncle Sidney." She hoped Sidney could hear the admiration in her tone. "You know, you were very cute in your embarrassment over the breastfeeding incident when you first arrived in town."

"Was not." His knee pumped up and down with a bit too much vigor.

"Slow down there, sparky, or she'll start rattling."

"Oh, man. Sorry." Sidney looked panicked and slowed to a crawl. "This better?"

"You're fine. Don't worry."

"You tried to fluster me," he teased. "Why *do* you do it, Isabella?"

"Because I like to see you blush. There's something so endearing about it."

"And you're irresistible when you ogle me."

"What?" She sputtered. "I do *not* ogle, thank you very much." Of course, she did. Isabella glanced in the opposite direction, pretending to watch the dancers. When he said nothing, she dared to look at him again.

"Gotcha. That was too easy." He laughed. "I like to see *you* blush. It's downright endearing."

"Touché. What's that song you were singing just now?" Pulling the burp cloth from the diaper bag on the bench beside her, Isabella wiped the drool beneath baby Paul's mouth.

"I have no idea. Something I made up. Ellie doesn't seem to be particular." He kissed the top of the baby's blonde head. "Must be my version of a Twitty ditty. Ever since you told me about that Conway Twitty song at the store, I can't seem to get away from the Twitty references. They apparently feed into my warped sense of humor."

Nearby, Bella burst into tears. Moving Ellie to his shoulder, Sidney half-turned on the bench. "What's wrong, Bella? Come over here and join us."

The little girl scampered over to them. After plopping on the bench, she settled between them.

"Why the tears?" Sidney said.

Using the opposite end of the burp cloth, Isabella carefully dabbed beneath the little girl's eyes.

Bella sniffled. "Katie had to leave."

"I'm sorry, kiddo. It is getting kind of late, and I'm sure you'll see her again soon." Sidney hiked his sleeve and checked his watch. Was that a Rolex? Wow. Why would Isabella expect him to wear a Timex? Talk about being born with a silver spoon. He'd probably had a Rolex from the time he was a teenager. Caroline had one, too, but neither one of them flashed it around. To them, it served a function. So what if it cost a few thousand dollars? Isabella couldn't begin to imagine that kind of reasoning.

"I saw you dance with your Mommy and Daddy," Sidney said. "That must have been fun."

"Uh huh." Bella pulled on the skirt of her pretty blue dress. "Mommy made my dress. Isn't it bee-u-tee-ful, Uncle Sidney?"

"It is indeed. I should call you Princess Bella."

She giggled. Isabella listened quietly as Sidney engaged Bella in a conversation of everything about her favorite doll to what she'd learned in Sunday school the week before.

"Are you coming to church tomorrow?" Bella wrapped her hands around Sidney's arm and leaned her head against him. "Please?"

"Say pretty please, and then I'll think about it."

"Pretty please?" Bella looked up at him with pleading eyes, and Isabella was all but forgotten.

"Okay. I'll be there," he said. "I'll have to make sure I set my alarm clock."

Bella slid off the bench. "Bye, Sidney. Bye, Isabella."

"You have completely charmed that little girl." Isabella watched Bella run to her parents. "I'll admit to a wee bit of jealousy that she calls you Uncle Sidney. You've obviously wiggled your way into her affections in short order."

"It's as much a mystery to me as it is to you. But I can't pretend it hasn't made me think about kids since I've been here in Evergreen. I don't have the opportunity to be around many children, at least not long enough to spend quality time with them."

"You've never dated a woman with a child?"

"No. At my advanced age, I guess you'd think I might have."

"Kids are so honest," she said. "They speak their mind without worrying if they've hurt someone's feelings. Sometimes I think they can see past the outside of a person and go straight to what's in their heart."

He glanced down at her. "That's a profound statement. I think you're right."

"Would you like children of your own someday, Sidney?"

He was quiet for so long she thought he might say no. "Yes," he said finally. "I never thought much about it until the last six months. I guess faced with the mortality of a parent, you realize that life doesn't go on forever like you think it will when you're young."

"I'll admit I'm a pushover for a strong man who likes kids." Isabella nudged Sidney with her shoulder. "They *gentle* you." Paul, Jr. had fallen asleep on her other shoulder, and Isabella was content to leave him there. His soft downy hair smelled so fresh. Was there anything sweeter?

Ellie had fallen asleep, and Sidney carefully lowered her into the baby carriage. "I ordered this carriage for Ellie," he said.

"I should have known. It looks top of the line. Like the Lamborghini of baby carriages."

He grinned. "That's not why I told you, but you can't fault me too much. I usually let someone else pick out the gift. In this case, I wanted the best. Ellie's my niece, after all. If I didn't have money, I'd figure out something. I'd probably make furniture. Make her a crib."

That surprised her. "Have you ever made anything?"

"No, but I went home one weekend with a roommate from school. He took me over to his grandfather's house in West Medford, a suburb of Boston, on Saturday afternoon. He had a furniture shop set up in the garage behind the house. It took me a while to get used to the fumes. Seriously, I thought I was going to get high."

Isabella wasn't sure whether to laugh or frown, so she bit her lower lip.

"I watched this man—Melvin was his name—work with his hands, and I admired the concentration, the skill, the effort that went into it. To think that he created something of lasting quality, an heirloom, that someone would have in their home for years, was so awesome. I know it's not the same thing, but I enjoyed helping to put together the dance floor earlier today."

Sidney moved his arm around the back of the bench. His hand rested behind her, and his fingers lightly caressed the top of her shoulder. Isabella wondered if he even realized what he was doing.

"You'll have to talk to Marty about making furniture. Remember, that's what he does for a living."

"Thanks for the reminder. I'll definitely ask him," Sidney said. "You look like a natural with kids, too. Witness the sleeping child on your shoulder. Do you see kids in your future?"

"I've always wanted to be a mother. I don't care if it's one child or five, but I want to be the mom who volunteers for things, drives the carpool, organizes the bake sales. All those things."

"Then I'm sure you'll be a big hit with all the other moms." Sidney's smile sobered and his brow creased. "I like talking with you, Isabella. I don't get the chance to do this often."

"What, talk? It's like anything else, Sidney. You have to make time and take advantage of the opportunities."

He shot her a grin. "This is the kind of honesty I need in my life."

"Just don't expect everything in your life to run smoothly once you go back to Boston," she said quietly. "Nothing there will have changed. It'll be the same people, the same cases with some new ones thrown into the mix, but the dynamics will be the same."

"Yes, but *my* outlook and attitude can make all the difference, Isabella. My life is very *ordered*. I go from one thing to the next. Others handle my schedule and make sure I'm where I need to be, whether it's in a client conference, a partner meeting, or in a courtroom. My responsibility is to research, study, and make sure I'm prepared to give my clients the best legal representation their money can buy."

"I'm sure they appreciate what you do for them."

"I used to defend some of the cases no one else wanted. I did it to prove my worth to my father, number one, and to anyone else who cared to pay attention."

"Someone has to defend them," Isabella said quietly.

"I'm not talking about being a public defender. I'm talking cases where the clients paid big money hoping to get either an acquittal or a verdict of not guilty. High profile cases with names in the high society of Boston. Rape cases, involuntary manslaughter, even murder." He gave her a pointed look. "But never serial killers. Just so we're clear."

"And what cases do you work on now?"

"I switched to the non-violent white collar crimes. For the most part, I deal with privileged clients who've messed up. Some acknowledge that truth and genuinely want to change their lives for the better. They're the ones who quietly accept their fate, so to speak. But there are others who can't see that they've done anything wrong. They're either in denial or refuse to see the truth, and they go kicking and screaming if they don't get their way. They demand to be heard."

"It could be that life's beaten them down and they can't differentiate black from white, right from wrong, anymore." Isabella frowned. "You do represent *some* innocent people, I hope?"

Sidney nodded. "Yes, but unfortunately, a majority of them are guilty or they wouldn't be accused of wrongdoing in the first place."

"What made you decide to switch to the non-violent cases?" A sense of relief flowed through Isabella.

He tipped her chin. "Because I wanted to look at myself in the mirror and see a man of integrity, a man I can respect. I used to have a recurring nightmare where the victims of the crimes my clients had committed all came after me. They converged on me and beat me to a bloody pulp. And the sad fact? I probably deserved it."

Isabella shuddered. "You're much too hard on yourself, counselor."

Sidney shook his head and scrubbed a hand over his face. "I don't know why I started talking about all that. I like how optimistic and upbeat you are. You see the best in people."

Isabella lowered her gaze. "You don't really know me all that well." He couldn't know how beaten down she'd been after leaving Hartford. She hadn't trusted anyone. Yet, his observation wasn't so far off-track now. She'd changed a lot in the past year alone. Living in Evergreen had afforded her the time to slow down and think about her priorities. Most importantly, it'd given her the time she needed to reconnect with the Lord.

"In my own way, I ran away too," she said. "As it turns out, I ran straight into my *future*. One that offered me sanity and the kind of inner peace I never had in Hartford. Worldly success meant nothing if it meant sacrificing my soul."

"That's what I was trying to say." Sidney shifted to face her on the bench. "I felt like I'd sold out my soul." Resting his hand on her forearm, he traced a light, circular pattern with his fingers.

If Paul, Jr. weren't still on her shoulder, Isabella felt sure Sidney would kiss her.

You can't kiss him. That would be the worst thing she could do. Where did the line of distinction lie between being the man's friend and becoming more? Talk about a conundrum.

In her heart, Isabella knew the key had to be self-control. Being able to resist the physical attraction in not allowing the lines between friendship and romance to become blurred.

No handholding, no caresses, no kisses. The long gazes were kind of hard to ignore.

Lord, please help me. I can't resist this man without your help. I need you!

He lifted the delicate necklace around her neck. "I recognize the handiwork."

"Yes," she said. "Caroline gave it to me earlier tonight. I'm pretty much pledged to babysit Ellie for the rest of my life in exchange for it. Your sister knows I love pink amethysts, but I had no idea she'd gift me with such an extravagant gift."

Sidney's fingers were warm on her skin as he released the necklace. "See? I learned something else about you tonight. I feel as though I already know you better than my last five dates combined."

"Thanks for that." Shaking her head, Isabella was relieved for the change in subject. "How am I supposed to respond? You keep me on my toes, that's for sure." She hadn't had a date since she'd left Connecticut, only those *just friends* dinners and movies with Joel.

"I didn't say over how long a period I had those dates," Sidney said. "You might be surprised. The women were beautiful, smart, successful. The last date I had was with Taylor Norman, an oncologist at Brigham and Women's. We went to an Andrew Lloyd Webber musical at The Wang Center."

Isabella shifted on the bench. Why on earth would Sidney think she'd want to hear about his date with a gorgeous doctor? "Your point?"

Sidney chuckled. "No need to be jealous. *None* of those women, including Taylor, are anywhere near as fascinating, as exciting, or as beautiful, as I find you, Isabella. After only a couple of hours in their company, I felt claustrophobic."

"You poor man." Isabella kept her voice light and teasing. "I'm sorry you had to suffer." Red alert flags were shooting signals right and left, but she pushed them aside. More like shoved them far, far away.

"They were focused on themselves, on what they wanted to accomplish. They didn't really care about me or what I thought about anything. Our conversation was all on a surface level."

"You have to give a relationship time to develop, Sidney. Most women aren't like me, you realize. They're not crazy enough to spout out their hidden fears and vulnerabilities early on. They don't say whatever's on their mind at the risk of sounding foolish."

"I like how your eyes sparkle when you're trying not to laugh," he said.

Okay, so the man wanted to ruminate on her finer points. Who was she to stop him? This little exercise might prove enlightening.

"You have a habit of smoothing your hand over your hair, on the top of your head, when you're nervous." He demonstrated, as if she needed to be reminded. "You chew on your adorable lower lip when you've said something and then wonder if you shouldn't have." Sidney smiled and ran his finger along the bottom of her lower lip. Goodness, that was a sensual move. Was he doing this on purpose, trying to seduce her?

Walk away now, Isabella. Even if she wanted, she couldn't easily walk away considering she had a sleeping, drooling infant on her shoulder.

Isabella stared at Sidney. "You're either way more observant than I thought, or I'm painfully obvious. I seriously doubt my eyes sparkle, and you're delusional if you think my lower lip is adorable."

"When you started yodeling that ridiculous song from *The Sound of Music*, that's when you had me. Your joy spills over, and it's completely infectious. I don't know everything there is to know about you, Isabella—I'm not sure that's even possible—but I can read your *heart*. You have a sweet, gentle, loving spirit that gets inside a man, grabs hold, and won't let him go."

"That's, um…" Again, the man had rendered her almost speechless. "I doubt I'll ever receive a higher compliment. Thank you."

Sidney slid closer on the bench. "Tommy challenged me *not* to fall for you by the time of the Twilight Dance."

Isabella inhaled a quick breath, hardly daring to breathe. "Is that right?"

"I told him it couldn't happen. Not to focused, inflexible, Sidney Jefferson Prescott. No way. I told him I'd only come to Evergreen to reconnect with my sister and her family." He chuckled under his breath. "Tommy's one of your biggest fans, and he was pretty sure of himself."

She *would* not ask. *Could* not ask.

"But you, Isabella…by the way, what's your middle name?"

"Marie," she said quietly.

"You, Isabella Marie Caccavale, made me lose that challenge. If you know anything about me, you know I don't like to lose."

They turned their heads as their friends came to claim their sleeping children and say good night. With a few minutes, she was alone again with Sidney. Perhaps she should have made her escape with the others, but something held her back.

Smoothing the skirt of her dress, Isabella rose from the bench. "This has been a wonderful evening, but I should say good night, too."

"Stay." Reaching for her, Sidney captured her hand. "Dance with me one more time."

A soft groan escaped her lips. "I'm not sure that's such a good idea. It's getting late, and we have church tomorrow morning."

"Then may I walk you home?"

Still holding his hand, they began to walk.

Chapter 23

Sidney glanced up at the street sign as he walked beside Isabella. "White Pine Street." She withdrew her hand from his. Not knowing what else to do, he shoved his hands in the pockets of his slacks.

"The white pine has been the state tree of Maine since the mid-40s," she told him. "I'm sure you know Maine is The Pine Tree State, and the white pine is on the state flag. The pinecone is our state flower, and it's not even a flower. Go figure."

When she started to pull her sweater around her shoulders, Sidney helped her into it. "Do you rent or own?"

"As crazy as it sounds, I bought my house sight unseen before I moved here. Aunt Clara and the Realtor—one of her most trusted friends—told me the former owners kept it in top shape for a house that's over 70 years old. The brownstone in Hartford was even older. Nothing wrong with new, but the older ones have a unique charm, I think. Most of the homes in Evergreen are older, anyway."

"Except for the suburban ones like Caroline and Seth's," he said. "The home in Beacon Hill is over 120 years old."

"That's what Caroline told me. It sounds wonderful."

Sidney shrugged. "A bit overdone for my liking. Compared to the warmth of Caroline's house, it's a mausoleum. That's what we used to call it when we were kids. We have some hard decisions coming up whether to keep the house or sell it. It's worth a large sum of money because of its location, and my parents maintained it well. But there's something inside me that hates to let it go."

Isabella nodded. "I can understand that, and I assumed you still lived in the house."

He shook his head. "I have a place within a few blocks of the office. With the unpredictable winters, it's nice to be so close." He didn't want to talk about the penthouse or Boston.

"You know what I like about your street? Everything about it is so New England—patriotic with all-American charm." He pointed to a home on the opposite side of the street. "You have a 17th century Colonial over there next to a Queen Anne Victorian. Then on the other side of the street"—he turned and pointed—"you have a Gothic Revival. What style is your house?"

"We're here." She led the way up a sidewalk to a small Cape Cod-style home. In the dim spotlights lining the front walkway, it looked like it was made from the natural, weathered gray cedar shingles typical of homes on the Cape.

"It's perfect. Even without seeing the inside, I can tell it suits you, Isabella. Requisite white picket fence included."

"If you'd like to talk for a few minutes, let's sit on the porch swing. It's more private." Isabella hesitated. "Did Caroline drive you into town tonight?"

"I brought the car and left it on the far side of Landon's." He gestured to the walkway. "After you." He waited for Isabella to take her seat on the double swing. Once she was settled, he sat beside her. Planting one foot on the porch floor, he gave them a small push.

"Sidney, we should talk about that conversation in the kitchen. I need to tell you more. First of all, I've felt the attraction between us from the start. I've tried to deny it, but it's impossible."

"I know you were hurt by Tristan, and that he betrayed you," he said. "I hate that he did that to you. No one deserves that kind of treatment. If I met him, I'd deck the guy into next year."

The tiniest smile lifted the corners of her mouth. "I appreciate that you'd want to protect my honor. I found out Tristan had traveled to New York several times with one of our account executives. They'd stayed in the same room. I need to be honest and tell you that Tristan and I were a couple for nearly five years, and we lived together for three of those years."

"Were you ever engaged?"

"No, but we could have been." Isabella stared straight ahead as though ashamed to look him in the eye. "Ironically, he'd asked me to marry him a couple of times, but I never felt as if he meant it in here." She tapped her curled fist over her heart. "When I finally confronted him, Tristan threw his own shortcomings back at me as if his actions were *my* fault."

"Classic defensive mechanism motivated by feelings of guilt," he said. "A man needs to admit to his own failures. That's hard to do sometimes."

"It took me a long time to feel like God had forgiven me, even though I was a Christian and had confessed everything I'd done. I missed my mom so much after the breakup. Aunt Clara has been there for me always, loving me in spite of myself."

Stopping the swing, Sidney angled his body to face her. She looked so beautiful in her pink dress. Her lovely eyes met his, shining, big, and trusting in the reflected moonlight. He never wanted to hurt her. Never wanted to tell her an untruth. Never wanted to say good-bye and not see her again. He *needed* Isabella Caccavale in his life.

"I'd never fault you for your past, Isabella. Ever. I've got too many sins in *my* life."

"There's more." She drew in a breath. "Tristan more or less forced me out of the firm."

Sidney hadn't expected that revelation. "How could that happen? You were a co-owner."

"I was, but he made my life miserable. He did some dirty, underhanded things that made me look bad to our clients and employees. Those who knew me well understood I couldn't have done half the things he claimed. Finally, I sold out my half and signed it all over to him. Let him have it. It wasn't worth losing my self-respect, or what was left of it. Believe it or not, Tristan came to Evergreen seven months ago. He wanted me back. Apologized all over himself. Seems a number of the bigger clients still wanted me to work on their accounts."

"What did you tell him?"

"My life is here now, and that part of my life is over. I told him I'd pray for him, and then I asked him to leave. He did. That's the last I expect to ever hear from him."

"How did you feel knowing that clients wanted you back?" Sidney loved this woman's forgiving spirit. Telling Tristan she'd pray for him was what he'd expect from her.

"I'll admit that part was gratifying," she said. "I could always freelance if I wanted, but at this point, I'm not ready. Those skills aren't going to go away. I'm happy running the store and painting my landscapes for now. I'm content in my *soul*, and that means everything."

Kicking off her sandals, Isabella propped one leg beneath her. "Your turn. How about you? Surely there's been someone special in your past?" She lowered her gaze. "More than one, I imagine."

"I've only had one relationship that lasted," he said. "When I was 15, I met Olivia at the prep school we both attended. We were the same age, same year in school. She was beautiful, smart, and we dated each other exclusively from my high school days until my junior year in undergrad. She went to Boston College, and we got together as much as possible."

Isabella remained quiet, waiting for him to continue.

"She went to Italy on spring break and met a guy from California. One of those blond, beefy, surfer dude types. You know, you're from California. She came back, told me it was over between us, and then she moved to California. I basically paid Olivia's best friend to tell me where she'd gone. Like a lovesick fool, I flew out to Los Angeles to try and win her back. I couldn't believe she'd ditch all that we'd shared for some guy she'd only known for a few days. But she turned me away and told me she never wanted to see me again, that all I cared about was becoming a power-hungry shark like my father. That cut pretty deep."

"I'm sorry, Sidney. Did you ever see her or talk to her again?"

"No." He shook his head. He no longer felt the pain of rejection he had for years. "For all I know, she married him, and they have a bunch of little surfboarders. I threw myself into my studies after that. Olivia taught me how fragile relationships can be. From that point on, I've poured everything into my career. There hasn't been time for anything else."

"Do you think what happened with Olivia damaged your ability to trust another woman?"

Sidney considered her question. "I honestly don't know, but in retrospect, I'd say it probably did to a certain extent. What I *do* know is that I haven't gone out of my way to actively pursue another relationship. There have been opportunities, but it's not something that's been a priority in my life."

"Thank you for sharing that with me," she said.

He needed to tell her the rest. "My dad cheated on our mom. A lot."

Isabella's eyes widened. "Oh."

"My personality is a lot like my dad's—driven to succeed. In Dad's case, it was at the expense of my mom's self-esteem. Infidelity is a horrible thing. Mom withdrew and was distant for a long time, even from her children. The affairs decimated her. I figured out what was happening, but at the time, I was 17 and heavily involved with Olivia."

When Isabella reached for him, Sidney took her hand in his. "Dad was my hero. I admired him for his brilliant mind, I was proud for his success, but I hated him for what he'd done to Mom. I was a messed-up kid for a while. I tried smoking weed and drank myself into oblivion a lot of weekends. No one was there to tell me *not* to do it. I'm just thankful I never got caught or hurt anybody else, especially Olivia."

Isabella squeezed his hand. "You're a very special person."

"You're already in my heart, Isabella." He looked into her eyes. "Is there a chance for us?"

When she lowered her gaze, his heart dropped to his feet. "I get it." After stopping the swing, he lifted to his feet. "I'd better say good night and be on my way."

"Sidney, sit down."

He did as she asked. Waiting. Wondering. Hoping.

"I like you more than any man I've ever met in my life," she said. "In the short time you've been here, you've made me mixed up, mad, confused, even a little angry."

"Sorry?" What did she expect him to say?

She ran her hand over her hair in the way he adored.

"You've also made me laugh, you've challenged me, you've given me ideas for the store, you've listened to me, and you've made me feel like a woman worthy of a man's love. The love of a genuine, good-hearted, compassionate, kind, completely wonderful man."

"Isabella—"

"Please let me finish," she said, her voice firm. "I may never get up the nerve to say these things again. After what happened with Tristan, I'd put up walls around my heart. I never expected to meet a man like you. All those things you said to me in the park tonight? You can't even *know* how special those things are for me, for my heart. As crazy as this sounds, I've fallen in love with you. And it *kills* me because I can't have you." Isabella's eyes filled with tears that spilled over onto her cheeks.

Sidney pulled her into his arms, thankful she didn't push him away. "Because I'm not a Christian?"

"Yes," she said, gulping. More tears fell, and she brushed them away with the back of one hand.

Pressing his lips to her hair, Sidney leaned his forehead on hers. "I've fallen in love with you, too. Seems to me if we care about each other, God will understand and want us to be together. Help me understand. Why is it so important that I'm a Christian?"

She pushed back and her eyes searched his. "Because at the end of my life, I want to have the assurance of your eternity in heaven. More importantly, I want *you* to have that assurance. As much as I care about you, as much as I might come to love you, God loves you more than I ever will." She leaned further into him and clung to his neck, her tears soaking his collar.

"Isabella, I can't leave you like this."

She pulled back and looked up at him. "What do you mean?"

"I can't leave you crying. Let me tell you something that might make a difference."

"Please do. I could really use something positive right now." She laughed a little through her tears. The sight of her tears tore him in two. He couldn't believe this woman could love him. He felt so unworthy.

"Caroline told me she felt God is preparing my heart. Softening me. That He's working in me through this trip to Evergreen, and that in time, I'll meet Him. I feel that it *will* happen."

Isabella started to wipe the dampness from her cheeks, but he brushed his thumbs over them and kissed her temple. "Shhh," he said. "I'm telling you there's hope. Don't give up on me."

"Never," she whispered. "You prayed for your meal the other day, and that was a *huge* step forward. You're seeking, and God knows that. Do you know one of the things I most admire about you?"

"What's that?"

"How you're so honest with me about where you're at spiritually. You could claim to be something you're not to be with me, but you're strong enough, *man* enough, to not lie."

"I'm not worthy of your love," he said.

"You don't need to prove yourself worthy of *my* love, Sidney. You're worthy to *God*. There's a verse that says, 'The one who does not love does not know God, for God is love.'"

He tipped her chin. "Will you wait for me? Give me time? I have no idea how long it might take, but please pray for me?"

"I've been praying for you since the first day we met."

"Thank you." Wrapping Isabella in his arms, Sidney held her for a long time.

Does God hear the prayers of those who are seeking Him but haven't yet taken the step of faith? In his heart, Sidney knew the answer.

God, I'm here. I'm waiting. I know you're waiting on me. Show me the way.

Chapter 24

"Uncle Sidney!"

Sidney's breath caught as Bella ran over to him and scampered onto his lap. "You came to church."

Forcing down the lump in his throat, he kissed her cheek. "Yes, sweetie, I'm here." His arms circled her. The warmth and closeness of this child stole his breath. When Bella kissed his cheek, he thought he'd blubber like a baby. Yeah, he was going soft.

He'd prayed with Seth and Caroline at the breakfast table. They'd had no answers, other than to pray. Not that he'd expected instant answers. Life didn't work that way, he understood that. Caroline encouraged him to keep reading the Bible, and to keep trusting in God to work out the details. Then she'd kissed his forehead and told him she loved him.

Liesel looked tired. So did Paul. Granted, they'd all had a pretty late night. Sidney had heard Ellie crying in the night. Seth and Caroline took turns getting up with her, when needed. Sacrifice. That's what parents do for their children.

He had perpetual bags under *his* eyes when he was in the midst of a trial, clear evidence of the long hours spent researching and preparing his opening remarks and summations. His face often revealed the mental and emotional stress. It was inevitable, no matter the case. He compensated by ramping up his workouts at the gym to keep himself in peak physical condition. What were a few bags around the eyes if he could bench press more than his body weight? Ultimately, it was about sacrificing for the good of the case and his client. Just as parents sacrificed for the good of their children. The end result justified the means.

Wow. Was he seriously comparing a trial to raising children? That thought sobered him. Yes, because in many ways, his cases *were* his children. They consumed him, held his full attention, *owned* him.

You are sad, Prescott.

Sidney's collar felt tight, as if it was closing around his neck, pinching him, making it difficult to breathe. Keeping one arm around

Bella, with his other hand, he attempted to loosen the top button of his shirt beneath his tie. He'd never hyperventilated in his life, and he didn't want to start now. Hopefully, he wasn't suffering a heart attack. Heaven forbid.

"Did you come to meet Jesus?" Blue eyes the color of a robin's egg peered up at him.

"Maybe," he whispered. "If Jesus wants to meet *me*." His answer was as uncertain as Bella's question was achingly innocent.

Sidney focused on the simplicity of the church with its wooden pews and arched windows. No stained glass. No elaborate altar or robes for the minister. But it was well-maintained, one of those churches where people could say *Jesus resides in this place* and mean it. Bella clearly believed Jesus was in the house today.

"I'm sleepy, Uncle Sidney." Resting her blonde head on his chest, Bella closed her eyes. The feel of her snuggled next to him swelled his heart. The inherent trust she placed in him completely blew his mind. Why did she feel so attached to him? Most children seemed to shy away. Thought he was intimidating or scary for some unknown reason. He tried not to bark too loudly or frown at them without good reason.

With her almost ethereal beauty, Bella looked like an angel. In fact, she reminded him of some of those cherubs in paintings he'd seen at The Vatican in Rome. What would it be like to have a child, his own flesh and blood? A little person who looked up to him, who asked him questions that challenged his beliefs and long-held misconceptions about faith? About love? For that's what they were. *Misconceptions.*

His return to Boston was imminent. He was expected back to assume his position and responsibilities at the firm. The inner nudge to remain in Evergreen longer threatened to overwhelm him. The situation with Isabella was such a mess, but did it have to be? He hadn't slept much the night before. He'd plopped on the bed and thought over the events of the evening, tossing and turning. Asking God for answers, trying to pray, ending up frustrated in the end.

Sensing that Seth watched, Sidney turned his head to meet his brother-in-law's gaze. The man was praying for him even now. He could *feel* it. He'd been praying for him, and he'd continue to pray. The same with Caroline.

Closing his eyes, Sidney lifted his chin. After a few moments, his lids fluttered open, and he stared at the ceiling of the small chapel. If it were possible, he wouldn't doubt his mother was also praying for his soul up in heaven. Could Mom see him sitting here now? On a wooden pew in Evergreen Community Church, with Bella on his lap, wondering if he'd meet Jesus today?

So many questions.

The worship service began, and something inside Sidney wanted to hold Bella's thirty pounds of sweetness, give or take, for the rest of his days and never let her go. Never subject her to the pain and ugliness of the outside world.

As the organist began the opening hymn, the biggest challenge of the morning was rising to his feet with the sleeping child in his arms. Seth motioned to him, indicating he should lift the little girl and rest her against his chest. With only a small amount of fumbling, he managed to rise to his feet, and with a gentle nudge, positioned her head on his right shoulder. Sidney blew out a breath of relief. He'd somehow managed not to wake her up, and she still slept soundly.

Bella shifted and nestled her head closer, burying herself against him, her hands clasped around his neck. Should he sing or not sing? He wasn't very good, but he'd sing along quietly if he even knew the tune. The tune of the second hymn was a familiar one he'd heard played at funeral services, "Amazing Grace."

"Amazing grace, how sweet the sound," he began to sing with the rest of the congregation, thankful for the words printed on a screen suspended from the ceiling. "That saved a wretch like me. I once was lost…but now am found." He faltered as a wave of something he couldn't define washed over him. Resting his head against Bella's, he felt the rise and fall of her soft breathing.

Sidney silently mouthed the words on the screen as the others around him sang. *T'was grace that taught my heart to fear, and grace my fears relieved. How precious did that grace appear, the hour I first believed.*

Settling back on the pew a minute later as the hymn ended, Sidney darted a glance at Liesel. She nodded to Bella and mouthed, *Are you okay?*

He smiled and nodded. His mouth might be dry, his throat raw with emotion, but he wouldn't trade this time with Bella for the sweetest courtroom victory. What he was missing in his life hit home—those same things he'd mentioned to Caroline that he could finally admit he wanted. Marriage, family, children. *Love.* But he wanted love with a woman who loved him for himself and not his position at the law firm or his family's wealth.

Isabella couldn't care less about those things. She loved him for who and what he was.

A light patter of rain began to beat on the roof of the church. The steady rhythm was a comfort in its own way. He could almost feel his heart softening and expanding. Ready to welcome the truth. Ready to welcome the man named Jesus.

In his heart, Sidney knew he was close to finding it.

So very close.

Yet so far.

"Sidney! Wait up."

At Isabella's call, Sidney turned at the front doors, umbrella in hand. He smiled at the sight of her. "Good morning. I looked for you before the service. I'd hoped you'd come sit by me, but I understand why you might not—"

"I ended up subbing in the toddler room this morning. I guess I subconsciously needed the extra hugs." She gestured to her dress with a small smile. "In spite of what you might think, I didn't miss my mouth with my breakfast. She pointed to an orange stain on her top. "This is courtesy of Carley Sanders, and this"—she held out a section of her skirt covered in what looked like smeared jam—"is the handiwork of Jackson Ford."

"Good morning, you lovebirds." Barbara flitted behind them.

"Morning." Sidney shook Darren's hand.

"Nice to have you join us this morning, Sidney. Hope you'll come again soon." Hattie Nelson gave him a friendly smile and waved as she headed out of the church with a couple of other women.

"Sidney, we'll see you at the house later," Caroline said. She gave Isabella a quick hug and whispered something in her ear.

Tugging him by the hand, Isabella led Sidney outside. She lifted her face to the sky. A few raindrops landed on her cheeks, making her laugh.

He stared at her. "Come get under the umbrella. Your hair's getting wet, and your clothes are getting soaked."

"I don't care," she said. "My clothes are already a mess. *This* is living!"

"Living?"

"What's that girl doing now, Sidney?"

Recognizing Millicent's voice, he smiled. "Apparently, she's *living*."

"You have fun with that one." With one hand on the handle of her umbrella, Millicent adjusted her glasses with the other. "I wanted to thank you for dancing with me last night. Hank asked me to dinner. We're going to Manelli's on Tuesday night."

A wide grin spread across his face. "Glad to hear it."

"Come around to the library again sometime."

"I'll do that. Have a good day, Miss Millicent." With a nod, she departed.

Sidney walked to meet Isabella on the front lawn. "What is Millicent's last name?"

"Ponds."

He laughed. If Millicent ended up with Hank, she'd be Millicent Ponds Jergens.

"Sidney, lift your face to the sky and open your mouth."

"Why?"

Isabella released an exasperated sigh. "Just *do* it already!"

With a skeptical expression, Sidney did as she asked. "Happy now?" He acted like he was choking and grabbed his throat.

"That came from the sky, from God!"

"That particular raindrop that landed in my mouth?"

"Yes, you infuriating man! Forget science. Forget trying to explain everything away to try and convince yourself that it's *not* God. It's not like there's someone up there with a big rain-making machine who decided he'd sprinkle raindrops on Evergreen, Maine today."

"You don't know that's what I'm thinking." *Was* that what he'd thought? In this moment, he wasn't sure of much of anything. But he wanted to be sure.

"Well, in any case, this, my friend"—Isabella opened her arms and twirled in a circle—"is the handiwork of the Master. The mountains, the trees, the storm clouds, the rain, *everything*."

"Isabella?"

She stopped. "Yes?"

"I'm going to drive you home now. You're going to change into something dry, and then I'm going to take you to lunch. If you can put up with me, I want to go to lunch with you every day until I leave town. I want to spend as much time with you as possible. As long as you'd like that, too."

"Of course, I want that, too." Her eyes clouded with understanding. "When are you leaving?"

"Bryce left me a voice mail message last night. There are pressing matters at the firm. I can't ignore them any longer. I should have known it was a pipedream that I could stay long."

"I repeat, when?"

He hated to tell her. "Tuesday afternoon."

She lowered her gaze. "I'm thankful we've had this much time together."

"Me too, Isabella. You can't even know how thankful."

She forced a bright smile. "Promise to think about what I said, okay? About the raindrops?"

"I promise. Now please get under this umbrella with me before you catch cold."

"You're bossy." Her eyes lit with fire.

"You're beautiful." How he wanted to kiss her.

"Sidney, what *am* I going to do with you?"

"I'm sure you'll think of something." He pulled her beneath the umbrella as he guided her to the Aventador parked around the corner.

"If this is a loaner car, should I ask what your regular car is?"

"Mercedes. Black S-Class Maybach."

"I have no idea what you just said."

"They advertise it as a private jet for the road."

"That helps. Thanks." She gave him a smile as he tucked her in the car.

What Isabella couldn't know was that never in his life had he faced a situation he didn't know how to handle. Until now.

After lunch at The Evergreen Inn's main dining room, Sidney took Isabella home. Her Cape Cod cottage was a reflection of its owner—warm, cozy, completely charming. She showed him her paintings and told him she normally spent Sunday afternoon napping, reading, or painting. He suggested she paint while he read and strolled over to her small bookcase. "Got any Dashiell Hammett novels, by any chance?"

"I think so. They're filed alphabetically by last name."

He laughed. "A woman after my own heart." Within seconds, Sidney pulled out a volume of *Red Harvest*. "Got it. This copy looks really old."

"I found it at an old bookstore in Hartford. I used to love exploring some of the antique stores." Isabella pulled a paint smock over her head and tied it behind her neck.

"Do you have a jaunty little hat to complete the look?"

"No," she said laughing.

"I'm sure they have a lot of antique fairs here in Maine, don't they?"

"They do, especially during the summer into the fall months."

"That sounds like fun. Are you willing to show me around? I'll definitely have to make it back for the Harvest Festival."

Isabella pulled out her set of paints and tugged a stool close to her easel.

"The master at work," he said. "I'll leave you alone."

"You can talk. Just don't expect an answer every time."

"You realize this is what we'd be doing on a Sunday afternoon if we were dating." Sidney flipped a page of the book and realized he needed to be careful since it was so old.

"I know. Please read, Sidney."

"Yes, ma'am. I'll try." He pretended to read his book but stole glances at her as often as possible. Although he tried to be nonchalant, he wasn't fooling Isabella any more than himself.

An hour later, after getting a glass of water, Sidney strolled back into the living room, trying not to peek at her painting.

"You can look if you want."

"Thanks." He took a step closer. "You're painting Caroline and Seth's house?"

"Seth commissioned it for her birthday in October. Even though it's not for a few months, I figured I'd get a head start. Seth's given me some photos of the house to use for reference."

"Looks terrific to me. Have you painted houses before?"

"A few buildings and the gazebo in the park, but no houses. Toby's going to help me with this one to give me pointers, advice, that type of thing. I hope she'll like it."

"Coming from you, I'm sure she will. I appreciate your support of my painting, Sidney." He figured Tristan must not have given her much encouragement.

"By the way, I met Toby at the dance last night," Sidney said. "I told him I'd like to help out with one of the church beautification projects while I'm here, but that was before I knew I'd need to go back this week. If I don't see him before I leave town, would you mind passing on my apologies? I'll plan on helping out at some point in the future if the opportunity comes up."

"I'm sure he'll understand." Isabella's smile was reassuring yet he detected lingering sadness. He felt it, too.

"Thanks. Toby also mentioned your Aunt Clara's vision to sell the store to you. I hope I can meet your aunt before I leave town. She sounds like quite a character."

"You could say that." Isabella's lips twisted.

Another half hour later, Sidney waggled his brows with a mischievous grin. "Care to join me over here on the sofa?"

She blew out a sigh. "You're tempting me again. Friends, remember?"

"Whatever you say. I enjoy being around you. On *your* terms, Isabella. Whatever you want, but I figure we're adults capable of self-restraint and discernment."

She was quiet for a long time as she concentrated on her painting. "How often do you plan on coming to Evergreen?" she finally said. She put her paintbrush in a jar of liquid and swirled it around.

"That's difficult to say. Depends on what happens, I suppose. Maybe once every couple of months?" He closed the book. No sense pretending he was reading anymore. "Say what you mean, Isabella."

Standing, she untied the smock and removed it. He could tell she was deep in thought as she draped it over the easel. "Are we crazy here? If you have the opportunity to date some gorgeous professional woman in Boston, can you honestly tell me you'll turn her down?"

"Come over here. Please?" He patted the space beside him. She curled next to him, leaving a respectable space between them.

"First of all, I know you heard what I said last night about my last few dates." Sidney shifted to face her directly. "One thing you should know about me is that I don't lie." He propped his right elbow on the back of the sofa. "I want to be with you, Isabella, but I understand I'm not the man you need at this point. So, if a man comes along you want to date, call me, and we'll talk about it."

She laughed under her breath. "You would hate that."

"You're right. I would. In some respects, maybe it's a good thing I'm going back to Boston. I'll go to church with Bryce and Tiffany. I'm going to keep reading the Bible. I'll keep praying and hope God hears those prayers." He shrugged. "That's all I can promise at this point. I want to keep in touch with you every day if that's not too overwhelming. Text, email, phone, Skype. I'll call you, you call me. If I'm busy, leave a message, and I'll do the same."

"I didn't say you're not the man I need you to be, Sidney. I said you're the man I love." She looked at him with a helpless expression. "So, where does this leave us? We agree to not date but be like best buddies for now?"

He scratched his head and gave her his best version of puppy dog eyes. "We'll fumble our way through this together, okay? We don't have to make any decisions today, or tomorrow, or before I leave."

"Right," she said. "We wait on God's timing. That's what we need to do." Isabella sounded like she was trying to convince herself.

He reached for her hand. "Hard, isn't it?"

She blew out a sigh. "Yeah. But you're worth it. Are we going to give this a time limit?"

Leaning his head back on the sofa, he laughed. "I'm not. The fact that I've resisted kissing the living daylights out of you this far should tell you something."

"We're both showing amazing restraint." She crossed her arms over her middle.

"Yes, we are."

She jumped to her feet. "It'll be time for a light supper in a little while. How about soup and a grilled cheese sandwich?"

"Shared with you? One of my favorite things in life."

Chapter 25

The next morning dawned bright and beautiful with scattered fluffy white clouds dotting the brilliant sky. Yesterday's rain had cleared the air. He loved Maine—no city fumes, no smog, no factory pollution. Sparkling and crisp. The backdrop of the majestic mountains surrounding them. No wonder the citizens of Evergreen felt closer to God here. Sidney felt as though he could reach and touch the sky.

Breathing in as he jogged down Elm Street in the direction of Mahoney's General Store, he drew fresh air into his lungs and then exhaled. A man jogged toward him. He'd been introduced to him at the church yesterday.

"Morning, Sidney!" He gave him a friendly wave.

"Morning, John." He hoped that was the man's name. Based on the other man's smile, he was correct.

The front door of Mahoney's was propped open. Isabella was busy with some of the local customers. He stood in front of the door and waited until he caught her eye and lifted the small bouquet of red roses in his hand, fresh from Seth's garden. She gave him a radiant smile, and Sidney gestured to the bench.

Humphrey lounged nearby. "Hello there." Dropping to the bench, Sidney pulled out his water bottle and chugged down half the contents. "I'm willing to share. Would you like some water, Humphrey?" He'd seen a bowl on the ground, shoved halfway beneath the bench. Sliding it out, Sidney poured water into it. "There you go, buddy."

An older model, white Oldsmobile rattled up the street and stopped beside the curb. A woman who appeared to be in her early 60s or thereabouts stepped out of the car. Dressed in her Sunday best, she closed the car door and walked around the back of the car. With her handbag clutched between her hands, she wore pearls around her neck and in her ears.

Sidney studied her under veiled lids.

"Morning, Mr. Prescott." Her smile was genuine, polite, and somewhat reserved, as though she were sizing him up in terms of worthiness. For what, he couldn't be sure.

Who did she remind him of? Ah, Aunt Bee from Mayberry, that was it. Even her voice somewhat resembled the actress who'd played the role.

Giving her a bright smile, Sidney nodded. "Morning, ma'am." He'd given up wondering how people knew him. For one thing, sitting in front of Mahoney's was a good indicator. He might as well pee like a puppy around the front step to mark his territory. No, not a good idea. Hamilton Watters would probably be around the corner and dash right over.

Oh, he was silly.

The woman peeked inside the front door. "Looks like Isabella's busy at the moment, so I might as well wait. Do you mind if I sit here with you and Humphrey? And your roses?"

"Not at all." He slid across the bench to make room for her, painfully aware of his sweaty clothes. Maybe he should have gone back to the house and changed before coming here. Humphrey jumped on his lap and stretched, nudging Sidney to rub his belly.

"I'm Isabella's Aunt Clara. I imagine she might have told you a thing or two about me."

"Nice to meet you." He gave her a friendly smile. Somehow a handshake didn't seem appropriate. "I know you and your husband owned Mahoney's for a long time, and that you sold it to Isabella a little over a year ago. You should be proud. She does a great job with it."

"Yes, she sure does. God told me to sell the store to Isabella, you know." After Sidney looked at her askance, Clara laughed. "I'm eccentric, but I'm not crazy, no matter what you've heard. I'm also a firm believer in the ways of God, and how He looks out for our best interests." She darted a glance his way. "Are you a believer, young man?"

He couldn't take offense at the question since Isabella's aunt obviously loved her niece and wanted the best for her—including a godly man. Maybe this is what Toby was referring to when he talked about Clara's vision and the sale of the store as providential. Clara must have a direct pipeline to God or else she thought she did.

"I'm a believer in a lot of things, Miss Clara," Sidney said. "May I call you that?"

"I didn't give you my last name for a reason, young man. Most people in Evergreen don't need last names. It's only when strangers come into town that we remember we even have them."

"Then I hope you'll call me Sidney. I've been in town a few days, and most of the folks use my first name. I realize it's not the same thing as living here, like Isabella, but—"

"But you're Caroline's older brother. Any relation of that wonderful young woman is all right in my estimation. Sidney it is, then." Clara smiled and, releasing her grip on the purse, placed it on the bench beside her. "God also told me a few things about you, too, you know."

"No, I didn't know, but I'm fascinated to hear what He told you."

"For one thing, He clued me in that you've come to Evergreen for a reason. I understand you're a successful lawyer, a powerful man." She glanced his way. "From what I can tell, you're also a bit evasive."

That made him smile. "Some people would disagree with you."

"I have nothing personal against a man in the legal persuasion, as long as he's honest and upright."

Sidney chuckled at her use of the word *persuasion* instead of profession. In Clara's case, he had an inkling that word choice might have been intentional.

"'He who profits illicitly troubles his own house, but he who hates bribes will live.' No doubt those words of wisdom came straight from the Good Book.

"I'm not motivated by money, and I never have been," Sidney assured her. "Neither have I ever accepted a bribe, and I never will." Why did he feel the need to justify himself?

"Good." Clara appeared pleased, but then she looked over at him. "I'm not necessarily talking about you."

Sidney would need to ponder that statement. Was she referring to his father? Lawyers in general? "That's from Proverbs, right?" When she nodded, he continued. "I've been reading the Bible, a little each day since I've been here. Caroline has an old Bible that Seth gave her—"

"I'm well aware of that Bible and its significance in your sister's life. Old things aren't any less valuable. God's Word is the same today as it always was, although a lot of people nowadays twist the Scriptures to suit their own purposes."

Clara was a straight-shooter. For whatever reason, that didn't surprise him a bit.

"'The mind of man plans his way,'" she said, "'but the Lord directs his steps.' Sidney, I know a little something about your father from what Caroline's shared. I'm sure it wasn't easy growing up in the shadow of such a man. You've had a lot of expectations placed on you through the years, haven't you?"

"Yes, but going into law was my choice. I mean, sure, my parents heavily promoted it. I followed that path willingly, and so did my brother, Bryce. I admire Caroline for balking the family tradition, moving here to Maine, and following her passion." He stretched out his legs and released a sigh.

"The Lord directs his steps," Clara repeated. "My dear Isabella thought she had everything she could ever want in Hartford, and then she found out differently. In the same way, I think you've believed you have everything you could ever want in Boston, and now you're questioning if that's true. Is that right?"

"I suppose that depends on what I've wanted. I think when things happen in our lives, it helps us refine that vision," he said. "I love practicing law, Clara. In my case, family tradition dictates that I practice in Boston. I've had no reason to doubt where I practice, but I've changed the focus of my personal caseload in the past couple of years to something more palatable."

"Maybe God's whispering in your heart."

"I've never thought of it that way. I just know that I started to wrestle with my conscience. Even now, I'm not where I want to be just yet."

Bribes. Sitting forward on the bench, Sidney dropped his head to his hands.

Clara placed her hand on his shoulder. "Are you all right?"

"Give me a minute, if you don't mind. I'm absorbing." What was that verse again? *He who profits illicitly troubles his own house, but he who hates bribes will live.*

"Take your time."

His clients accepted bribes. That's what a large part of his white collar defense cases involved. By extension, was *he* guilty of the same offense? What was it Seth had said? Something about taking his practice in a different direction. Caroline believed God was softening his heart, preparing the way. Hattie's hints that Evergreen needed a law office…

"Where do you *want* to be?" Clara said. "Maybe that's what you should ask God. You don't have to wait until you're in church, dear boy. You can ask Him anytime. Sitting here on this bench, when you're jogging around town, when you're in the shower. Anywhere. When you have a close relationship with Him, you can talk to God anywhere and He always listens."

Sidney lifted his head and glanced over at Clara. "I get that you're probably in cahoots with God, but are you also in cahoots with Hattie Nelson?"

"I beg your pardon?" Although she feigned offense, the corners of her mouth curved upward. "I don't *do* cahoots, thank you very much. I have no idea what you're talking about."

He laughed. "Spunk must run in your family, Aunt Clara."

"Sounds like you two are getting acquainted out here." Isabella stood in the doorway. Arms crossed, she leaned on the doorjamb. "Cahoots and all."

"Your Aunt Clara has given me some important things to think about." He leaned close and planted a gentle kiss on the woman's surprisingly soft cheek. "Thank you," he whispered.

She put her hand on the side of his face. "You're a good man, Sidney. I can't wait to see how God is going to use you, how He's going to work in *your* life, like He's worked in my dear girl's life. After all, God told me that she was—"

"Aunt Clara, I missed you in church yesterday morning."

"I drove over to Augusta to see Samantha on Saturday and ended up spending time with them. That's my oldest daughter and her family," Clara told Sidney. "Phil and I had five children. None of them wanted to take over the store, so you can imagine how thankful I am that Isabella wanted to keep the tradition going. And when she marries—"

"Clara, don't you have that meeting at the Bethel Historical Society this morning?" Isabella gave her another pointed look.

"Yes, well, you're right. I suppose I should be on my way now."

Taking her by the hand, Sidney helped Clara to her feet. "I'll walk you to your car."

"Be good, Aunt Clara," Isabella called. With her cheeks bright red—as red as he'd ever seen them—she turned and headed back inside the store.

Sidney almost laughed. He'd love to know what that was all about. He was surprised Isabella hadn't insisted on walking Clara to the car herself.

He looked at the older woman. "Why do I get the feeling Isabella was afraid of something you'd say to me?"

"You're a smart man. I have no doubt you'll figure it out. Just keep thinking, and I'll keep praying. I've enjoyed our chat."

"Wait." Running back to the bench, Sidney retrieved the roses and brought them back to Clara. "For you."

"Why, thank you. I'm sure you intended these for Isabella, but don't mind if I do. Seth Barnes does grow the most gorgeous roses." She patted his cheek and then climbed inside her car. "I'll hope to see you again soon, Sidney."

Sidney tucked the bottom of her dress inside the car and then closed the door. "I'm sure we'll see one another again, Miss Clara."

Tuesday morning, Sidney jogged near the center of town. He wasn't leaving Evergreen until after lunch, and Liesel promised to have a picnic lunch ready in a half hour. Isabella had agreed to meet him on the front porch of Landon's. She needed to go back to the store soon after, and in his heart, he knew she didn't want a prolonged good-bye any more than he did.

A large yellow ball rolling across the front lawn of the bed and breakfast caught his attention. Bella ran after it, giggling, and carefree. Sidney smiled. Then he realized that ball would keep on rolling, and Bella would keep on running, if no one stopped them.

Both were making their way to the curb.

His heart lurched. If she didn't stop, in only a few seconds, Bella would be in the direct path of an oncoming car, a blue Buick with an older woman behind the wheel.

He had to do something.

"Bella! Stop!" His pulse pounded. "Sweet Jesus!" That wasn't a curse. It was his *prayer*.

With a burst of energy, Sidney ran as fast as he'd ever moved in his life. As he ran, he yelled at the top of his lungs, waving his arms to try and alert the driver as to the imminent danger.

Oh, dear God, please keep her safe.

The yellow ball dropped over the curb and into the street. Oblivious to the danger, Bella was inches from the curb. Her eyes widened, and she teetered on the edge.

Chapter 26

Arms outstretched, lunging into the street, Sidney grabbed Bella and tucked her into his chest. Then he took a flying leap toward the grassy area beside the curb, covering her head with his upper body and arms and twisting his body like he hadn't done since his diving days.

As he intended, he slammed to the ground on his right side. Breathing hard, Sidney rolled over on his back as the car screeched to a stop. The driver cried out and slumped over the steering wheel.

He'd only had seconds to spare. The impact of all the *what ifs* bombarded him. He was banged up, bruised and scraped, but Bella was safe. That's all that mattered. He still held her tight, pressed next to him, unwilling to surrender his hold on her just yet.

Thank you, Jesus.

Sidney fought for oxygen, his breaths coming out in short gasps. The world was spinning.

Bella started to whimper for her mommy and then let out a wail.

"Ah, sweetie, it's okay." Sidney held the trembling child against him. His breath still came out in ragged spurts. She buried into him as he stroked her blonde hair and whispered, "I feel the same way. Your mommy is coming." He kissed the top of her warm head and blinked away the tears forming at the backs of his eyes.

A small crowd of townspeople gathered to form a human shield in the street to prevent other cars from passing until they could get the woman's car moved.

"You okay there, Sidney?" He couldn't identify the man who'd asked the question.

"Unfortunately for some of you, I'll live." A few people laughed quietly.

"I think he's gonna be just fine. He's ornery as ever." That had to be Millicent. The voice sounded like her, the sentiment even more so.

Turning his head toward their voices, Sidney tried to focus. "Someone please check on the driver." His own voice sounded muffled, distant.

Marty came into view and saluted. "Will do, Mr. Prescott."

Bella's cries dwindled to sniffles, and he leaned his head against hers.

"Bella!" Liesel ran toward them with Caroline trailing behind her.

"You break any bones?" He didn't recognize the man's voice.

"How does he know that without the doctor taking a look at him?" That was a female voice Sidney couldn't identify.

Liesel reached Sidney and fell to her knees beside him, her face pale. "Is she hurt? Bella, sweetie, Mommy's here."

"I think she's fine," he rasped. Man, his throat was dry, his head pounded.

Bella struggled in his arms, and he released his hold on her. Pushing off his chest, she fell into her mother's arms. "Mommy!"

Tears streamed down Liesel's face as she gathered her daughter in her arms. "Oh, baby, you're going to be fine." Her eyes wide, she stared at Sidney as though she was in shock. Maybe *he* was the one in shock. He didn't know anything at the moment other than his back and shoulders were going to hurt a whole lot tomorrow. Probably more on the following day.

"Sidney, you saved Bella's life," Liesel murmured. "I'll never be able to thank you enough."

He waved his hand. "Stop fussing over me. I did what anyone would do."

Liesel rose to her feet, Bella clinging to her. As if it was the changing of the guard, Caroline dropped to her knees beside him. "You okay there, sport? You did a real good thing just now."

He laughed a little. "You might hear me groaning all the way to Boston later today. And I might hobble around like an old man for a day or two. Otherwise, I'm good."

"You probably didn't ever think you'd put those diving skills to such good use," she whispered. "I'm proud of you." Caroline ran her hand over his hair and kissed his forehead.

"He ran like Superman!"

"That's faster than a speeding bullet, you old codger. Superman flies."

"I know that, but he still has to run to get up his speed before he can fly!"

"Stop it, you two," a woman chimed in. "Did you see the way he took that flying leap? Sidney is a regular hero."

By this time, Sidney had given up trying to figure out who said what. He closed his eyes, thankful his breathing had finally slowed. After a few more seconds, with Caroline's assistance, he slowly sat up as he tried to regain his equilibrium. He rested his elbows on his propped knees and raked both hands through his hair. Dizzy, he dropped his head between his knees.

All around him, Sidney heard others taking charge of the driver, and trying to calm the growing crowd. Still woozy, he waved off their offers of help. "Give me a minute to catch my breath."

"Remember what you used to do if you got dizzy after a swim meet?"

Sidney looked up at Caroline. "You remember that?"

Her smile comforted him. "Count to five as you inhale, count back from five as you exhale."

She *did* remember. Sidney did as she asked, trying to fill his stomach with air, concentrating on breathing deeply, and sending oxygen to his brain so it would relax his nervous system.

"Sidney? Want to go up to the front porch at Landon's?"

Isabella.

Lifting his head, Sidney stared into Isabella's eyes. So beautiful, those eyes.

"You okay, Top Dog?" Crouching down beside him, she pushed a stray lock of hair away from his forehead.

"Yeah. I think so. We can try this."

Putting a gentle hand under his arm, Isabella assisted him to a standing position. When he swayed a bit, she increased her hold.

"I'm a…little shaky, but I'll be…okay." He rubbed a hand over his brow. "Just had the wind knocked out of me, that's all." Then he attempted a smile. "What took you so long?"

"I couldn't leave Humphrey in charge of the store. I had to wait for Tommy to get back from an errand."

Several of the townspeople cheered, clapped, and chanted his name to see him on his feet, like the wounded athlete being led off the football field. The noise hurt his ears.

Bella! He glanced around the immediate area. "Where's Bella? Is she okay?" He'd feared he might have crushed her when he took the dive away from the street. At least he'd landed on the grass instead of the pavement. Bella had landed on top of his chest, not crushed beneath his weight.

Blessings all the way around. *God was here.* Sidney knew He was.

"Bella's not even bruised, thanks to you. She's just a little scared. I think you're a little disoriented, Sidney. It's time to take care of you." Isabella's voice was calm and soothing. "I've got him, Caroline. We'll meet you at the house in a few minutes."

Sidney nodded to his sister. "I'll be there shortly."

"Do you want me to call the doctor?" Caroline's concern was gratifying. "To check you over and make sure you don't have a concussion?"

"If I pass out or start acting crazy, then call the doctor. Until then, no. I've taken harder falls in racquetball." Hit his head on a diving board a few times, too. "I need to catch my breath, that's all. I'm surprised to see you here today. It's Tuesday, right?"

"Yes. Liesel made extra for lunch, so she invited me to come."

He chuckled and then groaned. "Admit it. You two wanted to spy on Isabella and me." From the corner of his eye, Sidney noted the abandoned car still sat in the street. "Is the driver okay?"

"She's shaken up, but fine otherwise. She lives over in Bethel," Isabella told him as Caroline headed toward the house. "Hattie's taking her for a cup of tea to make sure she's all right before she tries to drive home."

"Good," Sidney murmured.

"And then we're going to keep *you* here until we make sure you're okay to drive home."

His eyes unexpectedly filled with moisture. "Bella needs to learn she can't run after a rolling ball." His voice caught. "Things can happen so fast."

Isabella touched a hand to the side of his face as she studied him. "God knew."

He nodded, and trained his gaze on hers. "Yes, He did."

"Do you think you can make it to the porch at Landon's?"

"Yeah, but I won't win any races. Afraid I'm not up to speed."

"Come on. Let's get you moving." Behind them, the townspeople started to disperse as Isabella slowly walked beside him across the front lawn of Landon's. She had her arm around his waist, and he draped his arm over her shoulder. His right knee was scraped and raw. Both elbows and shoulders ached. Minor annoyances.

God knew. Stopping near the porch, Sidney swayed.

"You're fine." Isabella strengthened her hold on his arm. "Only a few more feet to go."

Pulling away, Sidney made his way to the front porch and collapsed onto a chair.

"I was so afraid for her," he whispered. "So afraid." The tears began to flow, and he was powerless to stop them. His shoulders shook. For a man who rarely shed tears or showed emotion, he'd never experienced such an overwhelming need to cry. His lips trembled, his nose ran, and then his entire body began to shake.

Was he having a seizure? *What's happening here, God?*

A light touch on his skinned right knee made him open his eyes. Bella knelt on one side of him, Isabella on the other. As he watched, Bella leaned forward and kissed his knee. "You have a boo-boo," she said.

"Yes," he said, more tears falling down his cheeks. "I do. But I think I'm going to be fine." Mopping his face with the back of his hand, he motioned to her. When she stood up, he tugged her onto his lap. The effort hurt, but he didn't care. "How about you?" He sniffled hard and pushed blonde hair away from her sweet face. "Are you okay?"

"Uh huh." She smiled straight into his heart. "You met Jesus."

Sidney's face crumpled, and he bit down on his lower lip. "Not yet, Bella. But I'm ready. Will you help me?" He lifted his shoulders as another tear streaked down his cheek. "I don't know what to do."

"I'll show you," Bella said.

With Isabella sitting at his feet on the porch floor, holding his hand, and Bella sitting on his lap, Sidney Jefferson Prescott confessed that he was a sinner. He acknowledged that Jesus died on a cross in his place, for *his* sins, so that Sidney might have a place in an eternity in heaven.

Jesus cleansed Sidney's soul, mended his heart, and filled the void.

When he finished his prayer, Bella kissed his forehead. "All done. I love you, Uncle Sidney." Sliding down from his lap, she darted inside the house.

"And life goes on. Lead a grown man to Christ and then go get lunch." Sidney wiped his eyes. "My life will be forever changed because of the faith inside that precious child."

"Praise God." Isabella wiped away her tears. "Welcome home, Sidney." Rising to her feet, she softly pressed her lips to his temple.

Reaching for her, Sidney rested his hand on the side of her face. His eyes met hers—searching, asking, waiting. *Wanting.*

Isabella slowly lowered her lips to his. A sweet first kiss, gentle as the rain. Full of promise, full of love, full of faith that the Lord would work out the details.

"I'll go get something to clean your knee and bring you a glass of ice water," she whispered. "Then we can talk and share lunch if you're hungry."

"Thanks, Isabella." Sitting on that white wicker chair on Landon's front porch, Sidney stared out at the expanse of the front lawn. He glanced down at his knee. No miraculous healing there. He winced when he tried to rotate his right shoulder. Yeah, that would still ache for the next few days. He might end up with a whopper of a bruise.

You belong to me. You are mine.

"I'm here, God. Use me. I am yours." Lifting his arms, spreading them wide, as if an eagle poised for flight, he smiled. For some reason, his shoulders didn't hurt in the moment.

An older woman walked past Landon's, someone he'd never seen before. Wearing a dress similar to what women wore decades ago, her graying hair pulled into a bun, she slowed her steps. Turning her head, she gave him a radiant smile.

As if in a daze, he nodded and returned her smile. Then watched as she resumed walking. Did she know who he was? Know of the amazing thing that had just happened in his life? He shook his head and scrubbed his hands over his face. He wasn't even sure what it all meant yet. It'd taken him years to get to this point, and it'd been a winding road full of many bumps. So, it stood to reason it'd take a while to understand how becoming a believer in Christ would impact his life.

All Sidney knew was, he was finally *home.*

Chapter 27

A knock sounded on Sidney's office door and Mikaela poked her brunette head in the open doorway. "I'm sorry to interrupt, but there's a messenger here with a delivery."

She hadn't interrupted anything. He hadn't been able to concentrate on work in over an hour, dwelling on thoughts of Isabella. He tossed his pen on the desk. No sense in pretending he'd been doing anything with it other than tapping it against the blotter.

"Why didn't you buzz me?"

"I did, but you didn't answer."

"Fine. Please have the messenger bring it in."

"Certainly." Within seconds, Mikaela stepped aside. A young man ducked inside his office wearing khaki pants and a delivery service uniform emblazoned with the company logo. Between his hands, he carried a wide, flat package wrapped in plain brown paper.

"Afternoon, Mr. Prescott, sir."

"Afternoon. What do you have there?"

"Delivery from… Hang on just a second and I'll tell you." He pulled out a small, handheld device. "Mahoney's General Store in Evergreen, Maine."

Sidney's heart jumped. Isabella had sent him a gift? Didn't look soft or big enough to be a quilt. He doubted it was a huge slab of fudge. That made him smile.

"Your assistant already signed for it."

Sidney stared at the package and then realized the guy was waiting for a tip. "Hang on a second." Walking behind the desk, he retrieved his wallet from the inside pocket of his jacket. He retrieved a crisp twenty dollar bill and handed it over.

The young man's face lit with surprise. "You're very generous. Thank you, sir. Have a great day."

"Same to you."

Lifting the package, Sidney walked across the room and carefully lowered it onto his desk. HANDLE WITH CARE was stamped all over the package in bold red letters. Based on the size, Isabella must have sent him a painting. One of hers? He could only hope.

With extreme care, he worked on one corner. Took some doing, but he finally removed the strong tape and tore off a small section of the heavy paper. And then more. A layer of bubble wrap sat beneath the outer wrapping. Ripping the brown paper across the front, he tossed it on the floor and began to work on the bubble wrap.

A minute later, Sidney stared at the painting. He sucked in a breath, his heart swollen with a love he didn't deserve. In beautiful watercolors, Isabella had painted Landon's in the summertime. The bed and breakfast was just as he'd always remember it—the trees surrounding the house in full bloom, the bushes lush and full, a row of bright flowers planted in the flowerbeds along the front.

A metal plate at the bottom read COMING HOME. He knew instinctively what this work of art—this work of *love*—symbolized.

Nearly two months ago, he'd first met Jesus at Landon's. Coming home in the most deeply felt, *spiritual* sense of the word, in the most important decision he'd ever made. The most important decision he would *ever* make in his life.

He missed Isabella with everything in him.

What's the answer, Lord?

He needed to make a way for a future with Isabella. Sidney's gaze fell on the Bible she'd given him. After he'd asked, Isabella had highlighted some of her favorite passages for him to study.

You love her. Find a way.

He'd spent a lot of time and miles on the road traveling the three-hour, one-way drive to Maine on weekends, even during the week, as often as possible. He'd flown Isabella to Boston, introduced her to Bryce and Tiffany, who'd opened their arms, their hearts, and their home to her. He wasn't about to show her the Ugly Penthouse. He'd taken her to the Beacon Hill mansion. Walked the halls of Prescott Tate Burnesse with her by his side. They'd cheered on the Red Sox at Fenway, taken long walks on the campus of Harvard, taken a duck boat ride, done all the touristy things he'd never taken the time to do. He'd introduced her to his father and taken her to see his mother's grave.

In Evergreen, he'd read her sections he liked from classic literature. She'd cooked for him. He'd fished with Toby, Seth, and Paul. He'd played checkers and crooned country songs with Hank.

He'd sparred with Millie. He'd gone with Hank to pick out an engagement ring for his favorite librarian. He'd ordered a specially designed engagement ring from Caroline. Bought his sister a quilt. He'd fed Isabella dill pickles straight from the jar. She'd fed him several varieties of homemade fudge. They'd taken Aunt Clara for a helicopter ride. Gone to antique fairs, art shows, and fun, small-town festivals.

They'd sat on Isabella's front porch swing and talked about the future. They'd already shared their dreams of how many children they'd like, what they'd name them, where they'd take them, what they'd teach them. Together they'd taken care of Ellie, Bella, and Paul so they could gain hands-on childcare experience and give their friends much-needed time together.

He'd given her flowers. She'd given him a tool belt.

They'd shared passionate kisses and sweet kisses.

All the while still trusting the Lord to work out the details in the way only He could.

Now it was time to put his ring on her finger. Claim Isabella and step into the future with her as soon as possible.

Isabella had graced him with the love he thought he'd never find. He'd promised her abiding love she could trust forever.

They'd attended church in Evergreen Community Church. They'd attended church with Bryce and Tiffany in Boston.

He'd broken down the first time he sang the lyrics of "I Surrender All."

All to Jesus I surrender
All to Him I freely give
I will ever love and trust Him
In His presence daily live
I surrender all
I surrender all
All to Thee my blessed Savior
I surrender all.

Seth's words from his first visit to Evergreen found their way back into Sidney's mind now. Something about taking his practice in a different direction. At the time, Seth wasn't suggesting Sidney move to Maine. After spending more time there, he knew he could be happy there. He didn't want to completely disassociate himself from the firm. Maybe there was a compromise that could work.

His mind swirled with ideas. Possibilities. The more he pondered, the more excited he became. It *could* work. He needed to talk with Isabella.

You love her. Make it work.

The painting had arrived today, and an email from Hattie had arrived earlier that morning.

Sidney lifted his face and closed his eyes. *Lord, if this is your answer, then I'm happy to follow your call. Lead the way. I am yours, and you are mine.*

Now, he needed to tell Isabella he loved her and share his vision with her. What God was telling him to do. That wasn't something Sidney wanted to tell her in a telephone conversation or in an email.

Grabbing his suit jacket, Sidney stuffed his arms into it and headed out of the office. "Mikaela, I'm taking off for an early weekend."

"What about your meeting with the Lawrence family tomorrow?"

"Oh." He paused by her desk and slid his hands to his hips as he contemplated the options. "See if Bryce can take the meeting and send me a text. If he can do it, I'll call and brief him. If Bryce can't, see if you can get me a shortlist of anyone who can. That's the only appointment until early next week, correct?"

"Let me check. Just a second." She moved her mouse and clicked something on her computer. "You're clear until Wednesday morning with client conferences. You have the partners' meeting on Tuesday morning per the usual."

"Not a problem. I should be back for the meeting. After that, be forewarned there might be some big changes coming. We'll talk next week. Thanks, Mikaela. Have a great weekend."

"Sidney?"

He'd already started to head down the hallway. At Mikaela's call, he stepped back to her desk. "Yes?"

"Go get her."

"Thanks." He laughed. "Am I that obvious?"

"Just a little. Drive carefully and don't break any laws getting up to Maine."

He waved his hand over his head. "No promises."

Chapter 28

A loud siren sounded behind her, making Isabella jump. The lights from the sheriff's cruiser flashed in her rearview mirror.

"Not now, Hamilton." Isabella pushed harder on the accelerator. If she was going to get her first speeding ticket in Maine, might as well make it a good one. The sheriff's car sped up, and he was behind her Highlander in seconds.

"Isabella, please pull your vehicle to the side of the road."

With an exasperated sigh, she slammed her fist on the steering wheel. Only in Evergreen would the law enforcement officer recognize her vehicle and call her name through his megaphone or loud speaker, whatever it was. Not to mention he'd actually said *please*.

Isabella pulled over to the side of the road. The Highlander slid a bit in the gentle rain, and the tires spewed gravel. After lowering the window, she opened the glove compartment. After rummaging through the sunglasses, a bottle of suntan lotion, and other assorted items, she located the white envelope containing her important paperwork. Opening it, she pulled out her license, registration, and proof of insurance.

Hearing a car door slam, she looked in the rearview mirror and spied the sheriff walking toward her.

"Afternoon, Miss Caccaroni." Pausing beside the Highlander, he tucked his thumbs in his waistband.

Isabella laughed. "That's a good one, Hamilton. Stick with Isabella."

"Sorry about that." He had such a pleasant face, round, kind, not at all harsh or forbidding. "My kid calls you Miss Macaroni, so it kind of slipped out."

"Not to worry. No one gets my last name right, anyway."

He planted a sturdy hand on the window ledge. "Where are you going in such an all-fire hurry today? The roads are a little slick. You need to be more careful."

She offered him the documents. "Look, I know I was speeding at least twenty miles over the speed limit. Here's my documentation. Go ahead and give me a ticket so I can be on my way."

"You've never been a lawbreaker before, so if you could answer my question, I'd be much obliged."

"I'm headed to Boston," she said, blowing out a sigh. "I need to talk with Sidney."

"Mr. Prescott, I presume? That Sidney?"

"Yes. Is there any other?" She'd leaned her head back on the headrest but at his question, she glanced up at him. "You presume correctly."

"You working things out with him so you two can be together, I hope?"

"We're trying our best."

"Funny thing about those Prescotts," he said. "They come into Evergreen, meet a local and stir up a friendship, get people talking, and then they leave."

"What do you mean?"

A wide grin spread across his face. "I gave Mr. Prescott a ticket when he was leaving town a couple of months ago. He let out the engine in that fancy red car."

"Probably couldn't get away fast enough." She was surprised Sidney hadn't mentioned being stopped by Hamilton.

"That might be true, but Mr. Prescott told me he was speeding home to Boston so he could figure out some things. Then he planned on coming back up here to Maine as soon as humanly possible. All things considered, I'd say you left a favorable impression on the man, young lady."

Isabella smiled. "Good to know."

"Which brings me to my other point."

When Hamilton paused, Isabella glanced up at him. "Yes?"

"The Prescotts always seem to want to come back to Evergreen. Permanently."

"Evergreen has a lot to offer," Isabella said. "Hamilton, isn't it a violation to tell me about your dealings with another motorist?"

The sheriff's hearty laughter dislodged his hat. When it tumbled off his head, he caught it by the brim and then held it by his side. "You're too smart for me. Tell you what. I don't want to stand in the way of young love. I take it you're going down to Boston for a good reason."

"Yes, sir. The *best* reason. I only hope Sidney feels the same way."

"Then, I'll tell you what I'm gonna do. I'll let you off with a warning this time. Be safe on these roads. It's raining all the way to the state line. All the way down to Massachusetts today from what I hear. Don't get distracted and keep your eyes on the road. Got it?"

"I'll do that. Thank you, Hamilton."

"You betcha." Patting his hand on the roof of her vehicle, the sheriff smiled. "I sure hope things work out." With a respectful tug on the hat, he gave her a nod and strolled back to his cruiser. "Have a good day."

"Come on, come on, come on." Sidney eyed the speedometer. If he knew Hamilton Watters, he'd be patrolling the outskirts of town today because of the rain and wet roads. Easing his foot on the accelerator, he adjusted the defrost setting since his window was starting to fog. When he glanced out the front window, he blinked hard. A white Toyota Highlander was coming toward him on the other side of the two-lane highway.

Slowing the Mercedes, Sidney blinked and narrowed his gaze. Was that Isabella? How many vehicles like hers would be headed out of Evergreen early on a Wednesday afternoon? Short of honking and scaring her, he wasn't sure how best to get her attention. His gaze fell on his cell phone parked on the console. Grabbing it, he tapped it, waiting for the connection.

"Hey, beautiful."

"Hi, Sidney. How are you?"

"Missing you." He tried to keep his voice steady.

"I'm feeling nostalgic," she said. "It's raining here. You know how I love the rain, but it reminded me of you." Her soft sigh about did him in. The Highlander passed him on the road. As expected, she didn't see him. She didn't even turn her head, sure didn't slow down.

"Sidney?"

"I'm sorry. What?"

"Get your head out of your work. I asked if it's raining there?"

"Um, yes." He needed to move this conversation along. With that brief glimpse of her, the need to feel her in his arms became more insistent. "It's raining against my window here." That wasn't a lie. "Isabella, do you have your umbrella?"

"I do, as a matter of fact." He could hear the curiosity in her voice tempered with faint amusement.

"Good. Then pull over by the Mahoney's sign."

"What? Why?"

"Just do it. You'll find out why in a couple of minutes." After disconnecting the call, he tossed the phone on the passenger seat. Maybe he was sneaky, but his anticipation was at a peak.

"Sheriff Watters, if you're nearby and see this, I hope you'll give me a break." Sidney turned the wheel hard and did a U-turn in the middle of the narrow road. Glancing in the rearview mirror, he breathed a sigh of relief and then pressed down on the accelerator.

"Lord, I love her. Give me the right words. *Your* words."

Two minutes later, he spied her Highlander sitting beside the sign, off the side of the road.

Pulling his car behind hers, Sidney pushed open the door and climbed out. Isabella opened her door and hopped out with the umbrella in her hand. In her jeans, a light blue top, and those white tennis shoes, she was adorable. Beautiful. Sexy.

His.

His future. His life. His *wife* if she'd have him. They'd talked about their future, prayed about their future, but now—faced with the reality—Sidney prayed Isabella wouldn't have second thoughts.

Please, God, let her want me. Let her allow me to have a permanent place in her life, her heart, her soul.

The rain fell around them, steady and sure, the same as his love for her. Spattering his hair, his jeans, his shoes. Wanting to run, he forced his steps to slow as he walked toward her.

"Sidney!" Isabella's exclamation was one of surprise, but the joy in her voice, her eyes, could not be denied. She hurried toward him, dropping the umbrella on the ground as she threw her arms around him. "What are you—?"

He silenced her words by caressing her mouth with his. "I love you, Isabella," he said between more kisses, soft and sensual. Drawing her close against him, Sidney wrapped her in his arms. "I have missed you," he whispered against her cheek. Then he kissed her nose, cheeks, temple, forehead, chin. "I want you in my life always, not just weekends or holidays."

Spying the abandoned umbrella, he retrieved and opened it, holding it over their heads. "I realize it's a little late for this."

"I don't care. Oh, my," Isabella said at length. Out of breath, she moved one hand over her chest. "What a nice surprise." When he arched his brows, she pulled him close, and lifted on her toes. She looked into his eyes and smiled into his heart. "I love you." Then she pressed her lips to his in a deep, soul-affirming kiss he was guaranteed never to forget.

The woman had many talents. He looked forward to discovering more talents in the days, months, and years to come. Whatever the Lord saw fit to grant them.

"If that's how you respond to a surprise, I'll try to do it as often as possible." He stroked his thumb over her damp cheek, loving her with his eyes, wanting her always. "I'm wearing jeans to the office, my shirts are untucked, my thoughts are scattered. I have this inexplicable urge to go outside in the rain, lift my face to the sky, open my arms, and tell God to bring on the storms of life."

He rested his forehead on hers. Raindrops mingled with his tears and *her* tears. "I'm ready to face those storms now in a way I never could before. I want to give you my name so the people of Evergreen can finally pronounce your last name."

Unable to resist her, Sidney fingered a few wet strands of her hair and tucked them behind her ear. "Do you mind holding the umbrella?"

"What? Oh, of course not." Taking it from him, Isabella gasped when he dropped to one knee. Sidney looked up at her, needing to see the expression on her beautiful face as he asked this woman to join her life with his. He prayed she'd love the ring Caroline had designed. Reaching for it, tucked securely in the front right pocket of his jeans, Sidney pulled it out and held it up for her to see. He should have thought to pull it out *before* he went down on one knee, but thankfully he was able to retrieve it.

"Isabella Marie Caccavale, I'd be honored if you'd agree to be my wife, and take me as your husband. I promise to make you happy always. If you'll have me, I want to make blueberry muffins for you, sing love songs until you beg me to stop, sit in church beside you, build you a home in the suburbs to put Caroline and Seth's to shame, make babies with you, raise a family with you, and love you with all of me and everything I am."

"I'd be honored to be your wife, Sidney Jefferson Prescott. Nothing will make me happier than to spend my days loving you." Isabella kissed him and then waited as he rose to his feet. Taking her hand, he slid the round cut diamond ring flanked by pink amethysts on her finger.

"Caroline designed the ring, of course. If you'd rather have another design, we'll work on it with her," he said.

"It's perfect and even more special knowing Caroline designed it for us." With an irresistible smile, Isabella tugged on the bottom of his shirt. "You know, Aunt Clara came to see me this morning."

He laughed. "Another prediction?"

Leaning close, she teased his bottom lip with hers, driving him crazy. "I think you'll like this one."

Swaying a bit, he blinked. Dazed, Sidney wondered how soon he could get her to agree to marry him. "What did she say?"

"She told me it was high time to go down to Boston and stake my claim on love." Leaning into him, Isabella snuggled against his chest. "I was following my heart and driving down to Boston to see you," she said, pulling back. Her gaze moved over his face, coming to rest on his lips. "To tell you that I want to be with you and that I don't need more time to realize that I want you in my life every single day. I want to see your smile, and I want to laugh with you, cry with you, *love* with you for the rest of my given days. I want it all. Do I sound greedy?"

"No, you sound like me. I want the same things. This has been the longest two months of my life," he murmured. "Please say you won't make me wait long to marry you, Isabella."

"I won't." Tilting her head, she smiled. "My parents were married in October."

"That's much too far in the future," he said against her lips. "I'm an impatient man."

"We're already in August." He kissed a sensitive spot below her right ear, and a soft, sensual sigh slipped past her lips. "You can be very persuasive. How about in two weeks? I should be able to find a dress and get all the arrangements made by then. That was Aunt Clara's vision, by the way. That we'd be married in two weeks. She has a pretty good track record."

"Now you're talking. We wouldn't want to disappoint Aunt Clara, after all. I'm sure Caroline and Liesel will help." Sidney chuckled and kissed her temple. He couldn't stop kissing her, but Isabella didn't seem to mind. "Who are we kidding? Everyone in the town will probably help out. I'll meet you at the altar in Evergreen Community Church in two weeks. Say two o'clock?"

"Agreed. That way we can have a short reception and then head off on a honeymoon." Isabella's eyes widened. "Two weeks! There's no way we can get reservations in that short a time."

"Leave that to me. I'll find a way. Do you have a preference where we go?"

Her eyes searched his. "As long as you're there, it doesn't matter."

She'd told him in one of their phone conversations that she'd love to visit Italy and see the village where her paternal grandparents had lived their entire lives. As soon as he could, he'd make some calls. The first night, they could stay at The Evergreen Inn. He'd already called Caroline and Seth earlier in the day and told them of his plans, ditto Bryce and Tiffany. They'd all been overjoyed and excited to officially welcome Isabella into the family.

"In other news, Bryce and Tiffany have decided to take up residency in the Beacon Hill house, so we can keep it for family gatherings. They're planning on redecorating. I have another announcement—they're expecting a little boy in about five months."

"Oh, that's such great news! All the way around." Isabella's eyes lit, and her smile brightened the dark skies.

"And then this morning Hattie sent me an email with a real estate listing for an office in downtown Evergreen. The ad mentioned how it'd be perfect for a family law office. Right off Elm Street."

"Sidney, are you saying you want to *live* in Evergreen?"

"I'm saying I'd like to maintain a presence in the firm, and I can burn the rubber between Maine and Boston, as needed. It'll take some planning, but I'll make it work. I don't have any upcoming trials. I've already transferred a lot of my caseload. Bryce has offered to help redistribute the work."

Isabella gulped. "To be clear, you're not leaving the firm?"

"I'm not. If anything, I'm thinking of transitioning into family law practice and establishing a branch of Prescott Tate Burnesse here in town. I hear Evergreen could use a law office. I don't need to jump through too many hoops to be admitted to the bar, so there's no reason I can't practice here in Maine."

"That sounds like a good compromise," she said. "Were you coming back into town to take a look at that office space?"

"Among other things. I thought I should put in my bid for that space as soon as possible. I didn't want anyone else staking a claim on what I want to be mine. Isabella, I want to hire more people to help you run Mahoney's. Let's make Tommy a manager. You can pop in anytime you want, but I want you to focus on your painting. And maybe work on starting a family." He grinned. "Has Clara made any predictions about that yet?"

"One thing at a time, but I'm not getting any younger, you know. Let's not wait long."

Sidney smiled. "It's uncanny how well you read my mind. If you get a craving for a pickle during pregnancy, I know a place you can get a lot of really big dills."

She tossed her head back with deep laughter. "Where will we live at first?"

His lips traveled to her neck. "Not a problem. One of us has a perfect little house with a white picket fence. Sounds like a great love nest to hole up in together, don't you think? I envision cozy, romantic evenings in front of the fireplace. Padding around in our T-shirts, flannel pajama bottoms, and bare feet. Messy hair, messy…everything."

He growled against her neck. "I'll drive myself crazy if I give my thoughts free rein. That can be dangerous." He laughed. "I'll be good. Promise."

"Two weeks, Sidney. Two *weeks!*" Her beautiful brown eyes grew wide again, as though the truth was finally sinking in that they'd be joined in marriage soon. Fine by him. He couldn't wait to make her his. *Completely* his.

The rain had stopped, and taking his hands in hers, Isabella lifted her face to the sky. "Don't you love how the Lord works, Sidney? I love how He revealed Himself to you. In His time, and in His way, and when you were ready to receive the gift of His love."

"That's because God knew that in your heart, and in Evergreen, Maine, was exactly where I needed to be. I love you, Isabella." Sidney caressed her beautiful face and brought his lips to hers.

"I love *you*," she whispered. "Welcome home."

About the Author

JoAnn Durgin is the author of the beloved contemporary Christian romance series, The Lewis Legacy Series, including **Prelude**, the prequel to the series. Her other novels include **Catching Serenity**, **Heart's Design** (the forerunner of **Gentle Like the Rain**), **Love So Amazing** and **Love So Divine** (The Wondrous Love Series, Books 1 and 2), **Perchance to Dream**, **Echoes of Edinburgh**, and the popular Starlight Christmas Series.

JoAnn loves to hear from her readers! Please feel free to contact her:

WEBSITE: www.joanndurgin.com

FACEBOOK: www.facebook.com/authorjoanndurgin

www.ingramcontent.com/pod-product-compliance
Lightning Source LLC
Chambersburg PA
CBHW020612180626
46810CB00007B/2736